THE TWIG LADY & A CRYSTAL FOR CHARITY

DONALD F. AVERILL

ISBN 978-1-958004-25-8 (softcover)
ISBN 978-1-958004-26-5 (ebook)

This book is a work of fiction. Names, characters, places, and incidents are the product of the author's imagination or are used fictitiously. Any resemblance to actual locales, events, or persons, living or dead, is purely coincidental.

Printed in the United States of America.

INK START MEDIA
5710 W Gate City Blvd Ste K #284
Greensboro, NC 27407

Books by Donald F. Averill

An Iceberg's Gift

A Professor's Affair

Detour in Oregon

Glacier Fires and Ornaments of Value

Missing Notes, Hidden Talents and Other Stories

The Antarctic Deception

The Bitterroot Fire

The Bitterroot Diamonds

The Kidnapping of Megan Isaacs

The Kuiper Belt Deception

The Lighthouse Library

The Lighthouse Fire

The Niffits

Wolves' Hollow Murders

Visit
www.authordfaverill.com

ACKNOWLEDGEMENTS

Thanks to Katie Lynch and Efren Sifuentes for finding typos, punctuation errors, and making suggestions to clear up confusion. Mary Stebbins did a thorough job of editing, and most of the time I followed her advice.

THE
TWIG
LADY

CHAPTER 1

I had waited until midnight before going to bed but fell asleep on the sofa while watching an old Cary Grant movie. I expected Ken's cruiser to pull into the driveway any minute. He must have gotten home around one o'clock, but I was in bed dreaming. I remembered him crawling into bed, but I just rolled over and continued my dream. I was walking in a stream in cool water up to my knees, watching a bird bathing in a calm shallow pool surrounded by mailbox sized rocks. That's all I remember.

Not wanting to wake my husband, I sneaked out of bed, dressed except for shoes and socks and tip-toed to the kitchen to start the Sunday morning coffee. There was something about the cold tile that felt good on my bare feet. Ken would bring me my slippers when he got up. I had to smile thinking about our Sunday routine. The first weekend in June had been forecast to be sunny and warm and so far had met predictions. At 8:00 am the kids were still asleep and Ken didn't stir when I got up since he worked late Saturday night.

As I pressed the start button on the coffee maker, I heard Sasha's toenails clicking on the tile floor. It was amusing to see her little belly barely clearing the floor as she walked toward her water bowl. She stopped, checking with me for permission to be in the kitchen before she started drinking. I nodded an okay. After breakfast, I wanted the family to walk to the park, giving Sasha some needed exercise. The kids, Douglas Mills, twelve, and Erica Ann, seven, hadn't had a chance to use the relatively new play equipment. Ken could watch them play like human pretzels while Sasha and I toured the grassy area behind the jungle gym, slides, and swings.

We left the house a few minutes after ten o'clock and arrived at the park a few minutes later. It was a short walk along the winding Salmon Creek Drive that followed the small stream. Sasha seemed to know where we were going and pulled me along tugging at her leash at the front of our little group. I wasn't going to use a tether on our littlest, but Ken reminded me of the local ordinance as we exited the house. Although we were all immunized against COVID-19, we wore masks, just in case we met people at the park having similar intentions for Sunday morning exercise. But we were alone, so our masks were poked in our pockets, handy if the need arose.

When the play equipment came into sight, the kids ran ahead with Ken jogging behind to keep an eye on them. Sasha kept pulling at the leash as if she were on a hunt. She and I weren't far behind the others. Erica had gone for the swings and Doug hung upside down from the monkey bars when I arrived. Sasha sniffed around the bright red equipment, and then began pulling me to the grassy region behind the swings. Still shackled, I had little choice but to follow her. Assuming she was going to leave a deposit somewhere in the meadow, I had two used bread bags for containment.

However, Sasha began to meander, releasing the tension on her leash and my right arm. As we toured the periphery of the large green meadow, moving slowly in a clockwise direction, Sasha would occasionally stop, sniff the air, and look to the right across the grassy expanse. As we kept moving, I thought she had been listening to the noises from the kids, but that wasn't what had been attracting her. It was a voice from a shaded area not far from the play equipment, behind a row of arborvitae. At first, I thought some people were in the backyard of a house that abutted the park, so I ignored the sounds.

As we got closer, I realized it was a woman's voice. She wasn't speaking English. When we lived in Portland, one of our neighbors was from Hungary and I detected what I thought were Hungarian words. Sasha suddenly stopped and barked. I kept going, wanting to see who was speaking, but Sasha had other ideas. I had to pull on her leash to get her to move forward. Barking was the first signal of danger our little watch dog presented, so when she wouldn't follow me, I had to carry her. I moved around the shrubs and saw an elderly woman sitting in the middle of a concrete bench talking to someone, but she was alone. Sasha squirmed violently in my arms and I had to put her down. As soon as she was on the ground, she bolted from me before I could get a grasp on the leash.

I took a couple of steps after her but stopped when I heard, "Oh, let your dog run! I'm sure it won't go far." The voice was potent and reassuring.

I turned around and peered into the shadows behind the arborvitae. My eyes slowly adjusted to the shady conditions. At first I saw a dark shape, almost like a shadow. "Who are you?"

"Come closer so we can converse without straining our ears and voices. I'm a bit hard of hearing."

I called to Sasha, clapping my hands together, but she refused to come to me. She stayed about twenty feet away barking and scratching at the grass. I had never seen her act like that before. I gave up and resumed looking into the shadowy area where I could see an elderly woman sitting on a bench atop a small berm. I stepped a bit closer, "I'm Katelin Sanders, who are you?"

"I'm Judy Morgan. Please move a little closer."

I considered calling Ken if she offered me an apple, but Sasha would come to my rescue. I surveyed the area, looking for the person Judy had been speaking to, but couldn't see anyone. I did as she asked and joined her in the semi-concealed area but stood about ten feet in front of her and the raised precast cement bench. This woman was dressed entirely in black. I had to assume she was in mourning over the recent loss of a loved one. Maybe she needed someone to talk to, so I stepped even closer so I wouldn't have to raise my voice. Sasha had stopped barking but was watching intently.

"I heard someone talking, was that you?"

"Yes, I was talking to my late husband, Charles. He's the one in the middle."

That comment surprised me. What did she mean by the one in the middle? There were no other people visible. Was she hallucinating? Perhaps this person had wandered off from a retirement community specializing with care for Alzheimer's patients, but I wasn't aware of any facility in this area. How far could she have ventured away from her residence? I gave her a blank look.

She responded, "You think I'm a little unhinged, don't you? Let me explain." She crumpled some napkins and stuffed them in what I considered her lunch sack and said, "My Charles left me two weeks ago and I was taking care of some last minute business with him. I know he can't hear me, but I had to say some things, for my own welfare. See that tree over there? The one in the middle. It reminds me of Charles, shorter than the others, and a bit stout."

I glanced where she pointed and could see a maple, crowded between two tall firs or pines. I never have been able to distinguish between those evergreens. I saw Judy begin a big smile forming amidst a few wrinkles. Her teeth appeared original.

"You're wondering how old I am, aren't you?" She nodded, "I'm eighty-four. My birthday was in April. Charles was eighty-nine in May." She sighed, "We got married when he retired from selling real estate. He was seventy back then. I had been his secretary for three years, then we became real estate partners, and a year later we married."

I calculated how long Judy and Charles were married. "You were married for nineteen years. That seems a long time. Ken and I have been married eight years. He's a policeman here in Timberville. We moved here from Portland when the city quit supporting the police. The protests and violence has gone crazy in the city. We had to get out. I didn't want Ken to get hurt. The kids need their father and I don't want to be a widow trying to support two children and seeking a good paying job."

"What are you trained to do?"

I chuckled, "I'm a nurse. I met Ken when he brought a gunshot victim into the emergency room."

"You quit working when you married?"

"No, when I was six months pregnant with my son, Douglas. I've been a stay-at-home mom ever since, but I'll have to go back to work soon. Our savings is almost exhausted."

Judy continued. "My first husband, Keith, was a firefighter and got drafted. I worked for a dentist. He was very tall. He's the one on the left." She pointed again at the trees. "He was a basketball player in college. I was in the band and played a trumpet, trombone, and baritone." She smiled, "Not at the same time, I filled in when needed, when someone was ill or drunk."

"How long were you married to Keith?" Judy seemed to want to tell me about her life, and I was curious. I suppose I should have changed the subject.

"Only two years. He was killed in Viet Nam. It was an accident. He was loading a bomb and it fell on him, a five-hundred pounder."

"I'm so sorry. That must have been terrible for you."

"Thank you. Things happen, you know. I lived with my parents for a year before I met Jason. He was tall, too, but not as tall as Keith. But he could reach the top shelf of all the cabinets."

"What did Jason do for a living?"

"Oh, my. Jason started off selling farm equipment, but that was seasonal, so he began working for a car dealership. He sold Cadillacs to rich people, and that was his downfall." Judy shook her head and focused on the third and second tall tree on the right. "One of Jason's rich customers owned a small airplane and got him hooked on flying. He took flying lessons at every spare moment and before long, received his pilot's license. We couldn't afford to buy a plane, so he bought the plans for a two seater and built a small plane for us. But I was too scared to fly with him, so after about a year, he sold it for a tidy profit and invested in a Cessna. I went up with him several times, but I had my own ideas about flying."

"I would be too scared to fly in a small plane. I'd be afraid to get airsick." Feeling more comfortable in the presence of Judy, I joined her on the bench. Sasha stayed where she was, reclining in the grass intently watching us.

Judy snickered, "That's what I thought, but Jason had some pills and I was able to enjoy the rides. I never got sick, but I worried about crashing. I didn't like the lack of control. Then, he had a terrible crash and he was gone."

"Oh, I'm sorry. Did you ever have children?"

"No, but we tried." Judy smiled and winked. "My doctor, a gynecologist, explained that something wasn't right, but she didn't have a cure, nobody did. We had tried many home remedies."

"When my last, my third, Charles, and I toured Europe after the cold war, we visited Hungary. What a special trip! I had my fortune told by a gypsy woman at a touring circus. She told me I was something special." Judy clapped her hands and laughed. "That's what Charles always told me."

When Judy smiled, her eyes twinkled. She seemed to be enjoying the memories.

I heard some crying and could tell it was my youngest. I turned to see Erica suddenly drop to her knees next to Sasha, and call out, "I fell and hurt my arm. Daddy told me to come see you."

"Did Daddy look at it, Erica?"

She nodded and stood up holding her left arm against her side.

I walked toward her and said, "Let me take a look, maybe Daddy missed something."

Erica released her right hand and lifted her injured arm. There was a spot about the size of a nickel near her elbow. I manipulated her arm but she didn't exhibit any pain. I concluded it was just a bruise and it would be gone in a few days. I took her right hand to lead her over to Judy to say hello, but Erica pulled back and motioned for me to bend down to hear her whisper.

"Is that lady a witch? Why is she in all black clothes?"

I suppressed a laugh and answered, "No, She's not a witch. Her husband went to heaven a few weeks ago and she is wearing those clothes to indicate she is feeling sorry he left her."

Erica frowned, "Why didn't she go with him?"

I took a deep breath, "Well, they were given only one ticket. God wanted her to stay here and take care of some things. She has to sell her house." I didn't know what to tell her, but I was sure she didn't know about death. "Come and meet the lady. Her name is Judy."

CHAPTER 2

I took Erica's hand, turned around to move closer to Judy to make introductions and was quite surprised. Judy was gone! The bench was bare. There was no sign of anyone having been there. Erica and I sat on the bench and Sasha joined us at our feet. I picked her up and set her on the bench, watching her tail wag, happy to be part of the family.

Erica looked at me, "Where did the lady go, Mommy?"

"I don't know. When I was checking your arm she vanished, did you see her leave?"

A shaking head was her answer. I looked at Sasha, "Did you see the lady leave?" I didn't expect an answer, but I got a whine and she licked my hand.

As I wondered how Judy had walked away from the bench without alerting me, we returned to the jungle gym to see what the boys were up to. Doug was swinging and Ken had climbed the support pipes to the top of the swings and was doing some chin ups. When I heard "thirty," he dropped about three feet to the ground.

He grinned and asked, "Is everything okay?" I think he saw my puzzled expression.

"I don't know. I was talking to an elderly woman and when I was looking after Erica, the lady disappeared. I didn't even see her leave."

Ken said, "I meant Erica. She's all right, isn't she?"

"Oh, she'll be fine. Just a little bruise."

Erica held up her arm, "See, it's only a little bruise."

I looked at the kids and asked, "Do you want to play some more or go home?"

"Go home," replied Erica. Doug gave his usual shrug, "Yeah. Let's go. It's getting too hot."

Our tribe had only gone about twenty yards when I had a thought about Judy's disappearance.

"Ken, I want to check something at the park. I'll catch up with you in a minute." I had a mental flash that Judy had vanished behind one of the three trees we had been discussing. I had to check to see if my hunch was true.

Ken didn't seem to be interested. He mumbled, "Okay," took the leash and continued walking with the kids and Sasha.

I ran back to the park, across the grass, and stood in front of the trees. I could see behind the trunks of the tall trees where there was a hedge about four feet high, but Charles, the shorter broadleaf could be concealing a pathway. I had to push my way through the branches to investigate. In spite of using both hands to keep the branches from hitting me in the face, a small branch slapped me on the forehead and I almost tripped on the uneven ground.

That's when I saw it, a small black spider on my blouse. I hate spiders, so quickly brushed it away, continuing my push forward. Just as I thought, there was an opening in the hedge, big enough for a person to pass through. The walkway seemed to lead farther into the woods, but I wasn't prepared to follow it any farther. I had to return to my family.

I worked my way back through the branches and broke into a run across the lawn. I stopped when reaching the street and could see Ken and the kids far ahead. There was no reason to run, I would just be uncomfortable, so I began to walk, following the others nearly a city block behind. When they turned the corner, I lost sight of them and began to think about Judy's disappearance. If she had taken the path behind Charles, how did she pass behind that tree without making any noise? Erica and I weren't so far away to keep us from hearing her push through stiff branches. But maybe I was so concerned with Erica, I didn't hear anything. When I get home, I'll tell Ken all about Judy and her three husbands. I doubt if Judy's life is more interesting than Ken's police work. I wonder if he'll be interested.

The last fifty yards to the house were strange. When I turned the corner, Ken and the kids must have reached home and gone inside, but I saw a figure dressed in black at the end of the next block. I was sure it was Judy crossing the street and I wanted to run after her to see where she lived. I thought we would visit again when the opportunity presented itself. Maybe tomorrow when Ken is at work, the kids, the dog and I would pay her a visit. We could take some cookies. I hustled past my house to the corner, but by the time I got there the figure had vanished. The kids and I would take a walk this way in a day or two and perhaps we'd see her again. From the corner, I saw only one person, an overweight man in shorts and white undershirt mowing his lawn three doors away. I waited a couple of minutes, hoping to catch sight of Judy, before deciding to give up and return home.

When I got back home, Ken met me at the front door. "Where did you go? I saw you following us."

I sighed, "I need a drink."

"Isn't it a bit early for that?"

I laughed, "Not that, dear, ice water. I'm sweating."

Ken started laughing with me and Doug said, "What's so funny?" Our noise had interrupted his TV program.

Ken replied, "Oh, nothing. I thought Mom wanted a beer, but she just wanted some water."

Doug swung his head back around to the screen, "Oh." Erica had ignored our laughter; she was engrossed in the program.

Ken and I sat at the kitchen table with our ice water and he inquired, "Tell me about the witch."

"So, Erica told you about Judy. I told Erica the lady was not a witch; she was dressed in black because of the loss of her third husband. I guess I didn't explain it very well."

"Maybe we should blame it on your mother. She gave us the Hansel and Gretel book."

"It was your mother, dearest. Have you forgotten?"

"Yeah, you're right," he chuckled. "I was joking to see if you remembered. So, tell me about this so-called witch."

"Her name is Judy Morgan; husband was Charles Morgan. He was her most recent husband and was in real estate. Her first husband was…" It took me a couple of minutes to relay all the information I had gotten from Judy, at least everything I could remember.

"Do you want me to do a check on her?"

"Well, if you have the time. I'd kind of like to know about our neighbors. I doubt if you'll find anything. She's just an old lady that wanted to talk. I'm guessing she lives alone. Oh, something else. She speaks Hungarian."

"You'd better write me some notes. I won't remember all you've told me. I have to go to the department for about an hour this evening to get ready for a Monday morning meeting. I'll run a check on Mrs. Morgan when I'm there. It shouldn't take long. One more thing, how old do you think she is?"

"Gosh, I don't know. She married her first husband during the Viet Nam days. I'm thinking she was about twenty in nineteen seventy, she would be in her early seventies now, maybe a bit older. But she doesn't look a day over fifty."

"Where was she born?"

"That never came up, but I couldn't detect any accent. Maybe somewhere in the western US. I'll find out more when I see her again."

Ken arrived at the department office at 8:05 and logged on his computer, read the email about the scheduled meeting, and began preparing his suggestions for combating the influx of drugs on the streets. Timberville had recently suffered its first death from a drug overdose. Sarah Jo Turner, his senior partner, and Ken were assigned to track down the source of the heroin and try to halt the influx into the community.

Sarah had been on the force for twelve years but had been in law enforcement for eighteen. She had come to Timberville from the Spokane Washington Police Department when her husband was transferred to assist in managing the Three Sisters Wilderness. The couple had lived in Spokane but Harold worked in the northern Idaho forests. They had two children, a girl and boy, both college age and working at summer jobs to help pay tuition. Sarah's experience with her offspring led her to believe the drugs had been carried into Timberville by college students.

Ken wrapped up the information for the meeting and started to click on shutdown but remembered at the last second to see what he could find out about Judy Morgan. He brought up the website for Timberville Real Estate and entered: Morgan, Judy.

The computer returned; No item found.

Ken entered: Salmon Creek Drive and Pine.

He expected a list of all the homes to be itemized from the three block expanse of Pine Avenue. He was correct. The printed list contained twenty-three addresses, including property owners and renters. But a scan of the printout gave no Judy Morgan. Inspection of the house numbers indicated there were three possible locations where Katelin suspected Judy lived, two on the north side of the street and one on the south. Two of the three homes were unoccupied, leaving the third, the one at 333 W Pine as the only residence for Judy.

Ken checked the owner listed and found Diana Sabbat, Inc. but still nothing under Judy Morgan.

A wider search for Sabbat, Inc. gave locations in Seattle, Portland, San Francisco, and Los Angeles. A window was present that asked for a password, but Ken had no idea what to enter. He decided to try Judy Morgan and the screen went blank. There was no response to the mouse, so a reboot of the computer gave him back control. He reloaded the police department program and went home.

It was 9:30 when Ken parked in our driveway and entered through the side door into the kitchen. I sat at the kitchen table with a cup of tea reading a magazine and munching on a cookie. I glanced up as Ken picked up the last cookie and sat beside me, leaned over, and kissed my cheek. I volunteered, "The kids are already in bed. Did you get your report finished?"

"Uh-huh. Any more tea? It's the kind that lets you sleep, right?"

"Sure, I'll get you a cup." As I poured a cup of tea and warmed it in the microwave, I asked, "What did your investigation turn up about my new friend, Judy Morgan?" I was being a little presumptive about the fraternization, having just met the elderly woman and could hardly classify it as a friendship. But I am quick to make friends, especially with people from the neighborhood.

"Well, I don't think she owns her home. It belongs to a company called Diana Sabbat, Inc. They own property in the big cities on the West Coast. I believe she's a renter."

I responded to the microwave beeping, brought the cup of tea to Ken, and sat down.

"Hmm. She said her husband was in real estate. I thought she owned her home. Maybe she sold to a large west coast company."

We were in bed by eleven o'clock and in what seemed only a few minutes, I heard Ken snoring softly; I smiled and tried to relax even further. I opened one eye a few minutes later; it was 11:13. Then, I was awakened by a piercing scream, "No! Go away, go away!"

Ken and I had both heard the outcry and knew immediately it was coming from Erica. We slid from bed and were in her bedroom in five seconds. I was first in the room and flipped the light switch to see Erica kicking at her covers. "Go away, go away!" I sat beside her and gave her a shake to wake her from her bad dream. She pushed away at my arms as if fighting something, but she opened her eyes, squinting at the illumination from the overhead light.

"Wake up, Erica. You're having a bad dream." Ken was in the doorway and Doug was behind him peering into the room from the hallway. I heard Ken say, "Erica had a bad dream, go back to bed."

I held her head. "What were you dreaming, dear?"

Erica put her arms out to hug me and said, "Cats, Mommy. A bunch of black cats were trying to get me. They were everywhere, all around me. They were big and had red eyes. The cats were all bloody."

CHAPTER 3

"She's upset, Ken. Let's move her to the sofa and try to avoid a fitful night. I'll get a sheet and blanket. Wait a minute and bring her in to the living room. Hopefully, she'll go back to sleep and won't remember anything in the morning."

That didn't happen the way I had planned. As soon as Erica was lying on the sofa she asked, "Can Sasha sleep with me? She doesn't like cats."

I glanced at Ken and nodded my okay. "Get Sasha. She'll enjoy a night on the furniture."

I watched Ken, in pajama bottoms and bare feet, amble down the hallway to the nook where Sasha slept. I saw him pick up our littlest and bring her back to Erica, who moved her legs so Sasha would have room and not be pushed off the soft cushions to the floor.

Sunday night Doug had gotten the least interrupted sleep of the family members and Monday he was in a rush to get outside to ride his bike, a used twenty-six incher brush-painted a tired green by the previous owner. When we moved from Portland, Ken had grabbed the bike when the city cleaned up an encampment of homeless people. The bike had only one wheel and the tire was flat. Ken and Doug worked on the two-wheeler when we first came to Timberville, rebuilding the bicycle for their first father-son project. Doug admired new bikes wherever he saw them but had grown to love his fixer-upper, oiling the chain and keeping the tires optimally inflated.

Ken was dressed in his uniform, ate breakfast quickly, and was off to the department by seven forty-five. Doug was out the door soon after, telling me he was going to ride to the public library to check out a book about chess. He had lost several games to his father and wanted to get some tips so he could challenge his dad. Doug thought he would be gone for about an hour. As he climbed aboard, I told him I would take Sasha and Erica for a walk but we shouldn't be gone awfully long. We were going to see if we could talk with my new acquaintance, Judy Morgan. Doug called out, "Okay," as he swung his leg over the seat and peddled away.

Erica weathered her nighttime disturbance without any obvious ill effects. After eating, she was attaching Sasha's leash before I could get my shoes on. She wanted to talk with Judy to ask if the elderly woman had any pets. I wondered what Erica was thinking and as we started walking, I asked, "What did you want to ask the lady about?"

"I want to know if she has any cats."

Erica was skipping ahead of Sasha and me until we arrived at the corner.

"Which way, Mom?"

"Left. Look both ways before you go!"

We crossed the street and started down the sidewalk toward the house I thought Judy either owned or rented. A next-door neighbor sat on his front porch watching a tree service truck unloading equipment in front of the home in question.

"What are they doing, Mommy?"

"I'm not sure. Let me ask this gentleman."

Sasha almost dragged me to the man who seemed to be watching the activities with great interest. Sasha wiggled up next to him and received a back scratch and I received an inquiry, "What's your dog's name?"

"Sasha. I'm Katelin and my daughter is Erica. We came over to see Judy. Do you know if she's home?"

"Nice to meet you. I'm Ed Henry. I don't know anyone named Judy. Are you sure you have the name right?"

"Yes. I met her in the park yesterday. She said her name is Judy Morgan. What is the name of the person that lives next door?"

"Heloise Allen. I've known her for a couple of years. She's gone a lot of the time. She left last night for a flight to Vancouver. I'm watching the tree removal guys take out that front yard tree. She said it's in her way."

"Did she fly out of Eugene?"

Ed shrugged, "I guess. She doesn't drive much. Maybe Uber picked her up. I was watching TV and didn't notice."

"So, she went to Vancouver. That's not far, just across the river from Portland."

"Oh, wrong Vancouver. She was going to Vancouver, BC. It was for some kind of initiation I think. She mentioned a member of her group had recently passed and they were meeting to accept a new member, a young lady from Calgary."

"What group does she belong to?"

"I believe it's a feminist club of some sort. She was kind of secretive about it, didn't volunteer any details."

I nodded, accepting the information from Ed. I noticed Erica was holding Sasha and sitting on the lawn watching a man climbing the next door tree, a fifty foot fir that dominated the landscape for an entire block. He had a chain saw hanging from his belt. Three other trees stood in the backyard of the home on the other side of Ms. Allen's, but they were much shorter, probably less than twenty feet tall.

I joined Erica, sitting beside her when the loud saw began cutting through the timber about ten feet from the top. The saw began idling, a whistle followed, a rope was pulled, and the top of the tree cascaded through the limbs thudding to the ground. Erica's enlarged eyes looked at me and she said, "Wow!"

More ropes were hoisted up, limbs were cut and more branches fell until ten more feet of the trunk were exposed. The chain saw rapidly cut through the column and it fell with a thud, shaking the ground. Sasha jumped to her feet and pulled on the leash for fear of attack from the tree. Erica laughed and hugged the dog, calming our pooch. The remainder of the tree hadn't a chance and was soon on the ground being cut into firewood sized pieces. A woodchipper made short work of the limbs; the more massive ones were also cut to firewood size.

The entire procedure took a little more than thirty minutes. As the workers cleaned the yard and removed the stump, one of the men approached the front door and knocked. I stood and was about to call out that the owner was out of town, but I was shocked to see Judy, or I guess, Heloise, come to the door.

From behind me, I heard Ed's baritone voice, "Well I'll be. I had no idea she was back from Vancouver."

The man at Heloise's door handed her a sheet of yellow paper, turned away, and walked back to his truck. She glanced at Erica, Sasha, and me and waved before withdrawing into her house and closing the door. I decided Judy didn't want to talk with me, so I grasped Erica's hand and Sasha's leash and we started our steps toward home. As we walked, I began trying to rationalize what had occurred at Ed's front lawn. I was still in a quandary when we were back home. Heloise Allen, if that was Judy's real name, was going to be the subject of further investigation by Ken.

I had begun to look over the paper for deals on groceries but had yet to start thinking of making lunch when the doorbell rang. We had a No Soliciting sign on the front door, and we rarely had visits from neighbors, but I went to the door, curious to see who couldn't read. I opened the door, just a crack, to see who might be there and I was genuinely surprised. Heloise must have followed us home.

"May I come in to talk?"

My first impulse was to mention her lies, but I wanted to find out what she had in mind before I formed any conclusions, so I politely said, "Yes, Judy. Please come in."

Judy was dressed in a bright summer short sleeve dress with a large front pocket and wore pink sandal shoes that added about two inches to her height. She was still about two inches shorter than me at five-six. In the park I hadn't realized she was such a diminutive woman. I hadn't seen her stand before except at her front door and that was at a distance. The other thing I noticed was that she was much younger than my original impression had been. This woman was probably no more than ten years older than I, maybe in her mid-forties. Of course, I could be mistaken, she might have had plastic surgery and been using some revolutionary cosmetics. I couldn't help but smile at my inner thoughts.

"I wanted to tell you my real name, but I think my neighbor, Ed, told you I'm Heloise Allen."

I indicated she should have a seat on our sofa. Erica and Sasha moved away from us, withdrawing to the hallway. Erica was hugging the hallway wall with Sasha at her feet.

I sat at the other end of the couch and said, "Yes. I've been wondering why you told me all those things in the park. I haven't come up with an explanation."

She tittered, "I was going over my lines for my presentation at my group's meeting in Vancouver last night. We each had to give a performance at our LARP event. I went as a grieving widow who had lost her husband and two sons in the civil war. I changed the words to make it three husbands."

"LARP? I don't know what that is."

"It's an acronym for live action role playing. You've heard of cosplay?"

"Oh, yes. I've heard of that. That's wearing a costume of a comic character."

Heloise was nodding and was going to say something when we were interrupted. Doug came into the house, obviously agitated. "Mom, I just saw something terrible."

I motioned for him to approach me, but when he saw our guest, he hesitated, "Who is that?"

"Doug, this lady is Heloise. She's the lady I met in the park yesterday."

"Oh." He moved closer to me and whispered, "I have something to tell you, but I don't want Erica to hear."

I glanced at Heloise and said, "This is my son, Douglas."

Heloise stood and they shook hands. Doug was about the same height as our guest. She said, "It's nice meeting you Doug. If you have something to talk about with your mother, I'll go now. Your mother and I can talk later. I came over to tell her that one of my cats is missing, a black one named Specter. He disappeared last night."

Doug gave me a troubled look, "Can you have Erica go to her room, or maybe feed Sasha?" He pulled my shoulder down so he could whisper in my ear. "It's about a cat, Mom."

I quickly glanced at Heloise, "You'd better stay. Doug might have something important to tell you."

Doug sat beside Heloise while I guided Erica and Sasha to my daughter's bedroom. "I'll come for you in a few minutes and we'll figure out what you want for lunch." I shut Erica's bedroom door and returned to the living room. I sat beside Doug and asked, "What did you want to tell me, dear?"

"I rode my bike to the park and saw a kid about my age. His name is Jimmy Kraybill. It turns out we're in the same grade. We were just talking when these two older boys rode up and started teasing us about how ugly our bikes are, but we just laughed. Then, they said they wanted to show us something. I didn't want to go but they said I had to go with Jimmy, so we went with them to the edge of the trees and they pointed at a dead animal. They said they had killed it, but it was just a cat, not a rodent or anything bad. They said they forced a firecracker in its mouth and lit the fuse. Mom, the eyes were gone. It was really ugly and all deformed."

I was getting disturbed that Doug had been forced to view such bestiality. Heloise reached over, grasped my arm, and said, "Can I ask a question?"

I nodded, "Sure."

"Did you get the names of the boys that did this?"

"Just their first names, Dennis and Roger. I think they're about fifteen or sixteen."

Heloise was obviously disturbed; her face was reddening as she pursed her lips and frowned. "I must go now. I have things I need to take care of." She stood up and said, "I'm sorry you had to go through this bad experience, Douglas. Try to put it out of your mind. It was good of you to avoid telling your sister about this."

CHAPTER 4

I watched Heloise as she walked away from the house. She seemed to be going in the direction of the park. I wondered if she was going to check the animal body to see if it was that of her pet, Specter. From Doug's description of the mangled body, I questioned whether she would be able to identify the remains. I would have to talk to Ken about this tonight. I'm positive that there must be some regulation about animal cruelty that would apply, even to minors.

Heloise set out from the Sanders', determined to find the remains of her beloved cat. Specter was the quietest of her helpers and loved to be cuddled by Heloise after the others, Amos and Astrid, were safely in bed. Specter loved to fly; the others could take it or leave it. They were there to do their primary job, that's all: eat mice and spiders, sleep, fly on occasion, and scare people. Of course, Halloween was their favorite day, but accomplished an adequate job when called on, the rest of the year. When October arrived, Amos and Astrid began sharpening their claws and staying up later and later every night, sometimes far into the morning hours. Specter was different, he was always ready for action at a moment's notice.

No one was in the park when Heloise arrived. She walked to the far edge of the grassy region and began to search along the tree line. She heard the buzzing of flies before she saw the grisly remnants of a black cat. She waved her hands above the body and knelt to inspect the remains. It was Specter, there was no denying it, each of his front paws had a small spot of white surrounded by black fur.

She retrieved a large plastic bag from her pocket and with tears in her eyes, carefully slid Specter's body into the container. She stepped farther into the foliage holding Specter in both hands and glanced in all directions to see if anyone was watching. The surrounding area was clear, and swoosh, she left the park and was home in two seconds. Heloise entered the back door, placed her package on the floor and calmly sat beside her procedure books, disguised as a set of encyclopedias. She opened Book 1 and leafed through the pages to 'animal burials: assistants.'

Any phase of the moon was appropriate, but Saturn had to be in the southern sky and the Perseid meteors were to appear in less than a month. Everything was in order; it was mid-July and the Perseids began the second week in August. The eulogy was not complicated but the interment had to be at a depth of three feet or more, but no less. Heloise had a small empty freezer, so she placed Specter on the bottom shelf. She would bury her loyal assistant after dinner.

Near the western edge of her property, in the shade of her neighbor's trees, Heloise began digging. When the excavation was finished, she went in her house to rest until after lunch. Then she began planning her evening activities. First was to bury Specter, and then she was going to the high school to look at records to determine where Roger and Dennis lived. She knew the records office would be locked, but that was only a minor problem that would only take a short time to circumvent.

Before napping for about an hour, Heloise inserted a new battery in her telescoping wand, laid out her dark clothing, and made sure her cell phone was fully charged. Just before lying down on her sofa, she inspected her collection of brooms, one of which she would need for the evening travels. She sighted down the handles and picked the broom that possessed a slight curvature. She might need some mid-course corrections but avoiding straight-line travel might be a good tactic tonight. Besides, she was very good at stellar navigation. As a youngster, Heloise had been drilled thoroughly on the north star and positions of the planets as travel aids.

Following a low calorie evening meal of mostly vegetables, Heloise buried Specter and planted a rose bush at the top of the grave in remembrance of her favorite and affectionate associate. The eulogy was given and she sat beside the grave site recalling several significant travels she had taken with Specter. As the sun went down, Heloise went to her bedroom and changed into her nighttime gear. In order to prevent ankle-burn she wore her lace-up high-top shoes and sprayed them with low friction low reflection black paint. Before slipping into the back yard after dark, Heloise attached a GPS assembly to her short-haul travel broom. She didn't think she would need the unit, but she didn't want to be away from home unprepared.

Her preflight routine completed, she locked the back door, mounted her broom, and swooshed into the sky heading toward the high school. The building was nearly two miles away on the other side of town, but she made the excursion in a leisurely twenty seconds. She circled the buildings looking for the main office and landed on the roof of the two story building beside the roof access ladder. With her wand and her cell phone her only tools, she climbed to the ground and went to the side door that led to the parking lot.

The door had a numerical keypad for entry of a security code. Using the ultraviolet light on her telescoping wand, Heloise perceived that the 2, 6, and 7 were the numbers used to open the door. Six combinations of the numbers were possible so she began moving her wand clockwise for even numbers and the reverse for odd ones. Two circles around the pad were tried first, followed by seven circles counterclockwise, and then six clockwise. That wasn't it, so she used a second combination: seven, two, and then six after tapping the keypad with her wand. She had to tap the lock between even numbers.

Success! The lock popped open and she entered the building. Fortunately, no motion detector was activated and she found the records office without difficulty. The light from her wand was enough to navigate around tables and chairs to find locked filing cabinets. A quick look into two desk drawers turned up a set of office keys. With the keys in her hand, invoking hocus-pocus was unnecessary for complete access to students' files. Heloise reasoned that the boys, Dennis, and Roger, were not old enough to drive so were about fifteen years old and probably sophomores.

A flurry of her wand over the files divulged the needed information, Dennis Michaels and Roger Swartz had unsavory school records ever since the fourth grade. Heloise photographed the records with her cell phone, put everything back in order and exited the building. She was sure no one would be the wiser. Climbing the ladder to the roof took but a few seconds. She sat beside her broom, read through the boys' records, and found their parents' addresses.

The Swartz family resided at fifth and Elm, only four blocks from the school and at the edge of town. Heloise expected to land on their roof and listen to the sounds from within. She was sure she could distinguish the boy's voice from those of his parents'. She hoped he didn't have a sibling to complicate the issue.

It was hardly worth journeying on her broom, but Heloise decided not to waste any time. The short hop was not without danger, she almost collided with a television antenna attached to the chimney, but her broom anticipated the structure and swerved out of the way at the last second. She hovered above one of the attic vents and listened.

A female voice said, "Do you think Roger and Dennis will have any problems staying in the meadow overnight?" Heloise assumed Mrs. Swartz was talking to her husband. The male voice replied, "No. They'll be all right. They have lamps, batteries, a radio, and sleeping bags. They'll be fine. Roger will check in with us in the morning."

"Did they take our camping tent?"

Mr. Swartz added, "Yes, dear. It has mosquito netting, too. Their bikes were loaded down."

"Well, I'm going to bed to do some reading. Finish your beer, take a shower and come to bed."

"Yes, dear," he grumbled.

Heloise had heard enough. The boys were sleeping in a tent in a meadow. It probably wasn't far from town, so they should be relatively easy to find. But not wanting to ride her broom for more than a few miles, she decided to visit the home of Dennis Michaels. Perhaps she would get more accurate directions about the location of the meadow. She mounted her broom and swooshed away, rattling the TV aerial on the Swartzs' roof.

The Michaels' home was located in Hall's trailer park in Timberville's southernmost edge. A pickup truck and two motorcycles were parked next to the double wide. Heloise circled the home and guided her broom to the ground beside the truck. She was afraid landing on the flat metal roof would be heard by the inhabitants. A trailer park streetlight cast a shadow which allowed Heloise to place her ear against the wall of the illuminated room where she could hear muffled voices.

She remarked, "Good insulation," and withdrew a stethoscope from her hip pocket and listened attentively.

"The boys should have an interesting night at the National Park. I've seen the meadow and it's a nice place to camp. Get me another beer, Dora."

"Oh, wait on yourself. I already made dinner for you and did the dishes by myself."

Heloise had heard enough and quickly climbed aboard her broom, pointed it southeast and "swoosh," was flying toward the park she knew so well.

As she approached the park, collision with a large owl was narrowly avoided as she dropped below tree level. She descended farther to ride about ten feet above ground as she combed the area at slow speed looking for a tent. The meadow extended over several acres including a small hill and a nearly dry creek. The grass had recently been mowed. Heloise glided over the mower and noticed two bicycles. She stopped for a moment and let the air out of the bicycle tires, then resumed her search.

She noticed a dark form at the top of the hill, but it was two cows huddled together, disguised as a tent. She laughed and continued on. Following the creek bed, she soon discovered the boys' tent. It was pitched on the western bank of the creek next to a barbeque pit. They were sitting in collapsible lawn chairs drinking beer, laughing at something, probably a dirty joke.

Heloise slowly circled at thirty yards, planning her assault. She would swoop over the boys, close enough to attract attention, but too rapidly for them to detect her form. Just as one of the boys tossed an empty can she swooshed by and grabbed the object from the air. She circled back and dropped to the ground out of sight behind the tent to listen.

"What the hell was that?"

"I felt the air blow by. It must have been an owl."

"Why would an owl grab a beer can out of the air, Rodge?"

Roger laughed, "Maybe it wants the ten cent refund."

"Yeah, sure. Tell me another one."

Heloise backed away from the camp, stomped on the beer can until it was flat, and took to the air. She flew at the boys, dropped the crushed can between them, and hid behind the tent as before.

"Hey! Somebody's screwing with us." The boys stood and began looking around the camp site for a jokester. One of the boys said, "Get a flashlight!" Heloise disappeared with a swoosh that shook the canvas sides of the tent.

She landed behind a bush hidden from the beam of light the boys guided around their camp. After a few minutes of searching close to their tent, they went inside, apparently preparing to go to bed. Heloise crept closer to hear what was being said.

"Hey, Rodge, what if your brother is fooling around with a drone? He might have one of those things from the air force. What d'ya think?"

"Nah. George just signed up. They wouldn't let him use anything like that. He's just a peon. It must have been some kind of bird. Ya know, some animals like shiny objects. Maybe it took that can, exchanged it for one that was smashed, and brought back the crumpled one."

"Yah. Maybe you're right."

CHAPTER 5

Heloise was ready for the next phase. She set the volume on her cell phone as high as it would go, selected a recording of Specter's screaming meow, and hovered over the tent. When she pressed play, she grinned at the expectations and darted out of sight when the sound ended. She watched as the boys exited the tent searching the sky. She heard one of the boys scream, "We shouldn't have killed that cat, Rodge. It's come back to haunt us!"

"Get a grip, Den. There's no ghost of a cat. Someone is messing with us."

"I'm not gonna be able to sleep. I'm goin' home."

"Well, damn, I'm not staying out here by myself. We can come back in the morning and get our stuff."

"Yeah, let's get outta here."

Heloise watched as the boys used a flashlight to illuminate the way to their bikes. She rode her broom, keeping at a safe distance, but close enough to hear what they were saying.

First on his two wheeler, Roger quickly realized his tires were flat.

"Damn! There's no air in my tires."

"Same here, dammit! Someone's out to get us, Rodge."

"We've got pumps. It'll only take a few minutes to reinflate them unless they're punctured."

The boys fumbled with tool containers hanging from their bike seats and extracted hand pumps. Both boys began to pump air into their tires as Heloise thought about her next move. When the boys had their tires inflated and were storing the pumps, she knew what she was going to do, an air strike as the riders left the meadow. She readied her phone for the hoot of an owl.

She gave the boys a chance to get on their bikes and ride about fifty yards before she began the first strafing run. Heloise followed about ten feet above Roger and Dennis, but about ten yards behind. Heloise increased her speed dramatically and caught up, striking Dennis in the head with a grazing blow from her broom. As she swept by, she played the owl sound.

"I just got hit in the head by an owl. Better keep your bean down, Rodge."

"Not funny, Den."

"I'm not jokin'. Something just hit me in the head. Didn't you hear a noise?"

"Yeah, I heard you make a sound kind of like a bird, maybe a fart."

"It wasn't me! What do I have to show you, bird crap in my hair?"

Heloise decided to give the same treatment to Roger, so she made a second pass, brushing his hair with the straw of her broom.

Roger looked to Dennis on his left side. "Hey, quit throwing stuff at me. You're messing with my hair."

"I didn't do a damn thing. Maybe you'll believe me now. It's gotta be a bird, a big one."

Heloise had one remaining trial for the boys. She followed for another fifty yards, snapped her fingers, leaned forward on her broom, and sped past the bike riders a few feet above their heads. The wind created by her passing caused the boys to lose control of their bikes and collide. She circled the wreckage to make sure an ambulance wasn't needed, saw that the boys were only scratched up and some minor bleeding. She left the collision site and returned home.

Heloise stored her broom in her hall closet and commented, "I'm glad I took the one with the curved handle. Circling around in that meadow was easy." After getting ready for bed, she prepared a cup of tea, sat at her kitchen table, and recorded the evening's activities in her logbook. As Heloise climbed into bed, she looked at her favorite picture of Specter on her nightstand, smiled, snapped her fingers to turn out the light, and went to sleep.

Just as Ken was leaving the house after breakfast Tuesday morning, the phone rang. I answered it and caught Ken before he was out the door. It was Police Chief Watters.

I gave Ken the phone and whispered, "It's your boss."

Ken pressed the speaker phone button so I could hear what Watters was saying.

"Yes, Chief, what is it?"

"I got a couple of calls this morning from Mrs. Michaels and Mrs. Swartz. Apparently, something attacked the boys in the park last night. The boys think it was a bird. I'd like you to interview them on the way to the office. The women and the boys are at the Swartzs'."

"Okay. I'll head right over there now. Is that all?"

"Yeah. See me when you check in."

"Ten-four." Ken hung up and looked at me quizzically, "I wonder what that's all about. Why would a bird attack those boys? Maybe they were poking around in a bird's nest and broke some eggs."

I shook my head. "I'm not familiar with those families. I wonder if they have some impressionable children."

Doug had been listening and laughed, "I don't think Big Bird can fly, Dad."

"I think those boys must have watched a scary movie and had a bad dream. I'll talk with them and see what happened. See you for lunch."

"Okay. I hope you can give us all the details of the bird attack. I hope we're not having birds gathering to attack people—like in that Alfred Hitchcock movie we saw the other night. Bye."

I watched Ken climb in his cruiser, wave, and drive down the street heading for the bird investigation.

Ken arrived at home for lunch a few minutes after twelve noon. Erica and Doug were helping me make some sandwiches and I had just given Doug some carrots to peel. He finished one of the carrots and was holding it like a missile on a launch pad. Ken was watching as Doug said, "This is Mission Control. Five seconds to lunch!"

Ken and I laughed as Doug raised the carrot off the counter making a rocket noise.

"How'd that interview go with the mothers?" I was curious about Chief Watters' early call.

Ken laughed, "Whatever it was they imagined, it really scared them. They must have been doing something stupid and wanted to conceal whatever it was with a wild story. They thought they heard a cat, and then an owl. They wrecked their bikes when an owl attacked. They had scrapes and scratches to prove it. I think someone ran them off when they tried to steal something."

"How old are the boys?" I asked.

"They're about fifteen, Dennis and Roger."

Doug stopped peeling and said, "Hey. those are the guys who killed that cat."

"They did what?" Ken asked Doug.

Doug saw that Erica was listening, so he motioned to me to talk to Ken and went into the other room with Erica.

I motioned for Ken to come close so Erica wouldn't hear about the cat killing. Doug had kept it to himself, not telling Erica about it. I related what Doug had seen when the older boys forced the two younger boys to observe the body of the executed feline.

Ken stepped back, frowning, "When did you find out about that?"

"Yesterday morning. I didn't think to tell you."

"I wish I had known that when I talked with the boys this morning. I'm sure their mothers didn't know anything about it."

"What did the mothers have to say?"

"They wanted me to check out the meadow area where the boys camped to see if there was evidence of other people picking on the boys."

"Find anything?"

"Nope. The tent was there and undisturbed. I couldn't see any footprints except those of the boys. I asked Sarah if she had experienced anything similar to what the boys described, but she said no. She figured like we did, the boys were covering for something else, but why would they bring up the bird attacks at all if they were covering for some stupid activity?"

Ken sat down, picked up a carrot stick, and bit off a chunk. I smiled when I saw his Adam's apple wiggle when he swallowed. I said, "Heloise was here when Doug told me about the cat. She left in a hurry, walking toward the park."

Ken stopped chewing, "You think she had something to do with the attack?"

I had to laugh, "No, but maybe it was her cat, back from the dead."

Ken nodded as he thought, "Well, I'll drop by her place after lunch and see if she knows anything."

"We'll all go. I want to ask Heloise if she can watch the kids on Thursday afternoon while I'm at the dentist."

We enjoyed a leisurely lunch and cleaned up the kitchen by one o'clock. Ken had the kids in the cage in the back seat and I rode shotgun to Heloise's place, less than two blocks away. As we pulled up in front of the house, I watched three women on the porch, starting to enter the front door. Although I couldn't see their faces, I was certain Heloise had entered last. She was holding the screen door open and turned to look at Ken's cruiser as he shut off the engine.

I got out waving at Heloise and she came out on the porch. She was smiling, apparently happy to see me. Ken had to open the rear doors of the car from the outside. Detainees had no way to egress from the back seat.

Heloise stepped from the porch and we met halfway to her home. She was the first to speak, "Hello, Katelin. I see you are with your entire family, except for your little dog."

"Yes. My husband wants to ask you a question and I have one also." Ken stepped beside me and said, "I'm Ken Sanders, Katelin's husband." They shook hands and Heloise commented, "It's nice meeting you. Katelin told me you are a member of the police force. Do you have something official to inquire about?"

"Katelin told me some boys might have killed one of your pets. What can you tell me about that?"

"One of my cats, Specter, strayed from here several days ago and I found his body at the park. I buried him in the back yard. I don't know who was responsible."

"We received a curious call at the station this morning. It seems two teenage boys were attacked by an owl last night at their campsite. Would you know anything about that?"

"No, but I know about owls. They will attack a person if he or she gets too close to their nest. They can hit very hard when they strike."

Ken nodded, "So it's not unusual, even at night?"

Heloise replied, "That's when they're hunting rodents and such. Maybe the boys disturbed an owl when it was hunting. Maybe they threw something at it."

"Yeah, you're probably right. Thanks for the information. I'd better get back to my regular patrol. It was nice meeting you."

"Likewise, Officer."

Ken turned to me and kissed me on the cheek. "I'll see you and the kids later, about six."

We watched him get in the cruiser, wave, and pull away from the curb.

"You had a question for me?" Heloise asked.

"Oh, yes. I almost forgot why I came along with Ken." I motioned for the kids to join Heloise and me while they walked from where Ken had parked to where we were standing. I put my right arm around Doug and my left around Erica and said, "I have a dental appointment on Thursday and wondered if you could look after these guys for about two hours." I glanced at Heloise and grinned, "I can pay you."

"Oh, my, that wouldn't be necessary. But, unfortunately, I have some other duties to perform on Thursday afternoon. However, I have another idea. Come in the house with me. I have someone in mind that might help you."

We followed Heloise to the porch and she ushered us into her living room where two women were seated on a large sofa. They stood as we approached. The older of the two appeared to be about Heloise's age and the other was much younger, I guessed a teenager.

Heloise introduced us and we all took seats. Doug, Erica, and I sat on a love seat, and the three women on the sofa, the youngster in the middle. Athena Hazelton was sixteen and liked the name Aty, instead of Athena, the Greek goddess of wisdom. She admitted that she still had much to learn and was certainly not a fountain of wisdom.

Her mother, Hedda Hazleton, had accompanied Aty to Timberville to enroll her daughter in a week-long summer camp for teen girls. Samantha Simms and Heloise were cosponsors of the event.

I was not aware of the gathering and said, "When does the camp begin? I would like to help if at all possible."

I watched as Hedda gave Heloise an uncertain look. Heloise commented, "Thank you for the offer, but the other mothers will be contributing just about all the help we'll need." Heloise glanced at Aty and asked, "Would you like to watch after Doug and Erica for a couple of hours on Thursday?"

Aty's face beamed with a big smile, "Sure. That would be fun. Camp doesn't start until Saturday. That would give me something to do rather than sitting around waiting." She looked at her mother and then Heloise, "I've almost finished with the encyclopedia. I'm tired of reading."

I thought for a few moments and replied, "I think it would be all right. Come over about a quarter to one. I should be home before three o'clock. I'll pay you ten dollars an hour, if that's okay with you and your mother."

Hedda responded, "That's more than generous, Katelin. Half that amount would be more appropriate."

Aty sighed in dismay, "Mother!"

CHAPTER 6

The Pinecone B&B and The Bear and Bark Motel gradually filled up and had reached capacity by late Friday afternoon. No one had cancelled their registration for the five day camp. Following dinner, Samantha and Heloise were examining the sign-in cards filled out by the girls and their mothers. Hedda was checking the totals and reviewing the completed forms.

"Perfect, Heloise. Ten mature women and ten novices. The young ladies are from sixteen to eighteen years old. Ursula Moberg brought her twins, Jean, and Joan, just like she promised. Joan is the more independent and she will be assigned to you."

"Good, did they bring their flight equipment as requested?"

"Yes. Each team indicates the presence of at least two flight sticks, uniforms, and a GPS unit. Looks like we are all set for a productive week," Hedda nodded and remarked as she scanned the colored sign-up forms. "Looks like all have flight boots."

"Thanks for the help, you're a time saver. We'd better get to bed; tomorrow will be a long day. We have to travel at least thirty miles to get to the Three Sisters Wilderness area."

Hedda commented, "It will be dark when we leave Timberville, do you anticipate having any problems?"

"Not really, but our caravan might attract some attention. I hope all our vehicles are in good repair. Everyone knows how to change flat tires. That's the only breakdown I foresee." Heloise stood and walked toward her bedroom. "Good night, Hedda. I hope Aty is in good spirits at four o'clock."

"Aty's an early riser. Night, Heloise."

Two hours before sunrise, nine vehicles started toward the Wilderness area. The string of five SUVs, three pickups, and a single jeep extended for a quarter mile as they entered the Willamette National Forest, snaking their way along little used roads to the Homestead park and campground. Headlights reflecting from sets of eyes caught deer and smaller animals moving along or crossing the forest roads.

Everyone wore jeans plus sweatshirts or jackets even though the vehicle's heaters warmed the ten women and their novice companions. The caravan stopped for leg stretching at the park where few patrons were present. The women gathered at one of the bathroom buildings and Heloise heard utters of hunger coming from the girls. The older women decided to use the camp site fire pits and cook breakfast for all. As soon as the mothers began preparations for breakfast, the youngsters began to volunteer their talents and in short order, breakfast was over and the caravan had resumed driving farther east.

Following circuitous roads, French Pete Creek and then Horse Creek were crossed. When the women were within six miles of the Three Sisters mountains, Hedda and Heloise decided they had gone far enough into the wilderness. The ladies circled their vehicles like covered wagons had done in the past and established a base camp in a relatively flat area near a small unnamed creek.

Prearranged groups set out to collect firewood, firepit rocks, and a location for the two porta potties that had been towed in trailers. One group of three girls removed trash and forest debris from the area. As the camp began taking shape, the members ate sandwiches and began considering topics to be covered in the afternoon activities. Jolene Arnot, a high school physics teacher, had prepared a lecture on centrifugal force.

The ten girls gathered around Jolene and sat on blankets laid out by the older women. When all were seated, Jolene began her talk. As she spoke, she began to see some looks of confusion on the girls' faces, especially the more immature.

"All right, I'll show you what I mean." She walked quickly to her SUV and pulled a long handled broom from the cargo area. She returned to the group and said, "We don't call this a broom, it is a long flight stick." She smiled, "We must not say wrong things in the presence of people that don't know us."

Some murmuring occurred from a few of the girls.

"One last question before I demonstrate. How many of you can ride a bicycle?"

There was a unanimous show of hands.

"When you make a sharp turn, you lean in that direction, right?"

All the girls agreed.

"Okay. Becky, please join me." Jolene's daughter tittered and stood beside her mother. Jolene swung her right leg over the broom handle and said, "Get on behind me, lean forward and hold on."

The broom rose vertically into the air to a height of ten feet and slowly flew from right to left over the circle of vehicles. Jolene called out, "Now I will increase our speed. Watch for the orientation of our bodies as we pick up speed."

The demonstration lasted for less than a minute before the mother and daughter returned to the ground after a brief hovering maneuver.

"Now for a very important item. You must learn to communicate with your flight stick. I can only compare flying your broom to riding a horse; slight pressure with your legs, mostly with your knees, will allow you to change direction. You will increase speed by your forward lean. But much of flying is mental, your flight log will learn from you also. You must practice to gain experience, much like playing a musical instrument."

One of the girls, Lois Langdon, overflowing with enthusiasm, asked, "When do we start?"

"Right now. Get the short stick from your vehicle and begin by practicing to hover. It might take several tries before you can rise above the ground. Don't expect immediate results. Those of us with experience will be watching and giving tips. Try not to get frustrated."

The ten older women and their charges positioned themselves around the outside of the vehicles to ensure there was adequate room for trials and failures, but no accidental collisions. They were too far from emergency medical help but, if necessary, they were prepared for first aid treatment.

Evelyn Simms and her mother, Samantha, were stationed adjacent to Heloise and Joan. Heloise leaned against the nearest vehicle, a red pickup, and watched as Joan and Evelyn began their initial attempts to rise a few feet above the ground. Both girls tried and tried with no success. After about five frustrating minutes of what seemed to the girls, extreme effort, Heloise motioned to Samantha, "Hold on for a moment. Let me suggest something."

Joan looked at Evelyn. They both shrugged their shoulders and stood beside each other holding their brooms like they had been interrupted when sweeping the floor. Joan saw her sister's torso rise above one of the cars. "Oh! Look! Jean's getting it!"

Heloise motioned for the girls to come closer. "I'd like you to try something. Hold your broom tightly against your stomach with the handle touching your forehead. Now, close your eyes and think of being in an elevator. You are on the first floor and you want to go to the second. Think of pressing the button for floor two. Don't reach for it! Concentrate! Let your mind do the work."

Samantha spoke, "You have to realize, these are not ordinary brooms. They have to get used to your thoughts, kind of like extrasensory perception, ESP. They know when you have gained confidence in your abilities."

Heloise said, "That's right. They will fly with you when you have become one with your flight stick."

"Exactly! Don't try to hover yet. Walk around the camp site with your broom for about ten minutes thinking of flying. Let your broom become acquainted with your thoughts. Then return to us and try again."

Evelyn and Joan came running back to Samantha and Heloise, excited to try the hovering procedure again. During their walk they had seen three of the other girls celebrating limited progress and had picked up more tips on flying. They decided to work side by side so they could immediately share successful flying details.

The girls were ready. Samantha said, "Okay, girls, clear your mind of all thoughts except hovering. Ready, set, hover."

A few seconds passed, no more than four or five, and Joan began to rise, as did Evelyn, but Joan's broom handle was pointing toward the ground and Evelyn's broom was pointing up, the sweeping bristles making ground contact.

Heloise instructed, "Evelyn, move forward a couple of inches; Joan, scoot back a little."

The girls made quick adjustments and both were suddenly airborne, hovering shoulder high. They both called out, "It's working, I'm doing it!"

Heloise coached, "When I tell you, lean forward slightly and use your right knee to tell your broom to circle to the right."

Samantha warned, "Don't lean too far or you'll go too fast and risk falling off."

"All right, lean and hang on tight. You're going to move slowly."

With their teachers walking beside them, the girls completed a circle successfully. Joan, gaining confidence decided to speed up and nearly fell from her broom when she doubled her speed. She hadn't learned to lean correctly to counter centrifugal force. Nearly falling, she completed the circle hanging white knuckled and inverted from her broom and turning to the left.

Heloise came to Joan's rescue, helping her to the ground. She admonished her, "You tried to maneuver without proper direction or sufficient experience. Please wait for us to give you more instruction before setting off on your own. Unsupervised flying at this point in your lessons can be dangerous."

Joan smiled, "Yes, I came back upside-down a minute ago."

Evelyn laughed, "Stick to the basics, Joan. Remember, we're just beginners."

"Okay. I've learned my lesson. Practice makes perfect."

Evelyn smiled, "No, practice so you don't kill yourself. We've got two or three more days of working with the short flight stick and then we'll try the two-seater. That's gonna be interesting."

Joan whispered, "Aren't you interested in those robes? They look kind of like something we might wear at graduation."

Evelyn grinned and spoke softly, almost in a whisper, "Maybe that's what they're for."

Heloise commented, "It's about time for lunch. Let's break for now and we'll take up something new after we eat. Place your brooms in the back of my vehicle. Always remember where you leave your flight stick. If a difficult situation arises, it might be life or death if you misplace it. Your broom can't come searching for you."

As the two older women set out for the vehicle designated as the chow wagon, they began a discussion of their progress with Joan and Evelyn.

Heloise was looking around the camp site for any mishaps. She didn't see anyone in trouble. "I'm pleased that Joan has begun to experiment, but she hasn't had enough flying time experience to anticipate the results of her actions. What do you think about Evelyn's progress?"

"Well, I remember when I was learning and was too restrained to try anything new without asking for assistance. Evelyn is not as passive as I was. She's going to be a fine flyer." They took a few more steps before Samantha continued, "Joan's mother will be asking about her daughter's progress. I'll back you up. We can ask her about Jean's development to change the subject if necessary."

"Good idea, Sam."

CHAPTER 7

Leeray Brown, Jeff Wheldine, and Barry Nexly had been travelling north along US 97 since passing through Weed, California. They had been having trouble with their 1993 Ford pickup, a small red preowned vehicle Jeff had practically stolen from a used car lot in Weed. He hadn't literally 'stolen' the dented, faded stick shift. He test drove it around the car lot and discovered the clutch was about to give out, but Jeff thought there was enough life in it to get them to Eugene, Oregon. The dealer wanted $495 for it, but Jeff offered him $250 and the guy took it. A tank of gas was included.

Jeff had been favoring the clutch as they made their way north. On Monday noon, they made a left at Diamond Lake Junction onto state highway 138. They had stopped for lunch and changed drivers. Barry had only driven a mile or so when the clutch stopped functioning.

Leeray called out, "Better pull over, the sign says the mountain pass is 5,925 feet. We won't be able to make it."

Jeff added, "He's right, we've gotta climb 1,300 feet, but not in this chariot to hell."

The three college-age men got out of the cab and leaned against the truck bed watching the traffic pass by. Leeray suddenly turned to Jeff. "Could we pay somebody to push us up the hill?"

Jeff started unfolding an Oregon map, "Then what, coast down the other side?"

Barry was pointing at the map unfolded on the hood of the truck, "Yeah. Look, we coast down to the Pacific Crest Trail and hike to state route 242. We can thumb a ride to Eugene, sell the weed and split up, unless you want to make another fun trip from Mexico with me."

"If this little venture generates four grand each, I'll think about repeating the trip, but not hiking through the mountains," said Leeray. "How far do we have to hoof it?"

Jeff shook his head, "Christ, I don't know. Let me look at the map." Jeff bent over the chart, measuring with his fingers, and glanced at the legend. About a minute later, he said, "I figure it's about sixty-five miles."

"You're shittin' me!" Leeray's irritation with the idea was beginning to show. "Hell, I've never even walked for more than a couple of miles in a day, and that was on flat land, on concrete. How far can we hike in the mountains in a day?"

"We'll be following a trail, Brown. You're a tough dude, you'll have to suck it up." Barry continued, "You and I will go back to the junction and get some things for the hike. Jeff will stay here with the truck in case a cop comes by to see if he can give him assistance."

"What if a cop searches the backpacks?"

"I guess we're screwed. Jesus, you worry too much. Nobody will search us out here in the boondocks." Barry looked up and down the highway. "Have you seen any cops in the last fifty miles?"

"No."

"There you go. Let's walk back to that market and get some stuff for our hike." Barry started walking, stopped and looked back at Leeray who was standing beside the pickup, "Come on, it should only take us about an hour. Maybe we can bum a ride."

Leeray said, "Oh, what the hell." He took a few quick strides and caught up with Barry. Jeff sat on the running board and watched his pals cross the road and begin walking toward the junction.

Barry and Leeray hadn't gone more than a few hundred yards before they were picked up by a trucker hauling groceries to the market at Diamond Lake Junction. Leeray was elated with their good luck and started a conversation with the trucker, Dan Wilkes, a tough looking forty-five year old with enormous biceps.

"What're you delivering to the market?"

"All kinds of goods, but mostly vegetables and twenty-four loaves of bread. Take a look at the bill of lading if you want. It's on that clipboard, on the dash, the yellow sheet."

Leeray picked up the clipboard and scanned the list. "Look, Barry," pointing at bottled water and cheese, "we'll need some of these for our hike."

Dan laughed, "If you're gonna go on the Crest Trail, you're goin' in the wrong direction. It's back thataway." With his left hand steering, he motioned behind himself with his right thumb.

Barry said, "Yeah, we know. We're goin' to the market to buy some stuff for the hike. Our buddy is waitin' at our pickup."

The truck rolled into the back of the market to unload. Leeray and Barry thanked Dan for the ride and walked to the front of the roadside business. They entered through automatic doors and Leeray grabbed a cart, pushing it toward the back of the shopping area where dairy products were located. Barry disappeared down an aisle and returned to the cart tossing two loaves of bread in the top basket with the two-pound package of cheese and a dozen eggs Leeray had pulled off the shelves. A jar of mayonnaise and a package of eighteen bottles of water were added, half filling the basket. A large bottle of peanut butter and a family size package of cookies were added and Barry tossed in a package of plastic utensils. They headed to the checkout counter as Leeray retrieved a credit card from his wallet.

The checkout clerk, a fairly young blonde lady smiled, saying, "Paper or plastic, five cents each."

Barry stated, "Plastic."

Leeray whispered, "We forgot asswipe."

Barry replied, "I've got that covered."

The credit card purchase was approved. Leeray sighed, knowing it neared the limit. They picked up the three full sacks and left the store.

Barry had expected Leeray to complain, but not so soon. Only ten yards from the store, Leeray whined, "I've got two heavy bags, you've got one light one."

Barry motioned toward the motel with a nod of his head, "Follow me."

At the end of the motel rental rooms close to the market was a bench. Barry placed his bag on the bench and said, "Sit here with our stuff, I'll be right back." Leeray put the heavier of his bags on the ground and set the other bag on the bench and sat down. He watched Barry disappear behind the building, then focused on the highway and watched the traffic coming down the hill from the Crest Trail direction. A couple of minutes later, boredom caused him to begin searching for the package of cookies.

Just as he was thinking of opening the package, Barry reappeared pulling a two-wheeled golf cart with a bag strapped to it. "Where'd you find that?" Leeray asked, letting the cookies slip back into the grocery bag.

"Made a dumpster dive. Take a look inside the bag."

Leeray commented, "It's full of golf balls?" He stood and looked into the golfclub bag. What he saw caused him to laugh. "Where'd you get four rolls of asswipe?"

"There was a girl emptying waste baskets from motel rooms and I swiped those from her cart. She caught me and I gave her a dollar. She seemed happy to get the money."

"Yeah, I'll bet you made her day." Leeray sat down again and said, "There's not enough room in that bag for all our stuff. We need another cart."

Barry replied, "Nah, we'll put the heaviest items in the golf bag and put the lighter items in plastic sacks. We can carry those. We'll take turns pulling the cart."

"Sounds okay by me. Let's repack and start back to the truck. Jeff will think we left him if we don't get back pretty soon." Leeray extracted the toilet paper from the golf bag and set the rolls on the bench. A few minutes later they set off at the side of the highway walking toward Jeff and the out of commission truck.

It took them half an hour to get back, passenger cars and a few trucks passed, usually honking and passengers waving, but oncoming traffic ignored them. Jeff saw them approaching, climbed into the truck bed, and waved. A few approaching cars slowed, thinking he needed assistance, but he waved them on. The first thing he said when Leeray and Barry were close enough to hear was, "Where'd you steal the golf cart?"

Barry replied, "We stopped at the golf course and had a few before we came back. One of the guys took pity on us and gave us his cart. He wanted the clubs."

Leeray jokingly added, "That dumpster had a lot of good stuff in it. Most of the food we got was free. It was only a week past the expiration date."

"Yeah, both of you are full of shit." Jeff laughed and jumped down from the back of the truck and grabbed his backpack from the bed. He tossed the other packs to their owners and waited for them to distribute the extra weight. He grasped the cart handle and started walking up the hill away from the pickup. Leeray and Barry followed carrying the plastic bags.

The trio had walked for about a half hour when Leeray stopped and asked, "How much farther, Barry? Seems like we've been walking all morning."

"It's eight miles from the junction to the Crest Trail. So, I figure we've got about six more miles to go; that's about two hours for Jeff and me," he grinned, "two and a half for you."

"Thanks, asshole."

"Hey, don't get mad, that's just the way things are. Jeff and I won't leave you."

Every twenty minutes or so, the guys traded off pulling the golf cart. As Leeray walked, he decided to keep his mouth shut and not complain again. They were walking single file and had little to say to each other, except telling some dirty jokes. For the first three miles, no one offered to give them a ride, but when they stopped alongside the road to eat, a flatbed truck pulled over. The woman driver climbed from the cab and said, "I'll give you boys a ride if you'll help me unload."

Laura looked to be in her fifties, wore gray work pants and a long sleeve pink shirt. Her grey hair was cut short and covered with an LA Dodgers baseball cap. Leeray glanced at the material on the truck bed and immediately said, "Sure, but we're only going to the trail." Jeff shielded his eyes and squinted at Barry; they each nodded.

She replied, "That's fine with me. I have to drop this load at a cabin nearby the trail."

The truck was piled high. About three cords of split firewood took nearly thirty minutes to unload. Jeff thanked Laura for the ride and she expressed gratitude for the boys' help in emptying her truck. She turned back on to highway 138 and drove off over the hill as the trio filled out the hiking registration for the Crest Trail.

Before the guys filled out the form, Barry looked over the information requested and talked with Jeff and Leeray. "Don't use your real names and put down that you expect to spend about a week on the trail."

Leeray was first to sign the log and discovered that taking any apparatus with wheels was illegal. They would have to give up the golf cart. He signed the register at the kiosk and stepped away to talk with Jeff and Barry.

"We have to give up the cart. How are we gonna carry all our shit?"

"You're sure about that?" Jeff inquired.

"Go sign in, you'll see."

Jeff and Barry registered and returned to the bench where Leeray was sitting.

Jeff said, "Okay, we lose the cart. We need to get a couple more back packs and a pole about six feet long. There's a note advertising hiking equipment at Jen's Retreat. Have you seen any signs?"

Barry answered, "I think that's where we unloaded the firewood. That old woman's name is Jeniece."

"Let's head over there and see what we can buy from her." Jeff started toward the large ranch house where they had been a short time ago; Barry and Leeray followed.

It wasn't obvious that Jen's Retreat was an establishment for hiking supplies, it looked more like a bed and breakfast site for weary travelers. Without the notice at the kiosk, a hiker would never have known of Jen's, unless alerted by one of the locals.

Ten minutes after entering the retreat, the three hikers had purchased two large backpacks and a nearly six-foot long pole which had been salvaged from a broken garden hoe. Jen charged a dollar for the pole and twenty bucks for the two packs. The guys were relieved to get out of the little store and start repacking their food and equipment.

Leeray watched as Jeff and Barry put all the weighty items in the new backpacks. He finally asked, "So who's gonna carry those heavy bags?"

"Two of us will haul them on that pole. We'll carry it on our shoulders. Barry and I will take the first hour's shift. After thirty minutes, you'll take over for one of us. When a person puts in an hour, he gets spelled. I'm figuring we will be able to travel about two miles per hour. Let's try to get about four miles before we stop to eat and relax. Tomorrow will be a full travel day, sixteen miles or more."

Leeray said, "Sounds like a damned safari to me. I'll lead and you guys will be my porters."

Barry looked at Jeff and grinned, "Don't sweat it, nobody will see us."

Leeray suggested, "Hey, why not buy a horse or a mule?"

"Jesus, Leeray, we'd have to feed and water a horse." Jeff shook his head, starting to lose patience.

"Well, how about a camel?" Leeray grinned.

Barry replied, "Enough joking. Just shut up."

CHAPTER 8

Tuesday morning, the camp near the Three Sisters was active with excitement. The young women had risen when the sun came up and had bathed in a nearby creek. In spite of the immersion in cold water, the girls cooperated, especially after their elders insisted it was a requirement to be admitted to the sisterhood, much like a baptism.

After drying their bodies and hair with plush bath towels, they donned clean clothes, but skipped applying makeup. Following breakfast, they spent fifteen minutes reviewing Monday's training, before gathering for a lecture concerning flight below treetop level. The trainees received particular attention to acceleration on takeoff and deceleration when landing, both processes requiring hovering expertise.

The girls and their mentors moved away from camp seeking more space for practicing new and more acrobatic flying than Monday's hovering and leaning techniques. The girls required more airspace in order to prevent mishaps, primarily accidental midair collisions. Subsequent to three hours of intensive drill, the group paused for lunch.

Heloise polled the instructors while everyone ate and after noticing all the women were jabbering about the enjoyment they were having at the camp, she announced, "We are going to do something a little different this afternoon. We are going to have a competition. Joan and

Evelyn are team captains. They will choose their teams, each selecting four novices and four elders."

One of the girls, Cindy Logan, called out, "Ms. Heloise, what is the game?"

Jean Moberg yelled, "It's got to be baseball, nine on a team!"

Heloise said, "You're partly right, Jean, it's called Wickonball; it's similar to softball but with a few exceptions. You can probably guess the differences, you must fly to the bases, and any hit to the outfield requires the fielder to fly to get the ball and return it to the infield. The ball can only be thrown in the infield."

Joan started laughing, "This should be fun. Let's mark off the bases and get started. My team will be first on defense."

Heloise walked to her SUV and brought back a bat and ball. Samantha got a tape measure and catcher's mask from her duffel bag and began pacing off the distances between bases and home plate.

The temporary bases were marked with used paper plates from lunch.

Mimi Preston, the tiniest of all the girls at barely five feet tall, came running to Samantha, "Can I help, Ms. Samantha?"

"Sure. I'll hold the end of the tape and you can walk out to…" Samantha gave Mimi a questioning look.

"I know, sixty feet. My father was a coach and I used to help him mark the bases on the practice field."

Samantha responded, "Great! This should only take a few minutes and we'll get underway. I believe we'll have some fun, a lot of laughs."

Heloise and Samantha were coach and umpire, primarily to enforce the rules of the new game. Heloise knew that rules would probably have to be made up as the game was played. She gathered the defensive players and explained, "Everyone has to play on the infield until a ball goes into the outfield. Only one of the three fielders can pursue the ball on their broom and carry it back. You'll have to take turns. No throwing the ball until it's back in the infield."

She swiveled her head around observing the excited looks displayed on her team's faces. "Got it?"

There was a chorus of "yeses" and the team took the field. Joan was pitching and Mimi was catching for the Owls. The opposing team, first at bat, was the Ravens. Joan appointed two novices and a mentor as outfielders and reminded them to carry their brooms until needed. "Better hold your brooms vertically when in the infield so no one trips."

The game proceeded with no score after three innings and the novices seemed to be losing interest. Samantha and Heloise put their heads together and announced, "Anyone on base at the end of an inning will be there the next time their team bats. They can only get off by scoring."

Two innings later, the score was Owls: 2, Ravens: 3. The excitement had returned to the game. At the end of the sixth period, the score was tied and both teams were worn out. Heloise called an end to the game and gathered the players.

"I want you all to rest for the remainder of the afternoon. Following our evening meal, the novices will take their first nighttime flight. You won't be going far from camp because you will lose your way without landmarks. I don't want you to lose sight of the campfire. Make sure to wear bright clothes, preferably white, so we can spot you in the moonlight."

Jeff, Barry, and Leeray ate a late lunch and continued making slow progress on the trail primarily because of the irregular rocky terrain. Jeff and Leeray were carrying the pole on their shoulders when Leeray stumbled and fell, scraping his left shin against a jagged volcanic rock.

As he sat on the ground lifting his pant leg to expose his injury, "God damn rock tried to trip me!" He chuckled and asked, "Have we got any antibiotics?"

Jeff crouched beside Leeray and commented, "Yeah, I've got a small tube of Neosporin in my backpack. Wash off the blood and dry your leg." He handed Leeray a half-filled water bottle and began to search through his backpack. Pulling a roll of toilet paper from his pack and checking inside it was time wasted. He felt around and found the small tube of medicine on top of the Ziploc bag of marijuana. As Jeff handed the ointment to Leeray, the sunlight dimmed as they were suddenly engulfed in shadow.

"Hey, Barry, I thought you were going ahead. Did you get lonely and come back for company?" Jeff turned and looked up, expecting to see their buddy behind them, but was surprised to see a woman dressed in shorts and a light-blue T-shirt. She had a large pack and sleeping bag strapped to her back. Then he noticed four other bronzed legs behind her.

Surprised, Jeff stood and said, "I'm Jeff and the guy on the ground is Leeray. Who are you ladies?" He couldn't help noticing the three wore white masks. He thought hikers wearing masks was a bit strange, but perhaps they were taking all precautions to avoid Covid.

The tallest of the three and the closest to Jeff replied, "I'm Loathese." She pointed at the shorter of the other two women and said, "That's Melas, and that's Hazelene." The women waved and Melas asked, "Where's Barry, the guy you mentioned?"

"He's scouting the trail a few hundred yards ahead. He'll be back shortly." Jeff glanced ahead on the trail where it dropped out of sight about ten yards ahead of them. He heard a whistle and turned toward the women. "That's Barry, he'll be here in a few."

Leeray had smeared a thin layer of Vaseline-looking ointment on his scratches and tossed the tube to Jeff as he got to his feet. As he dusted off his pants, he looked at the women, "Have you guys hiked this trail before?"

Loathese cleared her throat and said, "We trekked through the Smokey Mountains last summer and thought we'd try the western states this time. This trail is more difficult than last year's route."

Hazelene added, "We saw your names in the logbook back at the kiosk on Route 138. We didn't think we'd catch up to you until we were farther along the trail. You boys have been moving rather slowly."

Jeff conceded, "We know, but since two of us have to walk about five feet apart holding the heavy packs, it's understandable, isn't it?"

"What are you hauling that's so heavy?" asked Melas.

"Mostly food, extra shoes, stuff like that." Jeff pointed at one of the women's packs, "What have you got in your packs?"

Hazelene replied, "Necessities. Say, we're going ahead and setting up camp for the night. When you catch up, you can have a hot meal if you like."

Barry said, "Thanks. That would be great. We'll see you later."

Leeray chimed in, "How far ahead will you be?"

Loathese turned her head and looked back, "Three or four miles, depends on the trail."

Jeff, Barry, and Leeray watched the three women forge ahead on the trail. Hoisting their heavy packs on the pole, they began to follow.

Barry commented, "Nice legs, but why didn't they take off their masks to hike?" Barry was walking beside Jeff.

"How would I know? I bet they're so used to wearing 'em, they didn't think to take 'em off."

"Yeah, how old do you think they are? From the sounds of their voices, I think they're older than we are."

Leeray quizzed, "Think they're married?"

Jeff said, "Didn't see any rings, but Loathese has some tats on her fingers."

"Yeah, so does Hazelene. I think they're just symbols, but I didn't see any on Melas." Leeray stepped over a rock but didn't falter. He was aware of losing his balance and tried to keep his mind on stepping as near center of the trail as possible. His mind was now beginning to think about having a hot meal and resting, but he had to continue the effort to plod ahead. He was wondering if the girls would be waiting for them.

When they began passing through a wooded area, Jeff called to Leeray, "Let's stop for a minute. I just got an idea." Leeray didn't want to stop, but he couldn't move forward by himself. The pole locked the two young men in tandem. He stopped and they lowered their pole and heavy load to the ground.

Jeff moved off the path and withdrew his pocketknife as he approached a small fallen branch. Leeray followed to watch what was taking place. Jeff cut back branches to make two Y-shapes and handed one to Leeray.

"We're gonna make slingshots to hunt birds? I haven't even seen anything but hawks and an eagle. They're way far off from us."

Jeff sighed heavily, "No, we're gonna hold the pole to get it off our shoulders. I'm getting a sore spot where the pole rubs."

"Hey, great idea. I'm getting sore, too. Let's try 'em out."

"Yeah, let's get our asses out of here and try to catch up to Barry. We don't want him all alone with those women."

Barry had come to a small stream and stood there pondering whether to advance or wait for his buddies. He could see wet footprints where the women had crossed, so he thought he was no more than twenty minutes behind. He decided to forge ahead and waded into the swirling foot-deep water.

The cool water soaked his shoes immediately, but he was pleased that his feet felt cool as he stepped through the twenty-foot wide rivulet. He wondered where the water emptied into a larger river; it surely had a name.

He heard a squishing sound when he stepped from the water. Sitting down on a stump to remove his wet shoes and dry his socks, he thought the guys would catch up while his wet things dried. Barry wrung out his socks, wiggled his toes, and inverted his shoes on some large warm rocks.

CHAPTER 9

As the shadows were lengthening and there was a noticeable drop in temperature, Barry relieved Jeff from his porter's role. Barry moved to the front of the pole with Leeray in the rear. Leeray had been leading and now he was having to either take quicker steps or lengthen his stride to keep up. Jeff forged ahead determined to find the women's camp before dark. All three young men were getting hungry and tired of the near constant uphill climb through the forested area.

After fifteen minutes of a grueling climb, Barry and Leeray came to a break in the trees and thirty yards of level ground. Jeff rejoined his buddies as they trudged ahead and gave them some encouragement.

"The women are only about a quarter of a mile ahead. I can see smoke from their fire. They're camped less than five minutes away. We can all get a night's rest. Remember, they promised us a hot meal."

Leeray commented, "I could eat a couple of horses right now. That cheese sandwich was gone five miles back, turned into energy and farts."

Barry laughed, "For once, I can agree with you, Lee."

Just as Jeff had stated, approximately five minutes later the guys stumbled into the women's camp, sweaty and dog tired. All three young men were surprised at what they saw. In addition to the campfire, surrounded by rocks supporting a cooking compartment similar to a commercial pizza oven, there were two lean-tos ready to be occupied for the night. There were sleeping bags and pillows for six people, one structure marked 'women' and the other labeled 'men', separated by enough distance that prevented eavesdropping.

Loathese announced, "We were wondering when you would show up. It's good to see you again. We hope you are ready for some pizza and beer."

Barry revealed, "Sorry for our delay. We were getting tired climbing those uphill paths and took a couple of breaks. When we saw the smoke from your fire, we moved as quickly as possible to get here."

Hazelene pointed behind the lean-tos, "There's a little brook over there. You can wash up. The pizza is almost ready and the beer has been cooling in the water for the last thirty minutes."

"Yes, we're almost ready to eat." Melas tossed Barry a towel.

Barry laughed, "What? No soap?"

All six hikers were stuffed and happy after dinner, especially the men, having imbibed more than their share of beer. The women drank what they said was a special tea and talked among themselves paying little attention to their dinner guests. Everyone was wrapped in blankets as the temperature dropped and sound asleep before it was completely dark. The nearly full moon provided enough light for the young men to find a spot to relieve themselves during the night. The beer had done its work on their bladders.

Back at the Wickon camp it was completely dark, except for brief shafts of moonlight dancing through the swaying tree limbs. A light cool wind was coming from the mountains to the east. When the moon rose above the timber, Heloise gave a shrill whistle and the novices gathered around her for night-flight instructions. The mothers had taken appointed positions in a large circle, like numbers of a clock but missing three, six, nine, and twelve.

Samantha and Heloise stood near the center of the circle next to the campfire as observers, ready to yell out instructions if needed. Evelyn and Joan took the six and twelve positions respectively. They were to consult occasionally with Sam and Heloise when they had questions.

"All right, begin hovering and when everyone is airborne, I will call out for you to begin circling counterclockwise. No passing at the beginning." Heloise glanced at Sam and said, "They'll want to go much faster. I hope we don't have any collisions."

Sam suggested, "We can have them pair up, that might help."

"Good idea, Sam. Let's do that after they've made a couple of complete circles. Then we'll speed them up and have trials before the witching hour."

At 10:00 p.m. all the novices were soaring around the outskirts of the camp without incident, keeping from infringing on any of their neighbor's airspace. Heloise whistled loudly, the girls completed a final trip around the course, and coasted to their mentor's location.

When all the novice fliers were on the ground, Samantha gave the instructions for time trials. She had met with the mothers and discussed the individual girl's achievements and established a minimum performance level. One by one the novices circled the campfire six times. There were no failures, although two of the girls were somewhat slower than the rest. By midnight the trials had concluded, the campfire was extinguished, and everyone was in bed.

The following morning, the camp had a visitor, a Ranger from the Three Sisters Wilderness. It was early, a few minutes after six o'clock and the sky light gray-blue. Heloise and Samantha had just ignited the campfire and were rummaging through their supplies getting ready to serve breakfast. The two women were startled by a baritone voice. They turned away from the cargo door to see a uniformed man substantially over six feet tall.

"Sorry to have startled you ladies, but I'm responding to a report from last night." He stepped forward extending his right hand, "I'm Johnathan Biggs, Wilderness Ranger."

The women introduced themselves and Heloise asked, "How did you get out here? We didn't hear a vehicle."

The ranger smiled, "Good question. My horse, Diamond, is tethered a ways back. She refused to bring me any closer on her back. Very strange behavior. First time my mount has ever done that."

Samantha suggested, "Perhaps your horse saw a snake."

"No matter. What I came to check on was the shrieks some hikers heard from the Crest Trail. Noises carry quite a distance in the mountain valleys. I've noticed there are a lot of girls in camp, were there any problems yesterday afternoon?"

Heloise chuckled, "Someone must have heard the cheers from our baseball game. I must admit we were very noisy."

Ranger Biggs said, "That must have been the source of the noises. I must have you extinguish your campfire. We are in a drought season and there is great danger of forest fires. Can you use propane camping stoves? Those are allowed."

Samantha was a little annoyed, "We've been very careful, Ranger. We had the girls sweep the area from the firepit to the trees to remove any tinder."

"That's good, but I'm concerned with airborne embers that could travel to the tree line. Please douse your fire and use propane. I must insist. There is a hefty fine for noncompliance."

Heloise called out to Joan, who was approaching with Evelyn from the dimly lit vehicles. "Joanie, grab a bucket from the car and get some water from the stream. We have to put out our fire." She paused, looking at the ranger, "Better get two buckets."

"Thank you for the cooperation, ladies. Enjoy your stay in the wilderness." Giving a half-salute wave, the ranger backed away from the women, turned and left the campsite.

Joan and Evelyn appeared with buckets half full of water. Joan questioned Heloise, "Do you really want us to drown the fire? It's not very big, hardly enough for cooking breakfast yet."

"Go ahead and douse the flames. We'll do as the ranger said, get out the propane cook stoves. They'll be safer for the environment."

Back on the Crest Trail, Barry, Jeff, and Leeray were getting up as the sky was beginning to lighten. The guys stepped away from the lean-to to pee and wash up in the creek. When they returned to their belongings, all the materials given them by the women were turning shades of gray and black, decaying into dust.

Leeray stood there looking at the blankets and pillows crumbling. "What the hell is going on? Hey Barry, ask the women about the stuff they loaned us for the night."

"I can't."

"What? Go ahead and ask them."

"Leeray, they're gone and so is their lean-to. It's like they were never here."

Jeff sat down and started making a cheese sandwich for breakfast. "You guys want something to eat?"

Leeray and Barry both said, "Yeah."

Barry said, "But don't start a fire. Let's get going. We can eat as we hike. Maybe we can catch up to the women and ask them a few questions."

Jeff took a bite of sandwich and said, "I'll bet those blankets were made from a new polymer that decomposes after twelve hours of use. No need to recycle anything. No need to wash it."

Leeray added, "Probably made in China. Lots of their stuff falls apart after you buy it, but it's cheap." He finished readying his backpack and one of the heavier packs for travel. "Hey, what do we do with the lean-to?"

Jeff answered, "Just leave it. Somebody will make use of it. It wasn't made in China."

Barry agreed, "Yeah. That's our good deed for the day. Let's get out of here."

The three young men had been on the trail for nearly an hour when two hikers approached from the north, a tall middle-aged scholarly looking man and what appeared to be a slightly younger woman with gray hair and glasses. The man's waistline must have been neglected for a few seasons, perhaps years. They engaged Barry in a short conversation. Jeff and Leeray were following Barry about ten yards distant and quickly caught up to listen.

"How is the trail to the south of us?" asked the gentleman.

Barry said, "Not too bad, lots of switchbacks and some shallow creeks, but mostly downhill. Where are you two headed?"

"Crater Lake. We've rented a cabin for a few days. Getting away from the university for a breather."

"You're teachers at the university?"

"I'm a Professor of Geography and my wife works in the financial office. I'm working on a book about the lake."

Barry nodded and enquired, "Did you people see three young women on the trail this morning?"

The woman answered, "No, but we passed three older women going north. They didn't say anything, just ignored us as we passed. We waved and said hello. Tim and I thought that was a mite strange."

"Three older women? Not about our age?" Barry glanced at Jeff and Leeray.

Tim replied, "The women we encountered were at least in their sixties. They all had gray hair. They passed us about an hour back."

"Huh, doesn't sound like the ones we slept with."

"You slept with some young women on the trail?" The woman shook her head and wrinkled her nose.

"It wasn't what you think, we simply shared the same campsite. They cooked dinner for us last night. There's a lean-to waiting for you near the trail. That was ours. The women knocked theirs apart this morning and scattered the poles. My friends, Jeff and Leeray, and I are going to Eugene."

"Well, it was nice talking to you young men. Maybe I'll see you again in one of my classes."

Leeray commented, "Oh, we're not students. We're just passing through…on the way to Portland."

Jeff grinned, "Yeah, we're businessmen looking for new markets."

The professor and his wife waved and continued hiking south as the three men watched them disappear down the trail.

The trio walked together so they could discuss the information received from the professor and his wife. Barry encouraged his friends to pick up the pace.

"Let's try to catch up to those older women and find out what kind of enterprise they've got going."

All three guys lengthened their strides and picked up speed. Leeray mumbled, "I guess we know why they kept those masks on, huh?"

Jeff commented, "Maybe those raisins thought we wouldn't want to stop and talk with them if they were old."

"Not me," said Leeray, "I was so hungry I wasn't even thinkin' about chicks."

Jeff replied, "Me either. I've got one thing on my mind; four thousand dollars profit for my bag of weed."

Barry pointed out, "We've got to be damn careful. We'll be sent to prison if we get caught. One-and one-half pounds of grass has got to be enough for a stiff sentence."

"I'm gonna make sure I carry only thirty grams at a time, max."

Leeray howled, "Where you gonna put the rest? In a bank? Open an account for Mary Jane?"

Barry snorted, "You guys probably won't believe me, but I had a grandma named Mary Jane. Her last name was Bishop."

"She ever smoke it?" asked Leeray.

"Hell, I don't know. She died before I was ever born. Mom rarely talked about her."

"That's why. I'll bet she smoked pot."

"Maybe."

Back at the Wickon camp, everyone had gathered for an introduction to the appropriate clothing for night flight. Intensive training was to be conducted for high speed flight, including supersonic motion. The mentors had brought their own uniforms which had been worn for many years while traveling hundreds if not thousands of miles. Nadine Bowden, an aeronautical engineer, and Lavern Sounds, a clothing designer, were the instructors.

Nadine stated, "All of you that are shorter than five feet six will be dressed in the S size and those taller will wear the T size. The flight uniforms are not flammable; they are impervious to flames."

Lavern held up a uniform and tried to burn it with a blowtorch, but it wouldn't ignite or melt. She added, "Your traveling boots and hat are made of like material. Although you haven't had extreme flight training yet, the special properties of your uniform are important when you travel at speeds faster than sound."

There was a chorus of gasps from the novices. Joan looked at Evelyn and commented, "I sure didn't expect to hear that. Now I've got a question." She held up her hand and was recognized by Nadine, "You have something to ask me, Joan?"

"I do. If we travel faster than sound, do we create a sonic boom?"

"Ah, a very good question. The answer is yes. You should only travel faster than sound at night during a thunderstorm. The sound will be interpreted as thunder."

Evelyn slowly raised her hand, not very confident in what she had to say. "Something just now occurred to me. Maybe it's a dumb question. Can we be seen on radar when flying high in the sky?"

"Ah, another good inquiry. Most of the time you will be flying fairly low in altitude, under the radar, but if all ten of you flew in formation, you would be detected as a flight of ducks or geese. So, you don't need to worry about being seen by military or commercial radar."

Lavern added to what Nadine had said, "When you are flying, you are automatically in stealth mode. There are no flat surfaces to reflect radar, you and your uniform are irregularly shaped." Lavern put on a hat and pirouetted. Everyone laughed and she said, "Come to my vehicle and I will fit you for your headgear. Nadine will give you the correct size uniform."

Heloise completed the introduction to the topic of attire, "Your boots are one-size-fits-all and will be given to you when we fly Friday night. You won't need them until then." Heloise scanned the novice's faces, noticing the excitement and eagerness to get their garments for flying. "I will let you go now for practice sessions. You are dismissed."

CHAPTER 10

Barry glimpsed at the sun through his sunglasses when he felt and heard his stomach growling. The noise was so loud he was sure Jeff could hear the rumble. From the position of the sun, Barry reasoned it was close to noon. He was growing tired of watching Jeff's butt appearing in his forward view. The heavy packs swung from side to side as they forged ahead through the trees. There wasn't much else to see as he watched the ground every few seconds and tried to avoid tripping and dropping his end of the pole. He called out to Jeff and Leeray, "Let's stop for chow. If we don't soon, I'm gonna pass out. I need to eat."

Jeff took two more steps and stopped, "Good idea, it's about time for some more cheese and peanut butter." Holding his Y-shaped handle with both hands, Jeff turned around to face Barry. "On the count of three you can drop your end. One, two, three."

Leeray was approximately five yards ahead of the porters and had heard Barry's appeal for food. He rejoined his buddies, stooping over the closest heavy backpack.

Barry watched as Leeray opened the pack. "Any sign of those women, Leeray?"

"Nope. I've been watchin' but all I've seen is dirt, rocks and lots of trees."

Barry laughed, "That's a bit better than my view."

Jeff scowled at Barry, "Thanks, buddy."

Barry chuckled, "That's okay, you're the butt of my jokes, most of the time."

Leeray motioned to Jeff, "Here, catch," and tossed Jeff a large chunk of cheese.

Barry said, "Smear some peanut butter on mine."

The male trio sat eating sandwiches and junk food they had bought before entering the Crest Trail. They had some juice drinks and water to wash down the dry, mostly starch, edibles. For about five minutes, none of the guys spoke. Leeray began to tire of the silence and began to look around.

Leeray asked, "What sounds have you guys heard from the trail?"

Jeff replied at once, "Footsteps and farts mostly, growling stomachs, too."

"Before, when I was leading our little parade, I heard some birds and I think squirrels," said Barry.

Leeray leaned back and pointed skyward, "What about those planes up above, leaving those contrails?"

Barry looked up to see two nearly parallel contrails converging in the eastern sky. "They're too high up for us to hear them. I bet they're over six miles up."

They bantered for about fifteen minutes before continuing on. Barry set off leading at a rapid rate, leaving Jeff and Leeray far behind after hiking for what he thought was only ten minutes. Looking at his watch, he realized he had been marching on the trail for nearly an hour. Out of breath, he sat down on a rock formation below a small cluster of young trees, inhaled deeply and slowly exhaled. That's when he heard a sound, not like anything he and his buddies had discussed. At first, he thought it might be a bird, a parrot, making the mournful noise, but when he looked for the strange source, he saw it, a small kitten in the closest tree.

Barry shrugged off his backpack and moved slowly toward the tree. "What the hell? How did you get here, little one? Where's your mama?" He looked closer to see if there was a companion, an adult cat, perhaps a mother, but after scanning the area for at least a minute, he gave up.

The little black kitten was all alone sitting on a limb about ten feet above ground level.

The plaintive meows forced Barry to act; he had to get the kitten out of the tree. But what would Leeray and Jeff say? He quickly dismissed that consideration. He didn't care what they thought.

He began to formulate a plan. The kitten must be hungry. He unzipped his backpack and retrieved a can of tuna, opened it with his pocketknife and moved to the tree directly below the animal. Barry knew if he extended one hand above his head, he could reach about eight feet, so with a firm hold on the open tuna can, he lifted it above his head.

"Take a whiff, little guy. I sure hope you're hungry."

The kitten reacted quickly and began to back down from the perch, its little claws digging into the bark as it skidded downward. As the completely black kitten got closer to the tuna, Barry began lowering his hand, keeping the food just out of reach. When the animal was about seven feet up, he changed the tuna to his left hand and grabbed the kitten by the scruff and pulled it from the tree.

Despite the meows, Barry gripped the cat tightly and carried the animal to an open area away from the evergreen. He sat down with the tuna and the little cat on a large flat rock. He held the animal next to the tuna and slowly released his grip. There was no doubt the kitten was hungry. It began licking up the oil but wasn't able to get the tuna without help. Barry used his knife to lift some of the fish from the can and placed it on the rock's surface. The little animal had recoiled from the can, but eagerly attacked the freed tuna. Barry dumped the rest of the can's contents on the rock and sat back to watch his new friend scarf up the canned fish.

"What am I gonna call you, kitty?"

Barry sat there thinking of keeping the little cat as a pet, but the more he thought about it, the idea began to fester on his brain. He would have to feed it, take it to a vet to get vaccinations, get a license, and give it a home. The kitten pressed against Barry's leg. He reached down and scratched the tiny cat behind the ears. It rolled over and exposed its stomach, encouraging Barry to scratch some more.

"Hey! What's goin' on?" It was Jeff. His buddies had caught up to him.

Barry held the kitten up so Jeff could see it and called back, "Look what I found." He stood up holding the tiny cat against his chest and walked toward his friends.

Leeray dropped his end of the carrying pole and stepped closer so he could see what Barry was holding. "Where did you find the kitten?"

Barry pointed, "In that tree. It was meowing. I couldn't miss it."

"How in hell would a kitty get out here in the boonies? It must be with an older cat."

"That's what I thought. I've been looking around and haven't seen its mom. I'm thinkin' it fell out of some hiker's backpack…maybe one of those older women that professor talked about."

Jeff came closer, "I'll bet you're right. It must have fallen from someone's belongings and they don't even know it's gone."

Leeray reached out and Barry gave him the kitten. "Looks like you fed it, Barry."

"Yeah, I gave it some tuna. It was really hungry. Might have been out here for some time."

Jeff nodded, "Lucky a hawk or eagle didn't see it or it would have been a goner."

"I think it was well hidden in that tree." Barry took the kitten back from Leeray. "I just thought of a name for it: Moxie."

Jeff commented, "You wanta keep it?"

"Just for a while…until we catch up to those old women. They'll probably want to take care of it. What am I gonna do with a kitten?"

Leeray said, "We could just leave it here. Someone else might find it and want a cat."

"No way! That kitten is defenseless out here in the wild. I'm gonna take it with me in my backpack. I've got to cut a couple of holes in my pack so it won't suffocate. You and Jeff go ahead, I'll catch up to you in a little while."

The Wickon camp was humming with activity in the afternoon. The capes for the novices were being designed to minimize wind resistance and brightly colored ribbon was being sewn into each hem. The iridescent strip of material corresponded to the colored band on each novice's hat. Orange, purple, blue, and red were the novices only choices, matched to the different time zone of their residence.

Since Heloise joined the Wickon sisterhood, she had been extremely proud to have purple trim adorn her hat. She felt it was like a Heraldic coat of arms. Her forebears, from the time of landing in the new world, also showed decorated head covers, originally only trimmed with red or crimson ribbon. Purple was added later when the western regions of the United States became settled. General Grant had complimented her with regard to her decorative head gear.

She was working with Joan when Kathy Glazer approached with her mentor. The novice was holding her hat in one hand and her cape with the other. She was apprehensive, but her coach watched from a few feet behind her, ready to aid the beginner if she needed help deciding options.

"Heloise, I'm from Alaska and the colors available do not correspond to my time zone. What should I do?"

Heloise frowned and then nodded, "Joan, could you please hand me the abbreviated listing book from the glove compartment? I'm sorry, Kathy. That was my oversight. I'll have to look up your assigned color. I've forgotten some of the details I used to have on the tip of my tongue."

In a few seconds, Joan returned holding a compact book disguised as a Webster's Condensed Collegiate Dictionary. Heloise blinked three times turning to the letter C as Joan held the thick book.

"Ah, here you are. Your color is emerald-green, but you may choose another hue if you like."

"Oh, thank you. I've always liked chartreuse. Would that be all right?"

Heloise replied, "I believe that would work. The board of directors would certainly approve of your choice. They are fairly lenient when it comes to Alaska, we have few members that far north. I was pleased you and your mother were able to attend the camp."

Mrs. Glazer said, "I don't believe we have any chartreuse ribbon in our supplies. Do you have any that color?"

Heloise looked at Kathy's mother. "Use blue and make some adjustments. You know what to do."

Kathy's mentor said, "Come on dear, I'll show you how to make some color changes. It's a simple task." Kathy and her mother withdrew from Heloise and Joan, walking toward their red pickup.

Samantha and Evelyn had been sitting in the back of their SUV listening to some music on the car radio. When Samantha noticed Heloise was free to talk, Sam left the vehicle and approached her associate.

"When should we inform the newbies about the utility of their capes?"

Heloise grinned, "Let's do it after dinner tonight."

It was a few minutes after four o'clock when Barry looked down into a broad valley where he recognized three women hiking slowly, nearly two hundred yards ahead. Deciding to wait for Leeray and Jeff to catch up, he sat on the end of a cedar log that looked like it had been there for years. A shrill cry came from above the valley. Looking up into the cloudless sky he saw three birds circling. He didn't know enough about birds to tell if they were ravens or crows, but they were large and black.

Barry thought momentarily about letting Moxie out of his pack, but the sight of the birds caused him to change his mind. The birds were large enough to carry off a tiny kitten. His thoughts were suddenly altered when he heard Leeray call out, "See those women yet, Barry?"

"Yeah, they're down below in the valley, just ahead of us. At least I think it's them. They're too far away to ID for sure."

Jeff and Leeray dropped their heavy load and joined Barry on the log.

"Your turn to carry, Barry." Leeray grinned at his rhyme.

"Okay, Leeray. I won't delay." Barry laughed and slapped his thigh.

"I dare you to come up with one for my name," Jeff said. "How's your kitten sittin'?"

Barry chuckled. "I don't know. I was afraid to take him out of my pack when I saw those black birds swirling above the valley."

Jeff glanced ahead, looked down into the shallow valley and then up into the air. "I don't see any birds."

Barry scanned the sky. "They're gone. Probably taking a break like we are. Let's get out of here, it's downhill for about a quarter of a mile. Maybe we'll catch up to the women."

Leeray adjusted his backpack and started descending into the valley. Barry and Jeff hoisted their load and followed. They were almost matching their buddy's footsteps, finding it easy to move together when going downhill, only occasionally losing a stride to the slightly shorter Leeray.

Five minutes after relaxing on the cedar log, Leeray spotted the women. They hadn't moved from their previous position. They seemed to be waiting for the three young men. Leeray called out to Barry and Jeff, "We've caught up to them. They're just ahead."

Leeray waited for his friends to appear and together they walked into the women's camp. The three women were sitting on folded blankets in a triangle probing a small campfire with green twigs and looked up when the guys came into view. They were heating something in a pot.

Barry grinned and broke the silence, "Hello ladies. Whatcha burnin', water?"

Hazelene cackled, "Yes. We thought you might like some herbal tea."

Loathese added, "Take a load off and come sit with us. We'd like to talk; it's been a quiet day for us."

Barry answered, "Thanks. Some chatting and hot tea would be really great. It's kinda cool today."

CHAPTER 11

The three women looked as they had earlier, wearing masks and regular hiking clothes. One thing was different, they were all wearing black turtleneck sweaters. They each unfolded their blankets to make room for the three young men and indicated Jeff, Leeray, and Barry should sit. Before Barry sat down he removed his backpack and said, "I found a kitten on the trail today. Would you ladies like a kitten? We can't care for it and would like to give to someone." He unzipped the top of his pack and a large furry animal jumped out, but it wasn't a kitten, it was a full-grown black cat. He was shocked, as were Leeray and Jeff.

Jeff called out, "What'd you feed that kitten, Barry?"

"You saw that tuna can. That was all I gave it."

Barry watched the cat rub against Hazelene's legs. She reached down to pet it. She exclaimed, "Oh, you found Pernicious. Thank you."

Melas observed, "He must have wandered away earlier today. We're glad to have him back."

Jeff said, "Barry put a small kitten in his pack, not a grown cat. I saw it."

Melas replied, "You must be mistaken. You know, the high altitude does strange things to a person's sight if they're not used to the lower oxygen level."

"Yes, there have been lots of UFO sightings in this area," commented Loathese. "We're not too far from Crater Lake. Rumors of alien activity have been there for years."

Leeray had nothing to add, so he sat beside Melas and stated, "Nice fire."

Melas replied, "Yes, the tea is about ready. We have containers for six. You won't need your own cups."

Each of the women reached into their packs and withdrew a copper cup and a porcelain mug. Hazelene rose and removed the pot from the fire and began to pour the light-brown fluid into Barry's mug. She moved to Jeff, poured, and then to Leeray, filling each vessel half-full. Then she poured a generous amount into the women's cups.

Loathese spoke, almost commanding, "Drink up boys!"

Still wearing their backpacks, the young men began to drink, slowly at first, and then more rapidly until the mugs were empty. Barry looked at his buddies and gave them a thumbs up. They nodded and leaned back against their packs saying in unison, "Yeah, not bad."

The women had removed their masks and were sipping their drinks, looking at their male companions and winking to each other.

The last thing Barry saw before yawning and closing his eyes were the black teeth in the women's uncovered mouths. His final thought was wondering if they had ever been to a dentist.

Melas, Hazelene, and Loathese each poked the nearest young man and got no response; the three male hikers were apparently unaware of their existential being.

Loathese asked, "Are we ready?"

Hazelene extended her collapsible telescope and took a quick survey of the valley checking for onlookers. Not detecting anyone, she nodded to the other women and said, "We're all clear; let's proceed."

The women dragged Leeray's inert body close to a tall pine tree about five yards away from the fire. Then they alternated rocks and twigs surrounding his frame with his head pointing south.

Melas clapped her hands together like a little kid getting a present and said, "I want to do this one!"

Hazelene said, "I'll do the next one, if it's okay with you, Loathese."

Loathese replied, "My, aren't we eager today. Okay. Go ahead, Melas."

Melas walked slowly and knelt beside Leeray's head, "With the aid and wisdom of Satan we egnahcxe ruoy namuh ydob rof a raeb." She stepped away from Leeray and the three women watched as Leeray's body began transforming. Loathese watched for about a minute then became bored, "Come and get me in about five minutes. It's going to take all three of us to move him."

Melas replied, "Take your time, Nessa. He'll be rounder afterwards. Two of us can roll him back in place. Do you think we can handle him, Hazelene?"

"Sure, we can do it by ourselves."

Melas looked back at the body being transformed. "I didn't think he would be so hairy, and those claws look hazardous."

Hazelene licked her lips and sighed. "Well, he's almost complete, then I get to do mine. I can hardly wait!"

Loathese returned to the fire to get more tea and check that the other two young men were still incapacitated. Kneeling beside each man, she checked their pulse and respiration. All life forces were normal, the special tea in their mugs had been adequate. With some difficulty, she removed their backpacks and began sorting through the contents. She wondered what Melas had done with the other pack but then saw it laying on the ground, contents scattered. Loathese found nothing of use and began digging a hole near a large tree to bury the three packs and their contents. The new beings would have no use for the items. After the belongings were buried, she watched as Melas and Hazelene rolled the newly spawned bear back to the campfire. She was happy to have her friends complete the job. She disliked handling the furry beasts because of their disagreeable odors and didn't mind if rolling the animal across the ground got the fur dirty.

Hazelene began to pull Barry toward the transformation tree but called out, "Aren't you two going to help me? This one is heavier than the last one."

Loathese and Melas grabbed ahold of Barry's clothing and helped pull the body into position. Hazelene knelt as Melas had and chanted her spell, "Wondrous all powerful Satan, please assist us, trevnoc siht yob ot a flow."

As the three women stood over the body, foul smelling gases began to escape from the victim's orifices. The women stepped back and pinched their nostrils. Hazelene remarked, "Well, double-damn! I hoped the stink wouldn't happen to this one."

Loathese exclaimed, "Oh, grow up, Hazelene. It always happens for this type of conversion."

"Yes, Hazelene, just breathe through your mouth, it will only be for a minute," commented Melas, rolling her eyes.

Hazelene was paying particular attention to the appearance of the silvery hair, the dark black nose, and the highly developed canine teeth of her timber wolf. Melas volunteered to help Hazelene scoot the dog-like figure into position near the fire.

Loathese stated, "One more, ladies. Help me get him into position. I'm going to make this a special one, something unique."

Hazelene checked Jeff's pulse and respiration. "He's good to go," she announced.

Loathese queried, "His heart's all right?"

Hazelene replied, "Good strong pulse, Nessa. I'm sure he can adjust to double or triple his normal rate. His pump won't have to circulate as much blood, will it?"

"No. He'll be quite a bit smaller. Help me move him, he's rather tall."

When Jeff was moved into position, Loathese circled the body clockwise once and then counterclockwise, uttering, "Fly by day and night. Recite like a parrot for confusion of those that listen." She knelt near Jeff's head, touching his neck with her right index finger, and said, "King of Hell, adversary of God, nrut siht gnuoy nam otni a citsejam lwo."

Jeff began to shrink to about one-fourth his normal size and large wings began to form, enveloped with rather large feathers. His ears moved to the top of his head above his eyes and began to oscillate back and forth like old radar dishes. The conversion was very rapid compared to the others. Loathese carried the large bird back to the campfire and laid it on a blanket like the others to keep them warm during the cold nighttime temperatures near the high mountains. The women did not intend to have the new beings die of exposure. She didn't notice the owl's eyes flickering as she said, "Well, Leeray's a bear, Barry's a wolf, and Jeff's an owl. Three perfect transformations. I wonder if they'll get along?" But the owl, not yet completely asleep, as it closed its eyes shutting out daylight, heard a woman's cackle specifying the transformations.

Loathese stood beside the fire observing the women's creations. "Join me, Hazelene and Melas, to rejoice in our work. We have completed an exceptional task today."

The three women donned capes and uttered in unison, "High Lord, Satan, let these beings enjoy their new lives in the wild."

Loathese had one last utterance as she turned to her associates, "Pack your things, sisters. We must move on for other duties. There are novices we must deal with to the north near the Three Sisters." Ten minutes later, there was no sign of the women or their cat having been at the campfire, only a bear, a wolf, and an owl comfortably asleep on old, tattered blankets.

Twenty-three miles north, the Wickon campers were preparing their evening vegan meal. The novices had been gathering wild berries for dessert and the mentors had been sorting through an assortment of mushrooms collected earlier in the day, taking care to eliminate the poisonous items. Edible roots, onions, cauliflower, broccoli, peas, and mushrooms were then stewed in several pots on the propane fired cook stoves.

Novice Joan had been watching the sky to the south and questioned, "Heloise, is a storm expected tonight?"

"What gave you that idea, dear?"

"Look!" Joan pointed to a dark-gray, nearly black cumulus cloud, rising above the trees and then shrinking back out of sight. "Could that be smoke from a forest fire?"

"Oh, my." Heloise raised her palms to her cheeks and commented, "I don't believe that darkness is from a storm or a fire. I think it is a foreboding sign of the appearance of bad actors. I saw that harbinger come into view several times long ago, in the 1860s. We'll be getting some lightning and cold wind gusts accompanying several uninvited guests."

"Should I tell Samantha about it?"

"Yes, please do. She needs to know so she can alert the other mentors. We'll need to prepare for some unusual activity. Have Sam come see me after she gives the warning. We'll have a group discussion after dinner."

Heloise watched Joan run to the vehicles searching for the camp cosponsor until she heard Samantha blow on her referee's whistle and call out, "Trouble is on its way. We'll meet after our meal at Heloise's car. It's important, so make sure you come, everyone."

Forty-five minutes later, evening shadows lengthening, the campers began to gather around the original campfire which was nothing but ashes and a circle of rocks. Most of the women had donned sweaters and were murmuring, wondering what the meeting was all about. Apparently, only Joan and Heloise had seen the ominous cloud. A short distance away, Heloise related what Joan and she had seen earlier and what it meant. Most of the mentors had seen at least one such manifestation before. One of the women, Cybil Thompson, asked, "Do you think we should send out a scout?"

Heloise nodded, "Yes, would you like to accompany me tonight after dark?"

"Sure, I'll go with you. How far away do you think the wicked beings are?"

"Not more than a few miles. They have had several hours to travel since we sighted the cloud. But that's assuming they are travelling by foot."

One of the novices, Becky, nervously asked, "Could these crashers be watching us now?"

"I don't believe so, Becky. If that were the case, one or more of the mentors would have sensed a feeling of dread." Glancing around the group, Heloise inquired, "Has anyone had any strange sensations today?" Everyone shook their head; no one had perceived anything unusual.

"Okay. Now, I would like to give you a demonstration of the use of the colored ribbon concealed in the hem of your cape." Heloise tossed her hat on the ground in front of her. "Novices, I need three volunteers." Eager to take part, three of the young women stepped forward.

"I want you to stomp on my hat like you are trying to put out a fire, trying to kill it."

Everyone watched as Joan, Jean, and Kathy violently attacked the hat, treading it into the dirt making it into a dirty black pancake. After thirty seconds, in order to stop the activity, Heloise said, "That will do. Now watch."

She spread her cape over the crumpled hat making sure the ribbon in the hem made a complete circle and said, "Regenerate!"

The novices watched intently as the cape began to stir and expand, a small dust cloud escaping from beneath the black material. When the motion ceased, Heloise stepped forward and lifted the cape. Her hat reappeared in pristine condition as if newly purchased, never worn.

The novices couldn't believe their eyes and started cheering, delighted at what they saw. The three novices that had done the stomping rushed forward to Heloise, smiling. Eyes wide with excitement, Joan asked, "Are there other things the cape can do?"

"Oh, yes. I can think of at least twenty tasks without referring to the handbook. One is very handy, it's for tying knots, but the ribbon must be pulled from the hem, otherwise the cape will become a tangled mess. I'll go over some of the other commands tomorrow. You will have to commit them to memory. You shouldn't write them down or someone might use them maliciously."

CHAPTER 12

As the campers drifted back to their vehicles to begin preparations for sleeping, Samantha joined her close friend. Heloise had begun to don clothes for the scouting trip with Cybil Thompson. She was sitting in the car's back seat pulling on heat resistant knee socks.

Samantha stated, "I believe we should post sentries. What do you think?"

"Good idea. I hadn't thought of that. I guess the demonstration and the scouting trip with Cybil were on my mind."

"Well, it will be dark by nine o'clock. I'll have a novice and a mentor start two-hour shifts starting at ten o'clock."

Heloise thought for a second and replied, "Better make it three, Sam."

"People or hours?"

Heloise chuckled, "Oh, three people. Have them walk the perimeter about ten yards outside our vehicles. No talking or we might get some false alarms. Show them how to use their shoes as flashlights if they don't know already."

"When will you be leaving?"

"Cybil and I will start our patrol just as the sun goes down. I want to locate landmarks before it gets completely dark."

"You'll be gone for thirty minutes?"

"Yes, I'm estimating a half-hour. That should give us plenty of time, but if we find something of special interest, it might take longer. We might have to sneak around some."

"All right, have a safe probe. I'll check with you later for a report."

Just as Heloise was asking Joan to warn the other mentors if she hadn't returned from the scouting trip after an hour, Cybil showed up at Heloise's SUV. It was 8:25 p.m., and Cybil was appropriately dressed for undercover activity. They climbed aboard their brooms, hovered for a moment and then whooshed off above the trees to the east. Travelling side-by-side scanning the hikers' path took the pair about five minutes before they saw a campfire on the Crest Trail. Heloise motioned to her partner to slow down, she wanted to land and approach the encampment on foot. They dropped from above the trees and touched the ground about fifty yards from the flickering flames.

"I'll go straight in; you circle around from the opposite direction. Don't let anybody know you're there. Stay out of sight, no matter what." Cybil nodded, hovered a few feet above the ground and slowly began circling toward the camp.

Heloise leaned her broom against a large tree that was easily identified and began to carefully make her way through the timber toward the trail. Moving from tree to tree for concealment, she made only the slightest sounds. She crept behind a large rock thirty feet or so from three women enjoying the warmth of a fire. Heloise dropped to her knees, removed her hat to keep from giving away her position, and listened.

In only a few minutes, Heloise learned the identity of what appeared to be the group leader, Loathese, and her companions, Melas, and Hazelene. The voices of the three women were barely audible and Heloise wanted to move closer, but that was out of the question, she would be seen. But then she was surprised, Loathese stood and looked directly at the rock where Heloise crouched and said, "If you want to hear what we're saying, you must come closer. We know you are behind that big rock."

Heloise dropped her cape and hat and stepped away from the rock, glancing past the campfire to see if Cybil was in place, but in the darkness, couldn't see her friend. She hoped Cybil would stay in hiding and would only come forward if a situation demanded her presence. Cybil was mounted and could appear in a fraction of a second.

Loathese stood with her arms folded across her chest. "What are you doing out here. Who are you?"

"My name's Heloise. I got lost on the trail. It was getting dark and I saw your light. Before I barged in, I was listening to see if you were nice people."

"Why are you dressed in black?" Before Heloise had a chance to answer, Loathese said, "Hazelene, check behind that rock. See if this person left something we should know about."

Heloise was getting nervous, but she didn't want to show any agitation. She hoped Cybil was listening.

Hazelene stepped away from the rock and approached, "Look what I found." She held up Heloise's cape and hat.

Loathese blurted out, "You have been lying, you are a witch!" The three women glared at Heloise. "You know who we are, then, and we can't silence you, but I can make you uncomfortable for a day. Hazelene and Melas, take hold of her arms. Hold her near the fire."

The two women grabbed Heloise's arms and moved closer to the flames. Heloise resisted, but Hazelene and Melas forced their captive to kneel by the burning branches. Loathese declared, "As an outsider, with the power of Satan uoy era etum rof a yad!"

The three women laughed and Hazelene called out, "Uoy lliw klat sa a drib!"

They released Heloise and stepped back chuckling among themselves. A second later, Cybil swooped through the fire making the three evil women jump away from the flames, fearful that their clothes might burn. Heloise grabbed her hat and cape and climbed on Cybil's sweeper behind her friend. An instant later, they were back at the tree where Heloise had left her broom.

Heloise donned her cape and hat and turned to thank Cybil, but only chirps came from her mouth. Cybil said, "I know what you are trying to say. You are welcome. Let's get back to camp and let the others know what happened. You'll be all right tomorrow. I heard what that sorceress said."

Heloise nodded, climbed aboard her broom and they returned to camp.

Arriving in darkness, the moon's meager light beams passing between the tree limbs, Cybil and Heloise hovered above Heloise's SUV until several of the mentors and novices noticed they had returned. They had not set foot on the ground until they knew the camp had not been attacked. When Heloise realized it was safe to land, she motioned to Cybil and they settled to the ground.

Joan rushed to greet the two women and asked, "Did you find them?"

Heloise didn't answer but motioned to Cybil to get a pencil and tablet from her car. Heloise gestured to Joan indicating she couldn't speak. Joan frowned and shook her head indicating she didn't understand. Cybil returned with a tablet and ballpoint pen, handing them to Heloise. With the car dome light on, Heloise printed a message and showed it to Joan: "I am mute for 24 hours. Please have Sam come see me."

While Joan looked for Samantha, Heloise wrote a long note for her camp cosponsor explaining the situation. She wanted Samantha to inform everyone of Heloise's speaking problem and make sure all the campers kept their capes and hats with them as they slept.

In the early hours of the next morning, when only three guards were awake patrolling the Wickon camp outskirts, Loathese, Hazelene, and Melas had sneaked through the forest to observe the site. Concealed behind the largest timber, they watched the Wickon training camp.

"How many do you see, Hazelene?" Loathese queried in a whisper.

"Only three are up and about. They must be guards."

"How about you, Melas?"

"The same, but they have about ten vehicles, so there must be nine or ten of them, and maybe more."

Loathese thought for a moment and reluctantly said, "Let's back off a safe distance and formulate a plan of attack. If there are ten of them, we'll have poor odds. We'll have to take them by surprise."

Twenty minutes later, three new guards were on patrol wearing their capes and hats. Each carried a broom ready for quick travel. They stayed equidistant from each other moving in a counterclockwise direction. Jolene's daughter, Becky, was the first camper to hear a slight rumble of distant thunder. On guard for only a few minutes, she looked up to see filmy clouds drifting across the moon's face. She thought to herself momentarily as she kept moving, "Reminds me of Halloween, kind of spooky."

Jean Moberg, another novice on guard duty, noticed the slight dimming of the moonlight but thought it was just due to moon beams being filtered through foliage. Then she saw a flash of lightning and heard thunder. She recalled talking about the weather with her mother after dinner. No storms were expected, the only bad weather was farther north on the Olympic peninsula. She felt something strike her hat, but thought it was an object falling from a tree, perhaps a pine needle. She didn't stop to investigate. She kept on the move.

It had started to rain, an odd occurrence from the delicate clouds, and then a cold east wind began to blow the rain drops so swiftly they felt like hail stones when they struck Jean's face. She pulled the brim of her hat down for protection, leaned into the wind, and decided she should wake Samantha and Heloise. Her chief concern was, "Is this the sign of imminent danger?"

She ran to Heloise's SUV and pounded on the cargo door hoping to get the highest ranking mentor's attention. The driver's side rear window opened and Joan's face appeared. "What's going on, sis?" Raindrops began pounding at the vehicle and Joan said, "Get in Jean." The door popped open, Jean leaned her broom against the car, slid inside, and the sisters began to talk excitedly.

Heloise had been sleeping, but when the car door was opened, she fluttered her arms like a bird and tried to speak. A chirping sound came from her mouth and she stifled her voice, reaching for her pad and pen. As she began to write, she paused for a moment, listening to the wind and rain striking her car and then continued moving her pen across the page. She held her note near the dome light so the girls could read her writing.

"Wake everyone! We are all in danger! Honk the horn, turn on the lights and flashers!"

The third guard on duty was Laura Morfin. In her haste to warn her daughter, Marlene, Laura dropped her broom when it snagged on some shrubbery. When mentor Laura reached her car she found Marlene sitting patiently in the front seat grasping her broom so tightly she had white knuckles.

"Did you sound the warning, Mom?"

"No. It came from Heloise's car. Did it wake you?"

Marlene smiled, "Nope. When the wind hit the car, it shook and then the rain hitting made a terrible racket. I knew something was going on. I was sleeping in my uniform. All I had to do was put on my hat."

"You can straighten it when you get out of the car. It's crooked, tipped to the side."

"Yeah, there's not enough headroom in the car for it to be on correctly."

Laura said, "Let's meet with Samantha and see what's happening. Bring your broom. Let's get mine first." Laura and Marlene went back into the trees to recover Laura's broom, but when they reached the location where it had been dropped, it was gone.

"You're sure this is the spot?"

Laura directed the beam of her flashlight on a waist-high woody plant. "Positive. That shrub has broken growth where my flight stick was jerked away. Let's tell Samantha that somebody has my broom."

Marlene asked, "But why would anyone want it? It's tuned to you and me."

"I don't know, but we'd better alert Sam and Heloise."

Loathese, Hazelene, and Melas were watching the noisy activity of the Wickon training camp and laughing. Melas held the broom she had pulled from the underbrush and asked Loathese, "Let's gather these wooden sticks from them so they will no longer cause us any worry. These altruistic Wickons will no longer be able to become airborne."

"What'll we do with their implements?" asked Hazelene.

Loathese was quick to reply, "Burn them!"

"But it's raining so hard, they won't burn." Melas had a point.

Hazelene chuckled, "That's easy, we'll stop the rain."

The three devious witches grasped the stolen broom in the middle of the handle with both hands and said in unison, "Oh Satan, hear us. We beseech you to bring these implements to us. Gather them from this camp."

CHAPTER 13

Joan and her mother, Ursula Moberg, were in their SUV donning their capes and hats in preparation for any confrontations that might arise. Joan was sitting in the back of the vehicle when her broom began to move in an erratic fashion. The stick began to pummel the cargo door, harder and harder, and with one giant thrust, broke out the rear window and flew from the cargo area vanishing into the night.

Joan was startled and said, "Mom, I tried to hold onto my broom. But I couldn't do it. It twisted out of my hands. What's happening? How could it do that?"

Ursula was becoming irritated as she wrestled with her own broom as it tried to escape from the back of the car. She grasped onto the handle to keep it from rising to the opening in the cargo door, but she wasn't strong enough to overcome the rotation; it was burning her hands. She had to let go.

Throughout the circle of vehicles, the mentors and novices struggled to retain possession of their flight sticks. When the brooms became violent, most of the campers opened their car doors and let the sweepers escape the confinement of the vehicles. Heloise sat in the back seat watching and listening to the struggling campers. When the commotions began, she saw a broom fly from a car. Knowing the activity was originating from the three Satanic witches, she decided not to react, just observe. When her two brooms began to move, she let them go.

Jean was in the front seat, surprised by Heloise's reluctance to fight for control of the brooms.

She raised her voice in dismay, "You just let them go without a fight?"

Heloise tried to talk but could only peep like a baby chicken. She grabbed her pen and wrote on her notepad, *"I didn't have time to write you a note. I would have told you to relax. Let's see what happens."*

Jean nodded and they watched the brooms accumulate in an irregular cloud a few feet above the firepit and fall haphazardly into a pile. A flash of lightning occurred, striking the collection of flight sticks, causing them to burst into flame.

"Oh my gosh, Heloise. They will be destroyed! What will we do?" She waited for Heloise to write on her pad.

"Relax Jean, only the surface lacquer will get charred and the straw bristles will burn. The broom handles will not burn and we can replace the bristles. We'll let Satan's followers have some fun. They don't have the power to hurt us."

"But where are they? Are they hiding? Will we ever see them?"

Heloise responded, her pen moving with a flourish across her pad, *"When they think they have an advantage. They might not know there are twenty of us. But when they count the brooms, they will see our strength. I want you to tell all the novices not to eat or drink anything they are offered from the three women."*

Jean nodded and ran from Heloise to the next vehicle and the warning was quickly circulated to all the novices.

Satan's disciples were watching the activity, hiding in the trees outside the training camp's circle of vehicles. The three devotees were intent on counting the brooms as they accumulated on the fire pit and were overjoyed when the pile of brooms was struck with lightning and began to burn.

Loathese asked, "What is the broom count?

Hazelene replied, "I got nineteen, but I might be off by one or two. They came so fast."

"I counted eighteen. I think I'm right." Melas sounded very sure of her count. "I stopped counting when the lightning struck."

"Okay. That's too many for us to handle now. We'll make camp about a mile from here and prepare for some abductions when the sun comes up."

Melas reacted, "Good. I'll concoct a devilish brew for the Wickons."

"I'll help you. We'll have half the group converted by mid-morning," added Hazelene.

As the light of early morning brightened, the bear, wolf, and owl woke to find they were in a confusing situation. Dumbfounded, they looked at each other and then began to check themselves. Wolf was not aggressive toward the bear, and Bear had no fear of the wolf. Bear scratched his head sniffing the air, and Wolf had his nose to the ground searching for a scent. Owl took to the air and circled above the trees for a few minutes, hunting for people moving, then following parallel to the trail. His examination of the pathway was uneventful, so he returned to the vicinity of the bear and wolf. Fluttering his wings, he frequently touched down and hopped along the trail moving north.

Bear stood erect, huffing and growling. Wolf sat, tongue hanging, then jumped to all fours, howled, and began to follow Owl. Bear watched Wolf and Owl moving away and decided to follow.

Bear was having a difficult time trying to catch up to Wolf, who was following the scent of the three witches he guessed were responsible for these circumstances. As he ran ahead of Bear, the scent was becoming stronger. Owl was flying overhead, advancing out of sight, but returning to occasionally swoop down to encourage Wolf with a screech to continue the chase. Then flying back down the trail to see if Bear was still following.

As the scent grew in intensity, Wolf began to salivate, with the thoughts of warm blood in his mouth, he licked his fangs as he imagined ripping into the legs and arms of his prey. He wasn't sure of why he had such a strong desire to attack the women he was following, but he craved the excitement of the chase and the satisfaction of the conquest.

Bear was in no hurry. He could take his time and still follow the smell of the human women mixed with the odors of the wolf he followed. He was becoming fond of the owl that occasionally swooped down and screeched at him, apparently urging him to hurry up. He lumbered on, smelling squirrels, the perfume of wildflowers, the clean smell of cool mountain air, and even detecting the odors present from recent rain.

An hour passed, then two. Wolf stopped to drink from a stream and sniffed the air. He was still picking up the odors he had been following. The smells were growing stronger so his prey couldn't be very far ahead. He looked into the air to see if Owl was nearby, but didn't see the bird, and decided to sit for a while to rest. Wolf wondered if the bear was still following.

Wolf yawned, took another drink from the cold rushing water and felt the pangs of hunger. He patrolled both sides of the creek but found nothing to eat, not even one dead fish lying belly up on the rocks. Listening for squirrels as he returned to the trail, Wolf laid down and fell asleep on a large flat boulder warmed by the mid-morning sun.

The Wickon camp attendees had little rest after the storm and the broom roast. They huddled in groups of four in the SUVs as darkness gave way to a cloudless morning blue sky with a slight eastern breeze. A handful of novices had sustained slight bruises and scratches from trying to hold onto their brooms, but none of the injuries required even a small Band-Aid.

Heloise was escorting the novices from the SUVs to the pile of scorched handles so they could be reclaimed by their owners. The mentors were next to recover their flight sticks. As she pulled her broom handle from the fire pit, Samantha was the first to ask, "Where can we get some straw to fix our brooms?"

Heloise jotted on her notepad, *"Let's fabricate a broom from weed stalks and thin branches from young trees. We'll use your handle and a piece of my cape lining for binding. Then we'll fly back to the farming area at the edge of the park and bring back some wheat straw. It might take more than one trip."*

Sam nodded and replied, *"We won't be able to travel very fast with a broom made from poor substitutes."*

Heloise sighed heavily, chirped rapidly, and wrote with a flash, "We don't have any other options, do we?"

"I guess not. I'll get some help and we'll gather some raw material for our temporary fix."

Sam enlisted the help from an adjoining SUV where two mentors and their novices were waiting for directions. Fifteen minutes later, they returned with a bundle of straw-looking material. While Heloise waited, she removed about a foot of the lining from her cape. She began sorting through the accumulation choosing the best representations of straw, tossing aside things that would not suffice.

She hastily wrote a cursive note to Joan, *"Please cut these stiff fibers into thirteen-inch lengths and hand them to me. I will begin the assembly."*

As Joan passed the straw substitute to Heloise, they were bound in groups of five with rubber bands. When ten units were bound, Heloise packed them around her broom handle and had Joan hold the fibers surrounding the shaft. Heloise laid the piece of cape lining around the bristles and had Joan say, "Tie these fibers to this handle, tie them tight, use all your might."

Joan uttered a slight gasp as the cape lining began winding around the fibers without human intervention. She watched as the fibers were bound so tightly they almost appeared to be glued to the handle. Heloise jotted a note and gave it to Joan. *"See if you can pull the bristles from the handle."*

Joan clutched one of the fibers and yanked with all her strength, but it didn't budge. She glanced at Heloise and grinned, "It's like the handle wants to be a broom again. Do you think it wants to fly?"

Heloise nodded and motioned for Joan to get on and take it for a spin. As Joan mounted the broom, Heloise dashed off a short note, *"Ride ten miles and return as quickly as you can. I'll time you so we can figure out how fast we can travel."*

"Okay! I'm off!"

Joan left with a swoosh, barely clearing the trees, pinecones spraying the camp, leaving the evergreens swaying back and forth. Heloise looked at her watch to record the time. Nine minutes later, Joan returned to camp and hopped off her broom. Heloise peeped excitedly and wrote, *"Good work, Joanie! Your speed was 135 miles per hour. That will be fine for your trip."*

Joan knew that she had not gone as fast as she could have with her regular broom, but she was satisfied that Heloise was pleased. Joan thought, "What has Heloise got in mind? I guess she wants me to go alone."

Heloise was doing some calculating and looked up from her scratch pad. She shifted her eyes back to her pad and wrote, *"We'll need half a bale of hay to have enough straw for most of our flight sticks. I'm sending you for it. Here's a rough map; you can't get lost."*

Joan glanced at the crude sketch and gave Heloise a confused look.

Heloise realized she had forgotten the compass directions, and quickly marked them on the paper. The novice Wickon knew enough to fly low to avoid being seen by anyone, especially hikers and mountain climbers. She dismissed the possibility of encountering the satanists since she was flying in the opposite direction. She tucked the folded directions under her blouse and asked, "How long should the trip take?"

Heloise thought for a moment and replied, *"If you aren't back in about ninety minutes, I'll begin to worry. While you're gone, I'll make another temporary flight stick; just in case I need to come after you."*

"O.K. I'm leaving right now. Wish me luck."

Heloise gave a series of high pitched chirps and wrote a quick note, *"You'll do fine, break a leg."*

Joan frowned, not understanding, and didn't reply, mounted her broom and sped off to the northwest clearing the trees by only a few feet. She had been in the air less than a minute when she heard an airplane engine higher above her and to her left. She swept the sky with her eyes and saw a small plane moving parallel to her but about five hundred feet above the timber. An idea came to mind in a flash, "I'll ride along beneath the plane. No one will ever see me."

The plane was going faster than Joan, so she leaned forward to increase her speed and gain altitude. In a few seconds she was directly below the fuselage. She reached out and grabbed the left wing strut and relaxed, letting the plane pull her through the air. Her idea was to lessen the stress on her broom, having been through a fire that removed it's normal bristles. Being situated behind her cape and hat, the wind was calm, so she extracted the map Heloise had given her and watched for landmarks.

It hadn't occurred to Joan that she would be responsible for increasing drag on the plane and after a minute, the plane began to slow. She suddenly realized that she had caused a problem and the pilot was thinking something was wrong with his plane. Another minute passed but no further slowing took place, but another small plane was coming along side. Joan tucked her legs back, pulled her hat down over her face and concealed herself with her cape. At first, she was concerned, but then she decided the pilot coming alongside would probably think a piece of black material, like a sheet, had caught on the wing strut, certainly not a fledgling witch taking a free ride. She laughed and watched for the town of Timberville, where she could fall from the sky and find some hay. She would descend like a piece of material fluttering to the ground.

CHAPTER 14

Joan watched the ground for another five minutes. She took a deep breath when the plane was over the southern edge of Timberville. She released her grip on the wing strut, falling away from the plane like a piece of paper falling from a sanitation truck in a strong wind. She had to fight the broom's desire to glide through the air when she asked it to tumble until she was within ten feet of the ground. She almost waited too long before hovering and safely settling to earth.

She quickly reshaped her hat into a large handbag, turned her cape inside out so the crimson lining was exposed and carried her broom over her right shoulder like a hoe as if she were a garden worker. There were only two buildings nearby, a rustic looking log cabin and a modern metal barn. Walking purposely, she headed toward the barn, humming and swinging her broom.

As Joan cautiously approached the structure, she could hear two males talking and laughing. She stopped for a moment, built up her courage and proceeded into the barn. Two young men were on their knees working on bicycles; tools and bike parts scattered haphazardly around them. They didn't hear her, but her shadow announced her presence.

The heavyset one said, "Where d'you come from?"

The skinnier one said, "What d'ya want, sneakin' up on us like this?"

"I want to buy half a bale of hay. Do you know where I can get some?"

"I'm Dennis. Yeah, I know where you can get some." He poked his friend with a screwdriver and they both laughed. "What d'ya think, Roger?"

"That's not what I mean. If you can't help me, I'll go somewhere else. I don't have time to fool around."

Dennis said, "Half a bale of hay will cost you ten bucks."

Joan nodded, saying, "All right. Where is it?" She looked around the barn but didn't see any hay.

Roger pointed to the stall behind him to the right, "Over there. Come with me." He dropped the wrench he was holding and stood up, turned and motioned to her to follow. "Why are you dressed up in a costume?" Roger asked.

"I'm trying out for a part in a play. I'm playing a witch."

"Oh, I wondered why you were carrying a broom."

As they entered a stall, Joan could see a back wall stacked with baled hay. It looked very dry, just what she wanted. But she suddenly felt she was being attacked from behind and she bent down and swung her broom with all her strength. There was a thump as the handle struck something solid. Roger tried to grab Joan from the front, but she was too quick with the handle and she struck him over the left ear and jammed the handle into his crotch. Roger was yelling in pain, rolling over on the ground, and Dennis was lying in a heap, apparently unconscious.

"Smart-asses! Serves you right." She marched over to the hay, cut the twine bindings with a hand scythe that was hanging on the wall. She rewrapped the half-bale, dropped a ten dollar bill on the ground beside Dennis and peeked out the door to see if anyone was watching. She didn't see anybody, so she wrapped her cape around the hay, climbed on her broom and hovered for a few seconds to allow adjusting the center of gravity, leaned forward and swooshed into the air.

Joan found holding the hay awkward and decided to travel slower than she had when arriving in Timberville. She was on an important mission for the Wickons and she couldn't afford to drop the twenty pound bundle of hay. Her watch showed that she had been gone from camp slightly over an hour, so she expected to see Heloise on the return trip, especially since she was now flying at about half speed. She had been in the air a little higher than tree height for ten seconds when she looked back towards the small town. She wondered if all the young men of Timberville were as stupid as Dennis and Roger.

She soon dismissed the thoughts of the boys back at the barn when she saw a small black airborne object in the distance moving toward her. At first she imagined it was Heloise, but it was only a large bird moving slowly near the treetops. Not wanting any kind of confrontation, she climbed two hundred feet in altitude and avoided the fowl.

Another minute passed as Joan made the slow return journey. She switched arms holding the package of hay to avoid muscle fatigue. When Joan recognized a landmark from her earlier trip, she realized she had returned over halfway to camp. Just as she passed over a hill and dropped into a broad valley, a voice came from behind her.

"Let me help with that awkward load."

Without looking back, Joan recognized the voice immediately. Samantha was suddenly flying next to her. As they flew side-by-side, Sam edged closer, reached over and pulled the package to the center of her broom. Joan had finally released her death-grip on the valuable bundle.

Confidently, Sam said, "You can go ahead if you like. Tell Heloise I will be there directly."

Joan smiled, "I'll fly with you, if that's all right."

"Sure, that's okay with me. I'd appreciate the company. Heloise won't have to worry about either of us when we arrive together."

The local phone at the police station in Timberville rang three times before the police chief dropped his pencil and picked up.

"Hello. This is Chief Watters; how may I help you this morning?"

"This is Lila Swartz. I'd like to lodge a complaint. My boy Roger and his friend Dennis were brutally attacked out in our barn."

"Are the boys injured badly enough to require hospitalization?"

"Well, Dennis was hit on the head and was knocked unconscious. Roger was struck in the privates. I assume you know what that feels like."

"Yes, Mrs. Swartz. I played contact sports in school." The chief paused for a moment, thinking. "Did the boys see who hit them?"

"Oh, yes. It was a large woman dressed in black clothes and carrying a big broom stick. She told the boys she was trying out for a part in summer stock."

"Here in Timberville?"

"That's what she said."

"Summer stock is not being offered this summer; Covid and all."

"Well, she's also a liar then."

"I'm doing paperwork for the judge, so I can't come to see the boys, but I'll send Lieutenant Sanders out to interview them. Please have them stay on the property until noon."

"All right, I'll have them stay home this morning. Goodbye."

Before Chief Watters could reply, he heard a click as Mrs. Swartz hung up. He picked up the police broadcast microphone, set the frequency for Ken Sanders and said, "Ken, please go out to Swartz's and have a talk with their son, Roger, and his buddy, Dennis. Lila just called and said the boys were attacked in their barn by a woman dressed in a black costume. I'm a bit suspicious, those boys have a reputation for lying." The chief sat waiting for a few seconds and heard, "Ten-four." The chief shook his head and went back to the paperwork on his desk.

Samantha and Joan arrived at the Wickon camp, hovered next to Heloise's SUV and settled to the ground. Heloise was sitting in the cargo area of her vehicle sipping from a paper cup. She set the cup down and climbed out with her pad and pen. She checked her watch and realized her voice would be back in six hours. She was pleased there hadn't been any further attack on the camp and was happy to see Joan and Samantha.

Samantha dropped the bundle of straw to the ground, grinned, and sang, "We're back."

Heloise smiled and scribbled, *I assume the trip was uneventful?* She glanced at Sam and then Joan.

Joan had to tell her mentor of the boys' attack and Heloise smiled at how Joan had handled herself during the confrontation. When she heard the names, Roger and Dennis, she was ecstatic, but didn't want to show her jubilation, she just grinned. Heloise made a mental note to expound on one of the tenets of the Wickons: to only respond to hateful advances with appropriate defensive actions but not inflict permanent injury to the attacker.

Heloise tossed her pen and pad into her SUV and carried the bundle of straw to the firepit where half a dozen mentors and novices were busily preparing the scorched broom handles for new bristles. When she dropped the fresh straw to the ground a cheer arose, but Heloise waved her hands to silence the applause. She shook her head and brought Joan and Samantha forward to take a bow. Another round of applause occurred as Heloise gave her novice and coworker big hugs.

Joan and Sam knelt beside the pile of straw and began to sort the long strands from the chaff. Samantha established an assembly line of the mentors and as the handles were fashioned with new bristles, the refurbished brooms were claimed by the novice owners. Heloise handed each novice a slip of paper from her pad instructing the recipient to test her broom and leave the area to gather at The Husband mountain. The first novice, Joan, didn't bother to ask the reason for the apparent banishment, she followed orders without question. Aty was second in line and had to know more.

"Heloise, why are you sending us away?"

Heloise began scribbling on her notepad, the words appearing almost like magic. *Two reasons, Aty: for your protection and to keep the brooms beyond the retrieval ability of Satan's followers.*

Aty stuttered, "I, I should have figured that out. Sorry to have wasted your time. I hope your voice returns soon."

Heloise saw the embarrassment in Aty's face. She wrote, *It wasn't a waste. You can ask me anything. I hope these peeps leave before long too, thank you. I'm getting tired of writing things.* She watched Aty mount her broom, rise into the air and swoosh off to the mountain.

It took about fifteen minutes to complete the refurbishments for the novices and then the mentors began updating their own brooms. Heloise was monitoring the pile of straw and noted they would soon run out of bristles long enough for the brooms to fly adequately.

Samantha, carrying her broom, joined Heloise commenting, "I keep anticipating another attack, but nothing has happened. Should I go for more straw?"

Heloise nodded, peeped three times and jotted a note on her pad. She smiled as she wrote, *"You'd better wear your regular clothes. You won't travel as fast, but the others won't consider you a witch. Have Joan give you directions to that farm. I have some goggles for your eyes."*

Heloise retrieved a pair of goggles from her glove compartment, handed them to Sam and gave her a ten dollar bill. Sam straddled her broom, rose above the SUV, waved to Heloise, and swooshed away. Sam passed low over the trees, and was happy to be wearing goggles, as bugs were striking her face. She would have to clean the goggles before going back to camp.

Sam was in the air nearly half-an-hour before she saw the outskirts of Timberville. She saw the log cabin and barn coming into view so she landed, removed the goggles and hid her broom in the low-lying limbs of a large tree. She hung the goggles on the broom handle, straightened her clothes and began walking toward the cabin.

Two vehicles were parked at the large cabin, a newer model Ford pickup, and a large sedan, several years old. As Sam got closer, she noticed the car was actually a police cruiser marked with Timberville Police. From knowledge of Joan's earlier interaction with the boys, she concluded a policeman was talking to the young men. She hesitated for a moment and then rang the doorbell.

The door creaked slightly as it swung open to reveal a woman about Sam's age. She looked down at the woman, about five or six inches shorter than herself who asked, "May I help you?"

"I hope so. I'd like to purchase some hay from you."

The woman opened the screen door and stepped back. "Come in. There's someone here you should talk to."

Sam stepped into the foyer and then into the living room where two boys and a man in a police uniform were seated on a large leather-upholstered sofa. The policeman stood when Sam entered the room, the boys sat up, looked at each other, and then at Sam.

Mrs. Swartz introduced the males and asked, "We've never met, what is your name?"

CHAPTER 15

Sam smiled and said, "I'm Samantha Simms. I work with Heloise at the Sisterhood of Wickon training camp near the Sisters Mountains. I came in to buy some straw. One of our novitiates, Joan, bought some hay from your boys this morning, half-a-bale."

Mrs. Swartz, hands on her hips, commented, "Yes. We were just talking about that. She beat up the boys out in the barn."

"Joan? She's just a little bit of a person. How could she beat up these big strong boys?" Samantha gestured to Dennis and Roger who were glancing at each other, realizing they had been caught lying about their attacker.

Lieutenant Sanders gave the boys a questioning dirty look and said, "How about telling me the truth now?"

Dennis spoke excitedly, "We weren't gonna hurt her, Lieutenant. We were gonna tease her a bit."

"Sure, you were. Did you lay your hands on her?"

"Well, yeah. She turned around real quick like and her broom handle hit me in the head. It was kind of an accident, I guess."

Roger added, "I tried to grab her to keep her from falling, but she hit me in the balls with that broom. I'm still sore."

Lieutenant Sanders looked away from the boys to Mrs. Swartz, "I think I've got all the information I need. You might tell these two that if they don't straighten up, they'll end up in prison. They'll run out of chances if they continue this kind of behavior." Ken closed his note pad and started toward the door.

Mrs. Swartz followed him outside thanking him for coming to interview the boys. She went back inside as Ken drove away.

"Roger, go get Mrs. Simms a half bale of hay, no charge." She gave Dennis a disapproving look, "Dennis, go home." Mrs. Swartz ushered Dennis out the door and said, "Tell your mother to call me. We need to talk." She returned to talk to Samantha, "These boys! Tell Joan I'm sorry for the way the boys acted." She escorted Sam to the entrance, asking, "What do you need the hay for, if I may ask?"

"We had a small fire and our brooms were singed. We've been repairing them with new bristles."

"What do you do with the brooms?"

Samantha winked and replied, "We can't fly without good brooms."

Mrs. Swartz frowned and then laughed, "Oh, I could have guessed. How do you get back to camp? I don't see a car."

"Oh, I'm parked a ways off, under a tree."

Roger returned from the barn carrying a partial bale of hay. He had rewrapped it to keep the bale from disintegrating as it was being transported. Mrs. Swartz instructed, "Put it down here on the porch and go in the house. We need to have a serious talk."

Samantha thanked Mrs. Swartz, picked up the bundle and departed. When Sam had walked ten yards from the house, she could still hear Mrs. Swartz's voice, even though the door was closed. She couldn't help smiling at Mrs. Swartz's strong conversation with her son. Sam located her broom, donned her goggles, adjusted her position on her broom to compensate for the added weight, and took to the air. She was back in camp in exactly thirty minutes.

Sam dropped the new bundle of straw where the mentors were preparing the remaining handles for upgrading and said with an encouraging tone, "Carry on ladies." Sam wanted to change clothes so bug spots could be removed from her regulars. She turned around to go to her car and saw Heloise walking toward her holding up a handwritten message, *"You made good time, congratulations. Any problems?"*

"I met the two boys mentioned, Mrs. Swartz, and Police Lieutenant Sanders. I straightened out a few of the boys' lies. Mrs. Swartz was redressing Roger when I left. She has strong lungs."

Heloise smiled and started chirping. She scribbled a note, *The Satanists haven't reappeared. They must be planning something they think will be devastating."*

"That's good, we should be ready when they come back. Let's meet with the other mentors and plan our defense."

It was nearly noon when the Satanists had completed a plan to take over the Wickon sisterhood camp. Loathese sent Melas to observe the camp and report back right before they would barge into the Wickon facilities and spray the campers with a mist that would cause the members to freeze in place. Loathese had emptied the bear repellant from their dispensers and filled the spray guns with statue simulator for humans. After producing inertness, the three invaders would loot valuables from the Wickons. Maybe the campers would then consider changing their altruistic notions.

However, the three malevolent women had no inkling they were going to be attacked from their flanks and the air. They were concentrating on the Wickon encampment so intensely, they hadn't heard what was coming from the Crest Trail a few hundred yards away.

Bear, Wolf, and Owl had finally caught up with the sources of the scents they had been doggedly following. Bear and Wolf had an innate plan of attack, Bear, head on and Wolf crawling as close as possible to the ground, circling to take advantage of Bear's ensuing distraction. He would attack from behind, sinking his razor-sharp fangs into their unprotected legs. He was salivating as he imagined the warm blood gushing from shredded calf muscles. He wasn't hungry, he was angry, but he wasn't sure why.

Owl had been consuming fare all day that he knew would be easily converted to fecal material to be unloaded at opportune times. He had passed up consuming field mice, pellets would not be effective. Owl was a natural dive-bomber and would coordinate with the land attacks, swooping down from the air, spattering white feces on his prey. He knew his targets almost instinctively, expecting his droppings would be more disgusting in human hair than difficult to remove.

High above the forest to observe surreptitiously, Owl watched as one of the three humans began to separate from the others. He would have to be aware of her at all times. He could see Bear closing in on the other two women, edging closer and closer. He couldn't see where his friend, Wolf, was but knew his other companion was close by in the timber.

Bear was almost upon the two women when one of them turned and shrieked. The other one grabbed something and as she backed away, she extended her arm and a hazy cloud shot toward Bear.

Bear growled, continued his charge, took a swipe at the woman and knocked an object from her hand. The woman fell and Wolf was on her in a spit second, biting at her extremities. The woman who had screamed yelled, "I'm coming, Hazelene, try to climb a tree."

The screamer began dispensing another cloud of material at Wolf as she approached and he stopped biting, backed away, shaking his head and howling. The two women came together and helped each other onto a rocky outcrop beyond the reach of Wolf and Bear. When Owl saw the women evading his friends, he swooped down, clawing at their hair and releasing a glob of white poop on one. He flew to a high tree branch for a moment, focused on the other woman and made a second pass, discharging another blob of feces as he swooped past her head, claws extended.

Melas was too far away to have heard sounds of the attack from the bear and wolf and continued to observe the Wickon camp. When she saw the campers taking to the air, and no novices present, she withdrew into the woods, made a hasty about-face and started back to report to Loathese and Hazelene. Expecting to see her two companions preparing for their escapade with the Wickons, she was shocked when she saw them atop a large rock, shouting at a bear. She hadn't yet noticed the canine. A growl came from behind her and she spun around to see a large wolf, mouth hanging open, drooling.

Melas scanned the terrain and saw a three-to-four foot branch she could use as a weapon. She moved quickly, picked up the stout-looking limb and backed toward her friends, ready to strike at the bear and wolf.

Loathese called out, "There's only room for two up here, Melas. The wolf and bear can't bite, they've been sprayed so their jaws are frozen open. The animals' fur prevents the freezing potion from working on their bodies, but watch out for the bear, his claws can rip you apart."

Melas squinted at her devil-worshiping sisters, and asked, "What is that in your hair? Is that blood on Hazelene's legs?"

Loathese reached up to feel with her fingers and realized what had happened. "That owl pooped on our heads. He can attack with his talons and is big enough to knock you down. The wolf bit Hazelene before I could spray him to lock his jaw."

Bear and Wolf were slowly circling the rock outcrop watching for an opportunity to take advantage of the woman with the stick and making sure the other two wouldn't get away.

Loathese crouched down and whispered to Melas, "The animals will tire before long and we will sneak away when they fall asleep."

"I hope it's soon; I don't want to get clawed or pooped on."

Loathese had forgotten to ask for Melas' report about the Wickon camp, but as Hazelene sat atop the rock in slight pain, she asked, "What did you observe at the camp?"

"I returned quickly to tell you. All the mentors have repaired their brooms and resumed flying. The novices have apparently vanished."

Loathese and Hazelene had a short discussion. Afterward, Loathese whispered to Melas, "When we escape, we will travel to the Wickon camp spraying our trail with our scent. The animals will follow our odors and will encounter the Wickons instead of us. We will ignore the Wickons and leave the area."

Swinging the bare branch from side to side keeping the wolf away and evidently entertaining the bear, Melas whispered back, "You mean we will leave the Wickons to the animals and return to the East Coast?"

"Yes. Hazelene and I need to return to Salem, Massachusetts. There is a preacher we must deal with. He's spreading lies about us; saying we are good and mean no harm."

Melas laughed in delight, "Oh! I am going to warp his vocal cords so he can't talk any longer without great difficulty. His speech will be very painful."

Loathese grinned and nodded, "I'll let you lead our little group. You have very clever ideas."

The Wickons assembled for a group meeting to discuss their options provided the Satanists returned.

It was decided to send Samantha for the novices. She left immediately for The Husband mountain. As she flew near the mountain, she noticed a disturbance taking place not far from the coast trail. In order to avoid detection, she rose in altitude and circled the commotion. Possessing a pair of opera glasses, Sam took a closer look and spotted a bear and wolf threatening the Devil worshipers. Sam suddenly understood why the camp had not been further attacked by the Satanists; they were dealing with their own problems.

When Sam reached the southeastern side of The Husband mountain, she spotted the novices gathered in a tight group about fifty meters from the Coast Trail in a depression surrounded by timber. She decided to approach slowly to keep from alarming them. Jean was watching the sky in the direction of the camp expecting one of the mentors. Jean said, "We have a visitor, ten o'clock high." The novices glanced up and Evelyn exclaimed, "Relax, it's all right. It's Samantha." The girls waved as Samantha glided from the air to a perfect landing.

Samantha spoke, "It's time to return to camp, ladies. We're safe from the Devil devotees."

Several of the novices asked in unison, "What happened? Did the mentors chase them off?"

Sam grinned, "No, we haven't seen them at camp. The Satanists are preoccupied…with a large bear."

Jean volunteered, "We've been having a meeting and have chosen a name for our group, The NeoWics. I was chosen as president and Evelyn is Vice President."

"That's good to know. You have been busy when away from camp. Congratulations!"

Jean queried, "Has Heloise gotten her voice back?"

"I'm afraid not, but she should be speaking normally by the time we return to camp. Heloise gave me instructions for you for the trip back: She wants you to fly in formation, like geese; use your cape and blouse draped over your outstretched arms to resemble the birds; don't fly too fast, you might lose your balance."

Aty laughed, "Are we a gaggle of Wickons?"

Samantha grinned, "No, you're a woggle."

Jean giggled, "We're a woggle of Wickons! Let's fly!"

It took the young Wickons about ten minutes to get their flying uniforms prepared. When airborne, Samantha took the lead with five wogglers on either side, forming a nearly perfect *V* shape.

CHAPTER 16

Owl sat on a branch halfway to the top of a big fir patiently watching Wolf and Bear lose interest in the three women trapped on and next to a giant rock. He was sure that Wolf and Bear were getting tired and probably like himself, very hungry. Owl made two more fecal dropping runs and all three women bore streaks of white in their hair. He had noticed some activity of rodents during his last bombing run and decided he would go hunting; besides, Bear and Wolf didn't need his services. So, as the sun was dropping behind the hills, Owl went searching for dinner.

He flew back along the trail to the spot where both mouse and squirrel activity attracted his attention earlier in the day. The delectable little animals could hide effectively during the day, but Owl's hearing and night eyesight was like a destroyer sitting on top of a noisy submarine. The submersible would have no chance of escape. When Owl had a mouse and a small squirrel in his talons, he flew back to Bear's and Wolf's location. He took his former position in the tree and began eating supper.

The next time he looked down at Wolf and Bear, they were asleep and the women were gone. He felt he should have screeched an alarm to his companions, but he must have fallen asleep after eating and missed the human activity below. Owl was sure Bear and Wolf would resume hunting the women at first light, not enough blood had decorated the rocks and ground.

Satan's disciples spirited away from their tormentors when it grew dark. Melas focused on watching the animals grow weary. When eye lids were closed for several minutes, she considered the animals to be sound asleep. She reached up, tapped on the rock and whispered to Loathese and Hazelene. It was time to depart.

As the three women progressed through the timber, occasionally having to climb over rocks and around shrubs, they sprayed objects with their scent at seventy-five to one-hundred-yard intervals. When they approached within a hundred yards of the Wickon camp, they buried their spray bottles and began traveling due north to State Route 242 where they planned to steal a car and set off toward the East Coast to more familiar territory.

Heloise had gotten her normal voice back during the Wickon's evening meal. She was a little hoarse at first but following dinner was able to speak clearly with only a slight cough. With a canteen of water in her hand, she spoke to the campers, "If we are attacked, I want the novices to leave, load their hats with loose dirt and drop it on the Satanists from a safe distance."

The elder Wickons would follow by dropping their capes with commands to tie the attackers' hands and feet. With the Satanists disabled, they would be banished from the Oregon wilderness. Samantha and Heloise were to perform the banishment ritual with all twenty Wickons present. The combined strength of a score of like-minded Wickons would compel the Satanists to accept defeat and leave the area, forbidden, even for Satanists, to ever return.

The Wickons posted four night guards to watch for the Devil worshippers, but by morning no warnings had rung out. Heloise slept better than the night before, only waking twice when guards were changing. Joan slept soundly next to her in the SUV, snoring lightly. Heloise gently touched her novice's sleeping bag and the faint gurgling noises stopped.

The campers were all fed and policing the area by eight a.m. They were anticipating the last night in the wilderness when the elders would instruct the newbies about night flying at speeds faster than sound. The novices were making sure their garments were in good repair, especially their heat-resistant boots. Everyone coated their footwear with Abraz-Off, the anti-friction coating to reduce overheating at high speed. The campers conversed in small groups while they readied equipment, discussing the week's activities and the expectations of the impending flight.

Sudden commotion occurred when Aty came running breathlessly into camp yelling, "Bear! Bear! A bear is after me!"

The attention of everyone was briefly on Aty and then all eyes stared at the woods where she had emerged. From the noises issuing from the near forest, the Wickons could tell something big was approaching, but was it really a bear? Maybe an elk or a crazed mountain lion would make such noises.

Aty had been right, it was a bear. But it reared up on its hind legs and growled when it saw the group of women. A few seconds later, a large wolf appeared, tongue hanging out. It sat beside the bear slowly gazing at each of the Wickons. The bear dropped to all fours and sat beside the wolf. It too looked over the women as the wolf had done. The campers knew something strange was going on.

Jean gasped, "The wolf looks hungry."

Evelyn called out, "What should we do, Heloise?"

"Whatever you do, don't run. None of us can outrun a bear or a wolf. I suggest we move slowly back to our vehicles, climb in and lock the doors."

Instead of moving to her vehicle, Samantha followed Heloise, asking, "Do you think they're hungry? Maybe they smelled our breakfast."

"Great idea, Sam. I cooked extra bacon and ham this morning… for snacks. Let's use our brooms to serve them. That way we won't have to get very close."

Sam flinched when the wolf growled again. She grabbed at Heloise's arm and whispered, "You said we, don't you mean I?"

There was a fluttering sound and a large owl swooped over the Wickons and landed on the back of the bear. The bear seemed to ignore the big bird as it swiveled its head from side to side watching the campers.

Taken aback, Heloise whispered to Samantha, "There are three of them now. Could they be the Satanists in different forms?"

Sam thought for a few seconds and reacted, "If so, they would have to be females, just like the Devil worshipers, wouldn't they?"

"Yes, that's right! Get Katie Lynch, she's a biologist. Maybe she can tell the sex of the animals without getting too close. I'll get the ham and bacon. I'll have Jean get them a bucket of water."

Word was passed around the group and within thirty seconds Katie appeared beside Heloise and Samantha.

Katie asked, "What can I do? You've already said the right thing."

Sam whispered, "Are the animals male or female?"

Katie squinted and looked closely at the wolf, not as hairy as the bear. "I can't tell without seeing it walk or urinate. Have you given them any water?"

Jean was carrying a bucket half-full of water from the nearby stream. Katie instructed, "Put the water about ten feet from the wolf and move away. If he comes after you, have your broom handy and take to the air."

As Jean nervously placed the water near the animals and backed away, Heloise put the extra pork from breakfast on the bristles of her broom and approached the beasts. She extended her broom, ensured the scent of the meat was perceived by the bear and wolf, set her broom down and retreated. Before the wolf and bear had a chance to react, the owl hopped to the broom and took a piece of bacon. It flew to a tree, lit on a limb and made a strange series of noises, almost sounding like English words run together as it ate the bacon.

Everyone heard repeated garbled sounds from the owl, "Jebsaoul."

Katie was a little surprised at the character of the owl's gabble. It was a very strange sound to be coming from an owl. It was more like talk from a parrot. It struck her that the owl was actually trying to tell the Wickons something. As she watched the big gray wolf grab a chunk of ham, it seemed to swallow it whole and began moving toward the water. That was when she saw its genitalia. It was a male wolf. It couldn't be a female Devil worshiper transformed. She quickly informed Heloise.

Heloise had been watching the bear and wolf with great interest, noting they were not acting as wild animals. Normally, the wolf and bear would be antagonists, not sitting quietly side by side sharing the food she had given them. And the sounds from the owl were certainly strange, almost as if it was trying to say something in English.

The owl was repeating a different sound now, "Berysawoof." The bird would then reiterate the sounds, "Jebsaoul. Berysawoof." After four or five repetitions, the owl would seem to rest for about ten seconds and then start the noises again.

Jean and Aty rushed over from talking with a group of novices and mentioned to Heloise, "Some of us have been listening closely to the owl and we might know what it is saying. Aty came up with it first. She listens to rap and other pop songs and can understand most of the words. I don't get half of what the performers are saying."

Heloise and Samantha were engrossed with Jean's words. Heloise asked, "What have you girls come up with?"

Jean glanced at Aty, "Tell her, Aty."

Aty stepped forward and said, "I believe it said Jeb's an owl…but Jeb might be Jeff. The other sound is Barry's a wolf."

Heloise mulled over what Aty had said and it struck her that the three Satanists had transformed at least two unsuspecting people into animals, probably as a mean joke. The animals were undoubtedly males and young naive ones at that, probably hikers from the Pacific Crest Trail. But what about the bear? The owl hadn't mentioned the bear.

Heloise discussed her ideas with Samantha. Sam said, "I think you're probably correct. The owl is making sounds kind of like a parrot. Let's see if we can get the owl to mention the bear."

Samantha talked with the novices and told them to start talking about the bear, loud enough so the owl could hear the word *bear*. Perhaps hearing the word would trigger the owl to say something about the bear. Joan remarked, "Kind of like priming the pump?" Sam chuckled; surprised Joan had heard the expression.

Less than five minutes elapsed before the girls heard the owl utter, "Laroysabair." Joan ran to Samantha and said excitedly, "It worked! The owl said, 'Leeroy's a bear.' At least that's what Aty thinks the owl said. I think she's right; I truly listened closely." Joan was convinced that the novices had heard the truth about the bear, and so was Samantha. Samantha had to tell Heloise the news.

Samantha's eyes roamed the campsite and found Heloise getting closer than a broom's length to the bear and wolf, nearly feeding the animals from her hands. Sam approached slowly and watched the animals briefly focus on her and then back to the food.

"Heloise, the bear's name is Leeroy. The girls got the owl to talk."

"Good to know, Sam. That confirms what we thought. The Satanist's transformed three men into these animals. I guess it's our duty to reverse the spells."

"I don't think we have a choice. No one else on the West Coast has the knowledge or the constituents for the reversal. The good thing is there are twenty of us so the life force needed shouldn't harm us in any critical way. The youngsters should hardly notice any loss of function. However, the mentors might suffer appreciably. We have more to lose since it will take us much longer to recover."

Heloise observed, "You are right. Do you have any of the elements for the reversal with you?"

"No, I didn't pack any of the ingredients when I was leaving for your home in Timberville."

Heloise gave a heavy sigh, "I'll have to fly home and gather the materials. I'll take Jean with me. You'll have to handle the situation here while we're gone. Okay?"

Sam frowned, a bit concerned, "How long will you be?"

"It should only take an hour, barring any problems."

Heloise and Jean soared on separate brooms and were dressed in light blue clothing so they would be inconspicuous during their daylight flight. They flew a slight distance above the tallest trees and didn't encounter any birds on the way to Timberville. Jean followed Heloise at a hundred yards and landed a few seconds after her mentor.

The neighborhood was extremely quiet, no one was out doing yard work or walking their dog. Heloise watched for activity within a block of her home but was satisfied no neighbors had seen them land in her backyard.

"Let's go inside. What we need is in a small red case in my bedroom closet."

Heloise unlocked the back door and they passed through a utility room into a short hallway.

She pointed, "First door on the right."

CHAPTER 17

The sun was going down and the hallway was dimly lit but Jean could see the bedroom door. It was ajar about an inch. She took one more step, pushed it fully open and jumped back. Two fat little mice ran out and scurried down the hall into the living room. "Oh! I hate mice! I'll whack them with my broom while you get the case from the closet."

Heloise objected, "No, don't kill them, we need them for owl food. Owls don't drink water like other birds. They get water from their food. We'll load the rodents with a potion and let the owl have a snack." She walked quickly to her closet and pulled the red container from the top shelf and showed Jean its contents. Inside were six small containers that resembled chess pawns, in various shapes and different colors. In addition, there was a small rectangular wire cage for live food items, perfect for two plump mice.

"How are we going to catch the mice, Heloise? We need to get them quickly."

Heloise smiled and rubbed her hands together, "No problem, my two cats are at my next-door neighbors. I'll get them."

Heloise's neighbor, Ed Henry, had agreed to take care of her two cats, Amos and Astrid, while she was away for a week. There was one day remaining in the interval, but she needed the cats' assistance now. They could stay alone one more night in her house without any ill effects. She would leave them enough food and water to last until she returned the next day.

Ed saw Heloise approaching and assumed she wanted her cats. He wasn't sure the week was up, but he hadn't kept count of the days and didn't recall when she had brought them over. The cats had been fun to have around.

Ed was first to the front door and opened it before Heloise could ring the bell or knock. He was carrying Astrid.

"Hi, Ed. I've come to get Amos and Astrid; I've got a mouse problem…actually, mice."

"Come in, Heloise. I'll get Amos for you. He's in the kitchen." He gave Heloise Astrid, who was purring loudly.

"It's been six days and I've come home for only an hour. I'll be back permanently tomorrow afternoon."

Ed went to the kitchen and returned with the smaller cat, Amos. "Here you go. I enjoyed having them for the week."

"Thank you for taking care of them. You're a good neighbor."

"You're welcome. Bring them over anytime."

"Thanks again, Ed."

Heloise walked quickly back to her house and in twenty seconds, had two mice in the cage inside the red container. After setting out food and water and making sure the litter boxes were ready for activity, the women went out on the back porch and locked the door.

Jean inquired, "Won't Ed see us leave?"

Heloise nodded, "Maybe. We'd better climb over the back fence and leave from behind the trees. I don't think his hearing and eyesight are good enough to notice us."

On the return trip, Jean led and her mentor followed. It was a test of Jean's navigation skills which she passed without difficulty. The fliers made the reverse trip to camp quickly despite Heloise carrying the extra weight and the bulkiness of the red container.

Heloise removed the small colored bottles from the case and placed them on the cover of the propane stove. The Wickons gathered around to watch and learn how to make the potion. Since the animals had not made any antagonistic advances on the women, they were being ignored for the present.

Heloise inquired, "Are there any novices that enjoy baking?"

There were two "Yeses." Evelyn and Aty stepped forward. Aty said, "What can we do to help?"

"I need a quart of water in a mixing bowl. It needs to be accurately measured, so measure out four cups. That'll make a quart."

While the girls obtained the water, Heloise recited the recipe so all could hear: "All ingredients must be fresh; five drops each of purple, orange, and yellow; ten drops each of red, white, and blue; warm until the color fades, but do not boil. Do not use until cool."

Katie, the biologist, stated, "The wolf and bear can drink normally, but the owl is different."

Heloise nodded, "Yes, Jean and I brought two plump mice for the owl, we just have to have them drink some of the potion. Katie, how would you like to give the mice some water?"

Katie raised her eyebrows and grinned, "I'd be happy to. I don't like mice one bit."

A couple of other mentors set up another stove for warming the potion. Aty and Evelyn returned with the measured water and set it beside Heloise. "Thank you ladies. I'll watch you add the components and count the drops for you."

A number of the Wickons came closer and watched Aty and Evelyn remove the seals from the little bottles. The girls were to alternate adding the drops from the colored containers and Heloise kept track. Before Evelyn had added all five drops from the purple bottle, the other Wickons were counting in unison; "three, four, five." Aty continued with the orange container. Heloise let the others do the counting. After Aty had finished with the orange bottle, she whispered to Heloise, "They're making me nervous. I'd rather you did the counting."

"I can understand. Why don't you concentrate on your inner being and count for yourself, ignoring anything coming from outside your body."

Aty looked a bit confused but said, "Okay, I'll try that."

Evelyn finished with five drops from the yellow container and Aty carefully picked up the red vial. She unscrewed the top and began adding drops to the water, counting to herself, ignoring all sounds from around her. When she reached ten drops, she glanced at Heloise and winked, the suggestion had worked. Aty smiled and put the top back on the little bottle.

Evelyn and Aty finished with the white and blue containers, then Heloise warmed the solution until all color disappeared. Katie removed the wire cage containing the mice from Heloise's red carrying case and partially submerged the cage in the cooled potion. The mice swam for a few minutes, drank from the water and clung to the walls of the wire cage. Katie, who had been responsible for and watching the mice closely, announced, "I believe the owl's food is ready, Heloise."

The owl had been watching the feeding of his comrades by the humans. The bacon had lacked moister and he was thinking of going hunting again when he noticed one of the women walking toward his tree. She was carrying a small box, maybe something for him to eat. With his eagle eye, he noticed movement in the container. Yes! Mice! These people hadn't forgotten him.

His eyes were fixed on the box and when the woman put it down, two mice ran from the container. He was on them in a flash, one in each claw. He vanished into the timber for about five minutes and then returned to his perch.

Heloise and Jean had been watching the owl react. Jean asked, "Where did he go, Heloise?"

Heloise grinned, "I think he wanted to eat alone, perhaps he has poor table manners."

Jean laughed, "You know, you are very funny."

While the owl was away, the Wickons had placed a small container of potion near the wolf, hoping the bear would not attempt to drink. The bear's large broad snout would prevent him from slurping. Because of his large mass, he was going to need more life-force from the mentors, requiring several of them to postpone returning home for several days. Some of the mentors would have to drive several hundred miles with enough of their normal energy drained to possibly impair their driving and causing traffic accidents. Mr. Bear would be administered to later.

Heloise, Samantha, and Evelyn, Sam's daughter, decided to remain at the camp after the other mentors and novices had begun their return trips home. They would try to work out a plan to reverse transform the bear.

Nearly fifteen minutes after the owl had devoured the mice, he tumbled from the tree onto a bush, cushioning his fall. Katie and Samantha transported the big owl to the center of camp where the original firepit had been. Heloise, with Jean as her assistant, were preparing for the reverse transformation.

The mentors' manual warned that during the change, the patient might experience atrial fibrillation, so a defibrillator had to be available for emergency use. Therefore, it was necessary to construct such a device, using a car battery for voltage and two metal pancake spatulas as conductors. Jumper cables would carry the electricity for a brief shock.

The previously constructed firepit would be the site for the reverse transformations. But it would have to be enlarged to accommodate a human approximately six feet tall. The novices were assigned to expand the circular pit and place kindling at the east and west compass points. Pails of water were placed at the northern and southern positions.

The lifeless appearing owl was placed at the center of the circle, head pointing northward, and its form covered with a blanket. Then, the ten newest Wickons formed a circle and joined hands forming a human ring about the owl. Heloise stood outside the novice circle at the north, Samantha at the south. Directly behind each mentor was a flaming torch.

Heloise and Samantha held several sheets of parchment containing words written in calligraphy. As an integral part of the transformation, the artistically written words were to be read by each novice as the sacred pleas were passed around the circle.

Heloise started the process, handing the closest novice the first plea.

Novice Aty received and unrolled the first parchment. She read in a loud voice, "Angel of the Heavens, bring fire from the stars to this poor creature." Passing the written words counterclockwise, they were read nine more times before the kindling was set afire and thrown onto the blanket, where each ignited piece of wood brightened in a different color of the spectrum and as bright as a flare.

Aty gasped, and turning toward Heloise, said, "The blanket will burn and set the owl afire! His feathers!"

Heloise calmly replied, "Don't worry, Aty, the blanket is made of fire retardant material."

Samantha gave the next plea to Evelyn. She unrolled the sheet of paper and read, "Angels of the oceans, lakes, and rivers, bring water to this poor creature." The written words were again passed counterclockwise. Following the tenth reading, the pails of water were used to extinguish the still brightly burning kindling.

Heloise moved to the western compass point and presented Joan with the next parchment. Joan read with confidence, "Angels from the Earth's center and the deserts of Africa, bring soil to this unfortunate creature." Passing the paper clockwise, each novice read the words and flung a handful of dirt on the blanket.

Samantha held the fourth and final piece of paper, which she passed to Jean. Jean recited, "Angels of the sky, from the lowest deserts to the highest mountains, bring lifegiving air to this unfortunate creature." When the last novice read the words, a warm breeze began to blow from the mountains, unusual for this time of year at the altitude of the camp.

Heloise and Samantha remained standing and all novices sat facing the blanket holding hands, heads bowed. The standing mentors said in unison, "Following this verse, reverse the curse, which changed a man into this bird. Angels of the universe grant us this desire: convert this feathered creature to a human as he was before."

The blanket began to swell as if hundreds of birds were trying to escape from under the cover. A loud fluttering of wings occurred and then a piercing screech loud enough to hurt one's ears came from the center of the firepit. The novice's heads snapped back, fearful of what was happening, but they tightly grasped each other's hands. They held on to each other to keep the circle intact. The blanket continued to move, rising as it undulated, circular waves issuing from the center.

New sounds, clearly spoken words, were coming from under the writhing blanket. "Help! What is going on? I'm naked! Leeray! Barry! Where are my clothes? I'll get even with you guys!"

Heloise called out, "Young man…under the blanket, there are twelve women here. Cover yourself unless you don't think your nakedness will embarrass you."

From under the blanket came, "I need some clothes and something to drink. There is a terrible taste in my mouth. Where are my friends?"

Heloise said, "Wrap yourself and stick your head out. We'll talk."

The blanket rose two feet into the air and swirled around the figure beneath. A young man's head appeared, slowly turned three hundred sixty degrees to take in his surroundings. He asked, "Why are all these girls sitting in a circle?"

Heloise questioned, "Is your name Jeb?"

"Jeb? No, it's Jeff. Say, where are Barry and Leeray?"

Heloise pointed at the bear and wolf. "Over there."

Jeff jumped back, startled. "I don't see them, only a bear and a wolf, or maybe that's a malnourished old dog. Why are those animals here? It looks like the wolf is asleep, but that bear could be dangerous."

CHAPTER 18

Heloise addressed the novices, "Ladies, thank you for your presence. You are dismissed. I suggest you get some rest."
Jeff watched the young women break the circle and disperse to various sections of camp. He was still confused and asked, "Can someone tell me what is going on? Where are Barry and Leeray?" He turned toward Heloise and said, "You seem to be in charge. Can you explain what's happening?"

"My name is Heloise and I run a summer camp for girls to instruct them how to manage outdoor life in the woods. All together there are twenty members of our group. We are Wickons, white witches, that mean no harm. The young ladies just helped transform you from an owl to a human. Do you remember visiting three older women several days ago?"

Jeff, frozen in place like a statue, his eyes roving for what seemed a minute, said, "Yeah, but my memory is kind of hazy. I was with my friends, Barry and Leeray, and we drank some coffee. Maybe it was tea. I think we were with three women, not very attractive."

"Those women were witches, followers of Satan. You drank a potion and were turned into an owl," Heloise said. "Your friends were transformed into a wolf and a bear."

Jeff seemed slightly out of touch with reality, rapidly blinking, trying to make sense of the scene.

Samantha arrived carrying a shirt and pants, which she gave to Jeff. He put on the clothes shielding himself with the blanket and stepped away from the covering. He had no shoes, so he walked cautiously over to the wolf, avoiding rocks and thorns, and touched the animal with his right hand. He looked at Heloise, "Which one is this?"

"The owl told us his name is Barry."

"Can you get him back to being human?"

"Yes, you can help us."

"What can I do? I don't know any magic."

"It would help if we had some of his belongings. Where would we find them?"

"I don't know but I could make a guess if I had a map of the Crest Trail."

Heloise led Jeff to her SUV and laid out a map on the floor of the cargo area. She pointed out the Three Sisters and their current location. Jeff put his right forefinger on the trail and slowly traced southward.

"Here! I think this is where we were camped with those women. They built us a lean-to. I'll bet they hid our things nearby." He looked at the map's legend and said, "That's almost forty-five miles from here. That's three days of hiking."

Heloise smiled, "We can get there in less than thirty minutes."

"No way. You can't take a vehicle on the trail."

She grinned, "Come with me, Jeff. You're in for a little surprise."

Heloise extracted her double occupancy broom from her car while Jeff watched curiously and somewhat amused. What was this woman going to do with this long-handled broom? She called to Aty and Jean and said, "Suit up for a short trip. I need more eyes for a search. Follow this young man and me. We're taking a short flight."

Jeff was confused. What did this woman mean by a short flight? Did these women have a hidden helicopter nearby? His confusion was replaced by disbelief and a little fear when two young women suddenly arrived riding brooms like they were horses. Aty and Jean hovered head high about ten feet away from Heloise's car.

Heloise straddled her lengthy broom and said, "Climb on behind me, Jeff. Put your hands on my waist and hang on tight."

Jeff had never ridden a tandem bicycle before or even a horse and certainly not a broom flying through the air. He gulped and was nearly sick as the bad taste returned. He had antacid tablets in his backpack but that wasn't available. He took a deep breath, coughed and spat out a small piece of bone. His stomach seemed to calm down as he wondered if he had broken a tooth.

Heloise said, "Are you ready?"

Jeff was thinking this was all some type of trick but he decided to cooperate. "Yeah." Before he could think of anything else, he was in the air above the trees and accelerating. He slid back on the broom and held tighter. He looked down at the treetops beginning to flash by, shut his eyes, and intensified his grip on Heloise. He decided he was dreaming so he kept his eyes shut for several minutes, wind whistling and tearing at his borrowed clothing, mostly at his pant legs. His feet were getting cold. He tried to tuck them up against his thighs for warmth, but that was little help. Opening his eyes, he turned his head to the right and then to the left and saw they were being followed by two young women on brooms. This had to be a dream, but why wasn't he able to wake up? He wanted to pinch himself, but he couldn't release his grip on Heloise, his fear of falling was his biggest thought.

After what seemed to Jeff to be hours, but was only about thirty minutes of near agony, the motion slowed and he saw it, the lean-to. Heloise circled the area slowly and asked, "Is this the place?"

Jeff recognized some boulders and the lean-to, although the small structure had been damaged and rebuilt by other hikers. He saw a circle of rocks which he didn't recognize, but he remembered a tree where he had seen a kitten. No, that wasn't the same tree. This one was much larger and farther from the trail than the kitten-tree.

Jeff and the three women settled to the ground as if dropping to the main floor in an elevator, but with no sound or bumping. Heloise commented, "Let's look for any disturbed ground within ten yards of the lean-to. The Satanists wouldn't have exerted much energy to conceal three backpacks. Look closely."

Without shoes, Jeff remained on the trail and looked to either side for disturbed soil. Jeff's keen eyesight allowed him to quickly scan for small, raised portions of earth and when Aty was close to the large tree, he noticed the absence of weeds and grass at the base of the fir. He had focused on the young woman for a few seconds and almost missed the disturbed earth. She had caught his eyes when they mounted their brooms and left the camp area.

He pointed toward Aty and called out, "There!" She was surprised by his yell and almost stumbled over the small hump at her feet. She looked down and stepped back. Heloise and Jean joined her and began digging with sharp sticks they found lying near the trail. The backpacks, buried under only six inches of dirt, were pulled out of the shallow hole and carried to Jeff. Jean carried an orange pack with two purple stripes which Jeff recognized as Barry's. Aty had his black, blue striped bag and Heloise had Leeray's entirely red pack. The ladies dropped the dirty packs on the ground at Jeff's feet. He knelt, brushed off the dirt, opened his bag, pulled out a rolled up shirt, folded pants and a pair of sneakers.

Jeff carried his backpack and clothes to the lean-to, changed into his own shirt and pants and put on his shoes. He hadn't investigated the rest of his pack when with the women, but now his curiosity was overwhelming. The weight of his pack seemed about right, but he had to check on the integrity of his package of marijuana. He hoped the Satanists hadn't pilfered from his stash. Luck was with him; the grass was still sealed tightly as before. He assumed the other packs were in the same condition as his, so he would take them back to the Wickon camp unopened.

Jeff crawled out from under the lean-to and inquired, "Can we take these packs back to the camp with us? Will the added weight cause any problems?"

Heloise was quick to answer, "We'll just slow down a little, the brooms can handle the extra luggage."

Jean and Aty had already donned Leeray's and Barry's packs, anticipating the return to camp. Jeff strapped on his pack, climbed on behind Heloise and the three brooms and passengers took to the air. Jeff hadn't timed the first trip, but the return seemed to go faster. Maybe he wasn't as afraid of falling and was more relaxed even though they were moving through the air at nearly ninety miles per hour. His shoes were keeping his feet from getting cold as his shocked mind concluded that he was not dreaming.

Jeff and Heloise glided from the treetops to the ground next to the enlarged firepit where the nine other mentors were waiting. As they stepped to the ground, Heloise spoke to Samantha, "Is the wolf still asleep? If so, let's make the conversion quickly so we can conclude our camp experience and return to our homes. We'll dispense with the supersonic travel lesson. The mentors will have to carry out that instruction on their own."

Samantha said, "Mr. Wolf was snoring a few minutes ago. He isn't showing any sign of waking. We can proceed."

"Jeff, please put all of Barry's things in the middle of the pit. Scatter them about and we'll place the wolf in the center. Use the same blanket that was covering you."

When Barry's belongings and the wolf were in place and covered with the blanket, the reverse transformation began. Eight of the mentors formed a ring around the firepit with Heloise and Samantha outside the circle at the north and south positions. Each of the four parchments contained writings in Latin which were recited by Heloise and Samantha, then repeated in unison by the remaining eight mentors as they held hands and marched clockwise about the pit.

Jeff was watching the proceedings with Aty, Evelyn, and Jean. He glanced at Aty and asked, "Is this what the rest of you did to change me back from an owl?"

Aty, eight inches shorter than Jeff, looked up and said, "We said something similar, but not in Latin. The mentors are able to use a more powerful language to get more timely results. Each time this type of procedure takes place, some of the participant's lifeforce is lost."

Jeff was surprised and stammered, "Y…Y…You mean you donated some of your life to change me back to human form?"

"That's right. I hope we didn't make a big mistake. Don't worry, you won't have any female traits."

"But I thought you are all witches. Why would you do such a thing?"

"We're Wickons. We espouse women's rights and try to do good for those that need help. The witches that made you guys into animals are Satanists, Devil worshipers. They cannot fly."

Jeff pointed at the firepit, "Oh, look! Something is happening under the blanket."

A long mournful howl came from the pit, and then another, followed by movement that resembled a dog chasing its tail. The motion ended with a yelp and then a human voice called out, "Jeff! Leeray! What the hell is going on? Jesus Christ, I'm naked! Is this a joke? You guys are gonna get it for this."

Jeff yelled at the blanket, "Take it easy, Barry. You're under a large blanket. Feel around on the ground for your clothes. I'll take off the blanket when you get dressed. I'm with a bunch of women, so don't expose yourself."

"Dammit, Jeff, you've got some explaining to do."

Jeff and Aty watched Barry's movement telescoped through the blanket as he found items to wear. After two or three minutes of activity, Barry yelled, "Okay! I'm dressed, but I might have my sweater on backwards."

Aty bent over and took a firm grip on one corner of the big bedspread, pointed to an adjacent corner of the blanket where Jeff grabbed onto the material, and they folded back the covering to liberate Barry. He was sitting on the ground blinking his eyes at the sudden brightness and looking down at what he was wearing. He started laughing, "What a combination. This stuff was all in my backpack. Where is it anyway?"

Jeff pointed and said, "Look behind you."

Barry opened his pack and looked inside. Jeff knew what Barry was seeking, his pound and a half bag of pot. Jeff wasn't sure why the Satanists apparently ignored the presence of the weed and for all he knew the Wickons hadn't checked the contents of the backpacks. He wondered if they would have said or done anything if they knew the grass was present.

Finding what he was seeking in his pack, Barry said, "So, Jeff, tell me what the hell is going on."

CHAPTER 19

Jeff and Barry sat down at the edge of the firepit and talked for about five minutes. Jeff explained what had just occurred.

"So that bear is really Leeray?"

"Yep. I was an owl and you were a wolf. These women changed us back to humans." Jeff made a sweeping motion with his right arm toward the novices and mentors. "We've got to thank them for returning us to our old selves."

Barry said, "But I feel a little dizzy, not quite right." He rubbed the back of his neck as if he were trying to lessen a headache.

"I had that same feeling, but it will go away before long. I'm feeling fine now, after only a couple of hours."

Barry kept looking away from Jeff at the bear and frowning, "Are these women going to bring Leeray back?"

Jeff stared at Barry for a moment, blinked, and then said, "I don't know. The older woman, Heloise, seems to be in charge. Let's ask her." Jeff stood, brushing dirt from his pants, looking for Heloise. He saw her talking to a taller woman and pointed, "There she is. Let's see what she can tell us."

The two young men walked slowly toward the two older women. Heloise and Samantha noticed them approaching and met them in only a few steps. Heloise saw a questioning expression on their faces.

"I think I know what you're going to ask about. You want to know what we are planning for the bear."

Jeff wasn't surprised by Heloise's comment, she obviously knew what the young men were thinking. "Your Mr. Bear will have to wait until we have another opportunity for Wickons to gather."

Barry didn't like what he had heard. "You mean you're just going to leave him as a bear out here in the wilderness? He might be killed by hunters or by fighting with other bears or a pack of wolves."

Jeff had sympathy for Heloise, but he was disappointed. "We want to thank you for what you have already done. But do we really have to leave our friend out here by himself?"

"Don't you and these women apply black magic all the time?" Barry said.

"You don't understand. We don't perform black magic, we have limitations. We have all given some of our life force to reverse you from animal to human. We have all donated equal amounts. I can't ask anyone for more without endangering their life."

Barry said, "There's no plan *B*?"

Frustrated, Samantha pulled Heloise aside and they had a discussion which Jeff and Barry couldn't hear. Five minutes later, Heloise said, "We have an idea, but you two will have to help."

Jeff glanced at Barry. Barry nodded and replied to Heloise, "All right. What can we do?"

"There's a derelict barn south of the town, Timberville, where I live. You will have to care for your friend until I can make some arrangements. I'll help you until we can reverse the Satanist's curse."

Barry quizzed, "How much time will that take?"

"I'm not sure, Barry, maybe a week, maybe a month…or two."

Barry motioned for Jeff to come closer. They turned away from the mentors and talked, nearly whispering. It took them only a minute to decide what they were going to do. They didn't make any details known to Heloise and Samantha but Jeff said, "We'll go along with your plan. We think we can find something beneficial to do in your town. The barn you mentioned will be a good place for us to stay…especially since it will be cheap and out of the way."

All twenty Wickons gathered for a celebratory final goodbye. Heloise and Samantha each had a parting comment.

Samantha spoke first: "I want to thank all the mentors for their superior teaching. You novices have reached a transition point and are now classified as *A*-grade NeoWicks. If you do not falter in the next year, you will be accepted into the sisterhood as fully trained, proud, and capable Wickons. Give yourselves a round of applause."

When the clapping stopped, Heloise addressed the group: "Wickon is not a religion, we are an organization that delivers retribution to those that hurt humans or animals. However, we swear to never end the life of another, or deal them major physical harm. We strike at night and leave no traces. Do not divulge our methods or our identity to anyone. Maintain your anonymity at all costs. Continue to learn our methods and consult with a sister Wickon if you deem it necessary. Go in peace and safety."

Barry and Jeff heard the words of Samantha and Heloise and began to get suspicious. They were not members of the sisterhood and heard Heloise's statements about anonymity. They agreed that they would be subject to some sort of mental adjustment by the Wickons, but they would cooperate until Leeray regained human form.

The Wickons gradually dispersed to their vehicles and began to leave the camp following numerous goodbyes. Much bonding between novices caused the shedding of tears as friends separated.

Heloise hugged Samantha and they shook hands, but few words were said as they departed. Heloise signaled the young men to meet her by the firepit.

She addressed Jeff and Barry, "We're ready to start back to Timberville. I want you to help me get Mr. Bear in the cargo compartment of my car. The bear and you will ride with me. We'll be the last to leave for home."

Barry was quick to ask, "You mean that live bear is going to ride with us in your car? I don't think so. What do you think, Jeff?"

"It would be all right if he were anesthetized." Jeff looked at Heloise and asked, "Can you give him some water with the same drug you gave the wolf?"

Heloise chuckled, "I would only transport the bear if he were asleep. Let's get him some water with a little something extra in it. Once he's out, we'll have a difficult time getting him in my car. He probably weighs three hundred pounds."

Barry smiled and exhaled heavily, "Ahh, don't worry about that. Jeff and I can get him in your SUV. Just make sure he can't claw or bite us."

Heloise retrieved a small bottle from the glove compartment and, using a medicine dropper, added a few drops of a colorless liquid to a pail of water and put it near the bear. In ten minutes, Mr. Bear was drooling and snoring. He was ready to load.

Jeff hadn't questioned Heloise's preparation of the bear for car travel, but Barry was still a bit unsettled. "How long will he be out?"

"You young men can relax. He won't wake up until we have him in the barn in Timberville."

Heloise backed her SUV up to the bear and with some grunting and shoving, Jeff and Barry loaded the heavy animal. After closing the rear door, Barry commented, "What a stink! I never noticed Leeray having any body odor, but that bear smells like shit and vomit stirred together."

Jeff laughed, "Yeah, Mr. Bear doesn't use toilet paper on either end. I hope the car's AC works."

"We'll have to watch what we feed him in the barn." Barry wiped his hands on his pants and said, "I wanna wash my hands before I get in the car."

"Good idea, me too."

Even though Heloise was getting tired from a long day, she didn't want to allow either Jeff or Barry to share with driving, especially after they had been transformed earlier in the day. From experience, she knew regenerated humans did not have much endurance and concentration could wan while operating a car. After traveling for about thirty minutes, Barry and Jeff fell asleep, so she didn't have to take part in conversation. She looked at her watch and calculated they would arrive in Timberville at three in the morning. With all townspeople asleep, except for a few night owls, they would be able to unload the bear in secret, especially since they would be outside the city limits.

Heloise's estimate of their arrival time was off by nearly thirty minutes, but Jeff and Barry had awakened and were eager to locate the barn they had heard so much about. Heloise had only flown over the structure once and had paid only cursory attention. She remembered seeing the ruts cars or farm equipment had made, so with relative ease, she drove to the big barn door.

She backed to the dilapidated building and cut her engine and headlights. The new arrivals sat in the dark for a few minutes allowing their eyes to adjust to the dim moonlight. Her watch read 3:37 a.m. when they stepped to the ground and opened her cargo door. Heloise gave Barry a flashlight and said, "See if you can find a resting spot for Mr. Bear, something with some old blankets or hay for bedding."

Barry cautiously stepped into the structure, found an old John Deer tractor in the closest bay and farther inside a pile of hay and haybales, all covered with a thin layer of dust. He saw a pitchfork and moved the top few inches of hay to the side to expose cleaner material for the bear's mattress. He returned to the car to inform Heloise of his findings.

Jeff moved the three backpacks to the barn, leaning them against one of the old tractor tires that had gone flat. He could barely see where he was going in the dim light but found old bathroom facilities, similar to an outhouse, near the entranceway. He saw the hay pile and assumed the bear would be sleeping there until the drug wore off. He walked back out, pushing the barn door wide open so the car could back into the structure. He and Barry would have to roll the heavy body from the back of the SUV to the hay mattress.

Once the bear was removed from the SUV, Heloise gave Jeff and Barry a sack of leftover food, enough to carry all of them for a couple of days.

"I'm assuming you guys will be all right for a day or two. I'll be back to check on you tonight or tomorrow night." She smiled and waved, "I'll bring you some groceries. Stay out of trouble." She started to drive away, but stopped and called out, "Come here, Jeff."

Jeff jogged to the car. She handed him a blanket, then drove away.

When Heloise parked in her driveway, she remembered to make sufficient noise when entering the house so her cats wouldn't attack in the dark. She had trained them to repel any home invaders. She carried her two flight sticks into the house and dropped one on purpose to make sure her guard cats were aware of her entry.

She heard Amos and Astrid hissing and they ran to her when she turned on the lights and collapsed on the sofa. It had been a long day and she was dog-tired. The two felines joined her on the couch and were curled up beside her purring, expecting to be petted. It had been a week since they had received Heloise's attention, except for a few minutes the day before.

"I think, my little furry creatures, you're hungry. I'll get you something to eat and I'll have a snack. Then we're off to bed." She checked her watch and uttered, "I'll get up at noon."

Roger got up and dressed quickly. He had heard noises in the middle of the night and looked out his bedroom window to see lights at the old Wieselman barn. It was seven-thirty and his mom was doing something in the garden, his dad had gone to work. He jammed a piece of buttered toast in his mouth and dialed his buddy's number. He hoped Dennis didn't have to help at his dad's auto shop today. That barn was supposed to be off limits, but with Dennis as an accomplice, he didn't care. They had to investigate the source of the lights at Wieselman's. Since Roger was born, he had never known anyone to use that barn. That old tractor was rusted solid and should be sold as scrap.

Mrs. Michaels answered on the third ring, "Hello."

"Good morning Mrs. Michaels, is Dennis there?"

"Oh, hello Roger. How's your mother?"

"She's fine. She's out in the garden. Could I talk with Dennis?"

Roger heard some noises from the phone being laid on the kitchen counter and Mrs. Michael's voice, "Dennis! Roger wants to talk to you." Then he heard two sets of footsteps.

"Hey Rodge, what's up?"

"I need your help. I saw some lights out at Wieselman's barn last night. We need to check it out. Can you bring your twenty-two?"

"Grandpa's old single-shot? Yeah, I guess so. But not until Mom leaves this afternoon for her bridge club meeting. It's at one o'clock. She'll be gone for at least two hours. Is that okay?"

"That'll do. I'll keep an eye on the barn with my binoculars until you come out here. I've got some extra ammo. Dad has my gun; he's goin' after some rats. See you after lunch."

"Yeah. Later."

CHAPTER 20

Heloise woke up at two minutes past twelve, her internal clock was running slightly slow. She spent thirty minutes in the bathroom applying creams and lotions and dressed in Timberville civvies. Her mirror wasn't lying, she began to see the results of advanced age. She inspected the interior of her home checking for irregularities, sniffed her soiled Wickon outfit and tossed it in the washing machine for a deep water wash. Amos and Astrid wanted out, so she watched and played with the cats outside for a half-hour. It was 1:15 when she climbed in her car and started to the grocery store. Shopping was going to take at least an hour, perhaps longer. For a late lunch, she planned to pick up a six-layer Timberburger and fries at Pratt's Power Saw restaurant. She wanted to enjoy more of life on Earth before it was too late.

Dennis left home at one o'clock sharp with his .22 strapped to his bike frame. He was afraid the rifle might come loose when riding over bumps in the mostly unpaved roads he took to the Swartzs', so he rode slowly, keeping his eyes fluctuating between his cargo and the surface of the roads. Roger waited impatiently at the turn-off from the main road to the lane that led to his house. Dennis showed up at 1:21, riding slowly, and waving when he saw his buddy at the turnoff.

"Hey, Den, what in the hell took so long? Did your mom leave late for her meeting?"

"No. I don't have a scabbard for the gun. I had to be careful not to drop it as I rode out here in the sticks. It took a few minutes to get it tied down."

"My place is still in the city limits, it's not in the sticks," Roger rebutted instantly. "You don't even know anything about the sticks."

"Okay. I don't want to argue. Have you seen any activity out at that barn?"

Roger shook his head, "Nothing, but now I'm even more curious about what was going on out there with those lights."

"Let's go check it out; maybe some aliens landed," Dennis chuckled. "Have you got some bullets? I don't have any, Mom told Dad to keep them locked up so I couldn't get to them. She thinks I'll shoot someone." He rolled his eyes.

"She's probably right." He gave Dennis a .22 bullet from about a dozen he had in his pocket.

"Thanks, Rodge. You don't trust me with more than one?" He stuck the bullet between his lips like he was smoking a cigarette.

Roger smirked. "C'mon, let's check out the barn."

Dennis laid his bike on the shoulder, unwrapped the gun and loaded it. Roger moved the bike farther from the road to the top of the irrigation ditch and they started towards Wieselman's faded red barn. The old sun-bleached building was leaning sideways about five degrees and stood a good stone's throw from the road but it was easy for the boys to walk along the freshly made wheel tracks. When Roger was about a car's length from the barn door, he signaled Dennis, three paces behind him, to be quiet. He could hear two voices and heavy breathing coming from inside.

Roger withdrew to Dennis, still a couple of yards away, and whispered, "I think there are at least three people in there, one of them might be hurt. There's some heavy breathing."

Dennis smiled, "Romping in the hay?"

"Not that kind of breathing. It might be a big animal, like a cow or horse—or a big pig."

The boys scanned the closest barn wall and Roger saw an opening in the vertical siding. He said, "Stay here, I'm gonna peek through that crack in the wall."

Roger cautiously sneaked to the wall and pressed his cheek against the rough boards. He couldn't get a clear view of the occupants, but saw two young men sitting on the floor, talking and eating. He watched as they occasionally glanced toward a pile of hay and tossed food to someone they called Leeray. Whoever Leeray was, Roger couldn't identify, but he was definitely the heavy breather.

When Barry tossed a chunk of cold hamburger to the bear, his peripheral vision caught a change in light entering through an opening in the siding. He motioned to Jeff to lean closer. Barry whispered, almost inaudibly, "We have an eavesdropper."

Jeff rose and said, "I've gotta take a leak." Jeff darted to the barn door and threw it open. He had to shield his eyes from the bright outdoor light, but he immediately saw a shocked kid standing next to the barn wall.

Barry was right behind Jeff and squinted. He saw the kid and demanded, "What the hell do you want?"

Roger, although ready to run, stood his ground and said, "I'm just checking out the lights I saw this morning. I live over there." He pointed at his house. "What are you guys doing out here? This barn is on private property. Didn't you see the no trespassing sign on the road?" Roger stepped away from the barn toward the slightly older young men.

When Barry and Jeff left the barn, they were unaware Leeray the bear had slowly followed them. He was still hungry and hoped his keepers had more to eat. He saw his two friends standing outside and wanted to join them to get more food. Seeing another human, the bear began sniffing the air, wondering if the stranger had something edible.

Roger, a few feet from the door frame, had his back to the barn opening and was unaware a bear was approaching from behind, but Dennis saw the bear and shouted, "There's a bear behind you, Rodge, get out of the way!" Dennis reacted quickly, aimed his twenty-two and pulled the trigger, not knowing that a twenty-two bullet would hardly hurt a bear, unless the bullet hit a vital organ. Dennis was too scared for Roger to think about shooting the bear in the eye. He just aimed at the biggest part of the bear. He hit the upper hind leg on the right side of his target.

The bear felt a burning sensation where the bullet struck. He looked at his leg and then saw where the noise and pain came from. He saw a human pointing a stick at him. He had to defend himself and his friends and charged after Dennis.

Dennis quickly realized the bear was coming after him and dropped his gun. He heard Roger yell something but it didn't register. Dennis knew he couldn't outrun a bear and started racing toward his bike. His only option was to ride away as fast as possible. The bear was close, only five yards behind and closing, the chuffing getting louder. Dennis jumped the roadside ditch to access his bike. The animal lost ground when it had to climb out of the ditch, giving Dennis a chance to increase separation and get on two wheels. He didn't look back until he had frantically pedaled nearly half a football field away, but the bear was still following him. He continued to increase the distance from the animal and as the gap grew, he wondered if Roger was okay.

Heloise finished eating her high calorie lunch and bought a half-dozen glazed donuts for the boys at the barn. Rather than wait until evening, she decided to visit Jeff and Barry and discuss some possible procedures to return Leeray to human form. She was taking a leisurely drive out to the barn, approaching the turnoff to the Swartzs' when she noticed someone riding a bicycle and rapidly closing. It was a young man pedaling as if his life depended on escaping someone or something. As he passed by, he glanced at her for only a second. Heloise recognized the boy, she had seen him before when she punished him and his buddy for killing her favorite cat, Specter.

But why was the kid riding so hard? She slowed the SUV and directed her vision down the road. A large brown mass came barreling toward her, like a large boulder rolling down a steep incline. She looked closely and realized it was Leeray, the bear. What was going to stop the animal? Realizing she had to intervene, she slowed to a stop. Reaching into her glove compartment, she grabbed her telescoping wand. Somehow, she had to stop the bear.

Next, she opened the windows to let the aroma of the glazed donuts permeate the air, hoping the bear, smelling the sugar coated pastry, would be distracted from chasing Dennis. She would only use her wand as a last resort to cause the animal to stumble and come to a stop.

The bear slowed noticeably when it passed Heloise and halted about two car lengths away. Turning around, apparently forgetting all about Dennis, it lumbered back to the SUV. Donuts were the only thing the bear cared about.

Heloise held out a pastry, cooing, "Come on, big boy, climb into the car and have something to eat." She couldn't remember the magic words that would allow her to take complete control of Leeray, but as the bear climbed into the cargo area, she tapped it with her wand. It fell asleep after only one donut. Back in the driver's seat, she drove to the barn to find out what had happened. She wondered why the bear escaped from the young men and was chasing the kid on the bike.

As Roger watched the bear chase Dennis, he picked up the twenty-two and walked back to talk with Barry and Jeff. He felt that he was owed an explanation of why the two men were at the barn with a bear. If his friend got hurt by the bear, there would be hell to pay!

Roger demanded, "I asked you before, who are you guys and what are you doing here in Wieselman's barn with a bear?"

Barry stalled for a couple of seconds and then said, "I'm Barry and this is Jeff. We're with the circus and we're taking a stroll with our pet bear. He's been having some problems and we thought he needed some freedom in the outdoors."

Jeff added, "Yeah, Leeray has been cooped up for too long. He's normally pretty tame, but when your friend shot him, he became enraged. He's never been treated like that before. We don't use painful tactics when teaching him tricks."

Seeing an SUV appear, the boys watched Heloise entice Leeray into her car and drive toward the barn. Barry and Jeff worried that Leeray would venture into town and get shot by the police. That had a high probability of happening in this forested area. Roger watched the woman driver of the SUV stop, somehow get the bear in her car and was now transporting the bear, apparently bringing it to the barn. He had no idea who she was and he didn't know anyone who would put a bear in their vehicle.

When Heloise reached the barn, Jeff informed her that Leeray had been wounded. While Barry distracted Roger, Jeff updated Heloise about the circus cover story and that Dennis shot Leeray. She agreed to continue with the misrepresentation. Though Roger didn't recognize her, Heloise vividly remembered Roger, the other cat killer.

She approached Roger, introduced herself, and asked him if he could obtain some first-aid supplies.

Roger asked, "Are you some kind of nurse or a doctor?"

"No, I'm in charge of the welfare of animals in our troupe. Performing animals sometimes have injuries. I need to remove that bullet from Leeray. If I don't, he'll remain in a mean state. He could break into that home over there and tear it apart." She pointed at Roger's house.

"That's my house. I'll get our first aid kit; it's got all kinds of medical supplies." Roger, now motivated to protect his house and family, was eager to calm the bear down. "My dad was a corpsman in the Marines, so he's prepared us for just about anything."

"We'll get Leeray ready for some minor surgery while you get the medical kit."

"Okay. I'll be right back." Roger jogged toward his house, jumping over clumps of weeds and vaulted over the ramshackle fence separating the two properties.

Heloise motioned for Jeff and Barry to join her so they could find where Leeray had been shot.

"I think it's in one of his legs," Jeff volunteered.

They adjusted Leeray's body so they could inspect his lower anatomy and Heloise began to look through the hair on his left leg. She found the injury quickly, locating the bullet under the tough hide of the bear.

"How did you put Leeray to sleep?" asked Barry.

Heloise smiled, "I slowed him down with the odor of glazed donuts and put him to sleep with my wand. In the trade, we call it dream wand. He should be asleep for about an hour, long enough for us to remove that pesky bullet." Heloise kept looking back at the Swartzs' house to check on Roger's progress with the medical kit. She didn't want him to overhear her conversation with Jeff and Barry.

Roger returned with a green satchel emblazoned with a red cross and handed it to Heloise. "Let me know if you need anything else."

"Thanks, Roger. Stay here and watch. Maybe you'll learn something useful in case you or your friend ever get shot."

Heloise opened the bag, found a pair of sterile forceps, and began probing for the bullet. She located the slug quickly and pulled it from Leeray's leg. There was little blood loss and she tossed the piece of lead on the ground. She rubbed a pea-size blob of antibiotic ointment on the wound and declared, "He'll be good as new in a couple of days. Bears are tough customers."

CHAPTER 21

"Oh, I almost forgot," Roger told them, "When I was home, Dennis called and asked me if it was all right to come back. I told him he'd better not, the bear might remember his scent and go after him again. I told him we were going to remove the bullet."

Heloise grinned, "You did the right thing, Roger. You can take the medical kit back home now. Make sure you bleach the forceps or boil them before returning the instrument to the bag."

"Will you three and the bear be here much longer?"

Heloise hesitated for a moment and then replied, "No, we'll be leaving this afternoon. We have some activities that require our attendance. You might see us again though."

Barry and Jeff heard what Heloise told Roger and when the teen was out of earshot, Jeff asked, "Are we actually leaving this afternoon?"

"Yes. While extracting the bullet, it suddenly occurred to me that we don't need a group of people to donate some of their life force. There is another way to reverse a Devil worshipper's curse. I don't know why I didn't think of it before—I guess I'm getting old. Maybe I should retire."

Jeff commented, "You seem very mentally sharp to me, maybe you're just tired from being with all those women for a week."

"Yeah, I don't know how you were able to stand it," Barry grinned.

Heloise became very serious and ordered, "Get your things together, we're taking a ride."

Fifteen minutes later, Heloise backed the car into her driveway and cut the engine. She rarely parked so far back, but she wanted to get Leeray in the house without being seen by any neighbors, especially Mr. Henry. She mentioned her concerns to Barry and Jeff.

Barry suggested, "Can you wake up Leeray so we don't have to carry him inside?"

"Oh, sure, but I'll still need some assistance. You'll have to distract Mr. Henry so he won't see the bear coming in my home. He lives next door." She pointed out Ed's house.

"What do you want me to do?" Barry asked.

"Go over there and make up something, you're taking a survey—use your imagination. While you're doing that, Jeff and I will get Leeray in the house and into the basement."

"No problem. That will be easy. Should I do it now?"

"Not yet, follow me." Grabbing a plastic bag from her car, she walked away assuming Jeff and Barry would follow. "We need to pick raspberries from my patch first. Bears love raspberries. We'll lure Leeray into the house with the berries. I'll wake him once we've filled the bag with fruit."

With three pickers pulling the berries, the plastic bag was filled in slightly less than fifteen minutes. They liberally sampled berries as they picked, but it didn't slow them down appreciably.

"Ok, guys. Let's get Leeray in the house. Barry, it's time to go next door and talk with Mr. Henry."

Heloise and Jeff opened the rear cargo door as they heard Barry knocking on her neighbor's door. When they heard talking, Heloise waved her wand over the bear and said, "Evigitare faciatis."

Within seconds, Leeray began to stir. He opened his eyes and immediately focused on the stuffed sack of raspberries Jeff was holding. Suddenly, Jeff stepped back. "Whew! Leeray really stinks. Did he poop in your car?"

"I don't think so, my wand doesn't allow defecation when a subject is sleeping. Start moving toward my back door. He should follow."

Leeray reacted slowly, but Jeff held the sack of berries open so Leeray could get a strong scent of its contents. Ten seconds later, Leeray was in the house. Jeff led the bear downstairs and dropped the bag of berries in the middle of the concrete floor. While Leeray attacked the fruit, Jeff climbed the stairs, closed the downstairs door and asked, "Is that it, Heloise?"

"For now. I'll put him back to sleep when he's finished with the berries. I need you and Barry to do something else."

Barry returned from his visit with Ed Henry and commented, "That old duffer is pretty sharp. He wanted to know what I was doing at Heloise's house. I told him I was putting a bear in the basement and he gave a big laugh. Then I told him a lie, a buddy and I were selling magazine subscriptions. He believed the lie."

Jeff and Barry looked at each other and laughed. Heloise said, "Now we need to know where the city electric power station is located. I'll ferry you to City Hall and you can inquire. Tell them you want to avoid any high voltage wires when you go kite flying. As soon as you find out, walk in this direction, I'll pick you up. While you're doing that, I'll come back home so I can put your buddy back to sleep."

As they drove downtown to the municipal offices, Heloise answered questions, explaining how they were going to use the high voltage electrical wires to reverse the curse on Leeray. In her previous flights to and from town, she hadn't paid attention to the towers supporting power lines to Timberville. She wanted to know the specific location of the wires and their lowest height above ground.

Jeff asked, "Whoa! You mean we might have to climb one of those towers?"

Barry quickly added, "You actually think Leeray can climb up to those power lines?"

Heloise was surprised by their concerns, she had assumed the young men would want to do anything for their friend, without question. She suggested an alternative, "If we can access the area close to the voltage reduction transformers on the ground, I guess that might also work. See what you can discover without raising too many eyebrows."

Heloise double parked outside the City of Timberville Utility Office just long enough for Barry and Jeff to get out. She noticed a police cruiser approaching from behind and continued down the street. She turned and drove a few blocks toward home; occasionally glancing in her rearview mirror to see if the police car was following her. She finally relaxed when it turned off near the grade school.

As she pulled into her driveway, Heloise waved to Ed Henry. He had just moved a sprinkler in his front yard. She parked next to the back door, entered the house and went downstairs. Leeray was motionless sprawled on the floor. The raspberries were gone and the empty plastic bag only exhibited a few red stains. To make sure he wouldn't cause any trouble, she said a few words of dream wand and passed her baton over Leeray's sleeping body, pausing momentarily at his massive head, giving it extra attention.

Concluding Leeray was comfortable, Heloise stepped back toward the stairway and went up the steps. She heard a big sigh from the basement as she locked the cellar door. Back in her car, she felt some anxiety for the first time since being attacked by the Satanists at the camp. Jeff and Barry might be able to provide information to alleviate these feelings. She hoped they were successful obtaining answers to her electric power questions. She hadn't used electric fields to reverse a Satanist's curse since working with Nikola Tesla in the 1880s. He had provided her with great insight. She recalled feeling a tingling sensation on her skin and her hair standing off her head but felt no shocks of any kind when in his laboratory. It was an interesting time to experiment with something new to her and Nikola. A visionary man, he rarely smiled when experimenting with electricity.

She watched for Jeff and Barry but didn't see them as she returned to City Hall. There were several parking spots at the curb close to the municipal building so she pulled into the closest open space. After waiting about five minutes, she went into the building and asked about the young men. They had been directed to the WestCent Power Building two blocks away on the far corner of Main Street and Power Drive. She locked her car and walked to the building, hoping to find the youthful friends of Leeray as she made her way down Main.

Heloise smiled and nodded to people as they passed by but didn't stop to talk with anyone. Entering the foyer of the power company building, she paused to examine a map of the city power locations. Unfortunately, the high voltage feeder lines were not illustrated. She continued on to the Welcome Counter where a long haired young man wearing glasses was looking at a flat screen monitor. He wore a nametag that said smile.

He looked up and asked, "May I help you?"

Heloise smiled and said, "Gaming?"

Emile blushed and stuttered, "Y…you…you caught me." He took a deep breath, "What can I do for you?"

"I'm looking for a couple of young men that might have been here recently."

"Oh yeah, the kite flyers and hot air balloon dudes. Those the ones?"

"Yes. I'm here to give them a ride."

"They said they got what they wanted and left. They started walking up Power Drive. They couldn't have gone far." He pointed in the direction Jeff and Barry walked.

"Thank you." Heloise walked back to her car and began looking for her friends as she progressed up Power Drive. She was three blocks from the power company building when she saw the young men. One beep of her horn brought them to the curb. When she pulled over, they climbed in the car.

"So, how'd it go?" She asked.

Jeff answered, "I think we got what we needed."

Barry added, "Transmission line locations and power transformer sites. We didn't have to tell many lies but we thought they seemed plausible."

Heloise smiled, "The fellow at the power company mentioned you asked about kites and hot air balloons. The balloon topic was clever. What did you find out?"

Barry extracted a folded sheet of yellow paper from his shirt pocket and handed it to Heloise. "The voltage converter station is on this road. We were gonna take a look."

Heloise glanced at the city map, handed it back to Barry, stepped on the gas and pulled away from the curb. The power station was only nine blocks and two minutes away, right outside the northern city limits.

She parked next to the chain-link fence. At least ten feet high, the fence surrounded what appeared to be a standard city lot with a rectangular cement pad dead center. Danger and No Trespassing signs were conspicuous. Another fence, clearly marked as dangerous and topped with barbed wire, enclosed the pad. What looked like guardians from another world, four eight-foot-high metal structures with wires entering and exiting were bolted to the concrete block.

Jeff slid over to the back passenger window, looked out, and said, "Damn! I don't think we're wanted here."

"Yeah, Heloise, this place looks off-limits. How would we do anything here?" said Barry.

Heloise had a big smile, "Don't you worry, this is an ideal place for us. We will ignore the signs."

Jeff pointed at the tall metal structure nearest the station, "What if observation cameras are mounted on that tower?"

"I'll check for cameras in the dark of night and avoid the flood lights at the station." She grinned, "Stealth mode."

By nine-thirty, the only lights in the sky were from stars, a crescent moon, and city lights. Jeff and Barry watched TV in the living room and Leeray slept soundly in the basement after enjoying a satisfying dinner. Heloise took her warped broom and stepped into the darkness of her backyard. After scanning her neighbors' homes for undesired onlookers, she flew off to inspect the tower that contained the feed lines to the power station. A few seconds of hovering in the dark assured her no cameras were in the vicinity of the station. She returned home after being gone only ten minutes.

Heloise entered the living room and said, "Put on your dark clothing, boys. We've got a job to do." While Jeff and Barry donned appropriate attire, including masks, Heloise woke Leeray and enticed him into the cargo area of her SUV. The bear was a sucker for raspberries.

Getting to the power station took nearly fifteen minutes by car; most city streets did not intersect with Power Drive. Heloise had to drive to Main and turn north at the WestCent Building and follow Power Drive to the restricted location.

There was only one gate in the outside fence and it was padlocked, preventing access by unwanted visitors. It would be impossible to lift

Leeray over the fence and he was too heavy and ungainly to ride Heloise's broom.

Jeff commented, "We're screwed. We can't get past this fence and then there's another locked gate on the inside fence. I can see it from here. We're prevented from getting in."

Barry added, "That's right, I saw the locks this afternoon. Nothing has changed."

The boys' frustration was evident, so Heloise assured them, "The locks are not a problem. They are nearly insignificant." She smiled, exited her car and approached the exterior gate. In a blink of her eye, she waved her wand over the lock like she was conducting an orchestra and the lock sprang open.

CHAPTER 22

Barry opened the front passenger seat door shaking his head, "We should have known you had this under control."

Jeff began to laugh, "That little maneuver of Heloise's was wanderful! Get it? Wand-erful? Hope she does it again."

Barry elbowed him, "Jesus, Jeff. Get serious. Cut out the dumb jokes."

Heloise grinned and waved her wand over Leeray to wake him. She instructed, "Get Leeray inside the outer fence. I'll open the lock on the inner gate." She hustled ahead and released the mechanism on the inner protective fence lock.

She led the group to the exact center of the four megalithic transformers and using her wand, indicated where Leeray should be placed. Heloise turned and looked at Jeff and Barry, "We've forgotten something."

Jeff and Barry simultaneously said, "What?"

"A blanket and his backpack. He needs something to cover his nakedness and he will want his personal belongings."

Barry tittered, "You wouldn't be embarrassed seeing a naked man would you, Heloise?"

She smiled and replied, "I was thinking of Leeray's feelings, but you know more about him than I do. Would he want to be seen in his birthday suit by an old woman?"

Jeff said, "He'll be so disoriented when he reverts back, I doubt if he'll even care. I'll get his things, and a blanket just in case." He started back to the car, barely exiting the outer fence when an armed policeman seemed to appear from nowhere.

"Hold it, right there. Put your hands up. Lean against the car. Don't move."

The officer gave Jeff a quick pat down and ordered, "Turn around. What's your name?"

Jeff wanted to warn Barry and Heloise, but reluctantly, he complied. "Jeff Wheldine."

"I heard voices. Who are you with?"

Deciding not to lie, Jeff said, "Some friends of mine, Barry Nexly, Heloise Allen—and a bear."

The policeman said, "Heloise Allen?"

"That's right, she's in there." Jeff nodded toward the power station interior fence. "Can I get a blanket and a backpack from the car?" Jeff saw the identification tag on the officer's shirt: Lt. Sanders.

"All right, but I want you to ask them to come out from the power station."

Jeff opened the cargo door, reached in and extracted Leeray's backpack and a blanket. Sanders watched closely with his hand on his holstered gun. He followed Jeff to the opened gate and said, "Stop! Call to your friends."

Jeff stood frozen in place and yelled over the hum from the transformers. "Heloise, a policeman wants to talk to you."

Lt. Sanders asked, "How did you get in here? These gates are checked twice daily and are locked tight."

Jeff shrugged, "You'd better ask Heloise. I think the lock just popped open."

Heloise appeared from the fenced transformers and said, "Hello Lt. Sanders, we haven't met but I know your wife, Katelin. How may I help you?"

"This is a prohibited area. How did you and your friends get in here? This young man said you have a bear with you. Is that right?"

"Well…yes. We are rescuing the bear from the power transformers—to prevent electrocution. I'll show you how we found the gates when we saw the bear."

"Wait a minute. Don't you have someone else with you…and a bear? Where are they?"

This was Heloise's opportunity to divert the mind of Lt. Sanders and have him assist with the reversal of the bear to human form. She instructed Jeff to lead the way and motioned the lieutenant to follow. She followed the officer and as the policeman went through the opening to the transformers, Heloise waved her wand over his head and said, "Collaborate and misremember what you see tonight."

Sanders turned toward her, "What was that?"

"Oh, nothing important. I was just talking to myself."

When the lieutenant saw the bear and Barry, he said, "I'll help you carry the bear out of here. The three of us should be able to lift the animal, it's not too big. Heloise can lead the way and close the gates."

"Lieutenant, I've done this before so please follow my directions."

"All right. Whatever you say."

"Barry, cover Mr. bear with the blanket after Jeff puts the backpack beside him. Lieutenant, move to the foot of the animal and you boys take the sides." As the men were getting into position, Heloise stepped back, grabbed her broom and in three seconds, circled the four transformers accumulating static charges until her hair was standing on end. She dropped to the ground and touched the blanket with her wand saying, "Beast begone, young man return." There was an electric discharge, sparks flew from the blanket to the transformers, and a roar came from under the cover.

The blanket churned and shook for about twenty seconds like two wrestlers were fighting, rolling on top of each other under a canvas, followed by a loud yell, "What the hell? Where are my clothes?"

Jeff laughed, "Hey! It's Leeray—he's back."

Barry called to Leeray, "Your things are in your backpack, you are covered with a blanket. Get dressed, Leeray."

"I can't see what I'm doing. Do you guys have a flashlight?"

Lt. Sanders volunteered, "I've got a pocket light. Give him this." Sanders gave a small flashlight to Barry, who lifted the edge of the blanket and gave it to Leeray. It took about two minutes for Leeray to dress and come out from under the cover.

Lt. Sanders said, "Pretty neat trick, Heloise. I wish you would have informed me that this fellow was in a bear costume. I don't understand why you people are practicing tricks in the power station. As long as no one has been hurt, I won't cite you for trespassing, but please refrain from doing these things in restricted areas."

As Heloise was folding the blanket, Sanders inquired, "What did you do with the bear costume?"

"We can't divulge all our tricks, lieutenant. That is privileged information," she replied.

Lieutenant Sanders shook his head and smiled, "That's about what I expected. Let's get out of here and lock the gates. You people should go home. I need to continue my night patrol."

Heloise, Leeray, Barry and Jeff climbed into the car and drove away. The lieutenant snapped the inner and outer gate locks shut and walked to his patrol car parked in the shadows.

Leeray sat between his buddies in a state of confusion, "Tell me what just happened? Why were we here?"

Barry and Jeff brought Leeray up to date about the activities of the last two weeks. When they finished explaining, Leeray rolled his eyes, "I know you guys are screwing with me." Then he whispered, "What happened to my weed?"

Jeff looked ahead to see if Heloise was listening and quietly replied, "What? Your package of grass is gone? What was in your backpack?"

"You don't know? My clothes, a piece of ceramic tile and some dried cow shit!"

Barry offered an explanation immediately, "When the bear was chasing that kid, the other teenager must have taken your grass, Leeray. That's the only explanation I can come up with."

"Yeah, I'll bet that's what happened. We'll have to pay those two boys a visit," said Jeff. He gently nudged Leeray with his elbow and said,

"We'll get your stuff back, pal." Leeray didn't hear anything his buddies had said, he was sound asleep.

Barry observed, "Leeray's out of it. He's had a tough day. We'll have to go through all this again tomorrow after his brain's in better shape."

Heloise heard only bits and pieces of what the boys in the back seat were saying. She was excessively tired and was concentrating on driving. As she approached her house, she spoke loudly, "I'll let you guys sleep at my place tonight, but tomorrow you'll have to find a place of your own."

Jeff leaned forward, "Thank you. You've done enough for us. We'll find some wheels and a place to crash. Is there a used car dealer in town?"

"Yes, but I've never gone there. It's on the eastern edge of town, Otto's Autos."

Ten minutes later, Heloise had the young men settled on the living room floor in sleeping bags on air mattresses. After she yawned and crawled into bed, she said good night to Amos and Astrid. The cats were purring and curled up at the foot of her bed.

The living room guests were awakened in the morning by noises from Heloise's kitchen and odors of toast and coffee. When Leeray opened his eyes, he saw two eyes staring back at him. Startled at first, he realized the eyes were from a cat and he relaxed. The purring body brushed against his head and tried to crawl into his sleeping bag.

"No, you don't, you little bugger. You stay out of there." He gently pushed the cat away, tossed back the top of his sleeping bag and said, "Jeff, is this the cat we found on the trail?"

"No, Leeray. This one's different. Barry and I have a story to tell you that you might not believe, but we're not kidding, it's true." As the boys got dressed, Barry and Jeff rewound the clock on the past days since meeting the three women on the Crest Trail. Leeray was told about the three young men being transformed into a wolf, an owl, and a bear. Leeray had difficulty accepting that he had become a bear. He had no recollection of that existence.

"So, I was a bear from the time we met those three women until last night?"

"Exactly," said Barry. "Do you remember yesterday eating a half-gallon of raspberries in the basement?"

He grinned, "No, but I like raspberries on my cereal." Then he became serious, "What are we gonna do about my weed?"

Barry replied, "We need wheels and independence, so we're gonna rent a vehicle. Heloise will take us to a dealer after we have some breakfast. Get your things organized, wash up and let's eat."

Heloise dropped her overnight guests at the edge of town at Otto's Autos. Otto greeted the trio and asked, "What can I do for yah?"

Barry was the only one with a valid credit card, so he said, "We'd like to rent a small pickup—something like that one." He pointed at a slightly-dented dark-blue Ford F-150 parked behind several newer cars at the front of the dealership.

The three young men followed Otto, dressed in slacks and a light yellow dress shirt. He stood about five-eight or nine and looked to be about fifty pounds overweight.

Jeff asked, "What are your rental charges?"

"How long will you gentlemen need the truck?"

Barry replied, "We're not sure. We've got some business to take care of, so it might be just a couple of days, but it might take a week."

"O.K. The deposit is fifty bucks and twenty-two fifty per day. Mileage is extra and I'll apply your deposit to that when you return the vehicle."

Barry nodded, "That seems fair."

"All right, come into my office and we'll take care of the paperwork. I assume you want this on a credit card?"

As the trio followed Otto into the remodeled filling station, Barry replied, "Yeah, I've got a VISA card." He fished a bright red plastic card from his wallet and handed it to Otto.

When the papers were signed and the three guys were driving away from Otto's, Jeff commented, "Where are we going to stay, that old barn? If so, we'd better find out if it's legal. We don't need cops coming out there and searching our stuff."

"Good point. Let's go down to city hall and find out about that barn. I think it would be a good base of operations for selling weed," said Barry. "There are lots of hiding spots in that old cow house.

Leeray added, "And we can start looking for the thief that took my grass."

Jeff stepped on the gas and drove toward Main.

While Jeff, Barry and Leeray were renting a vehicle, Lieutenant Sanders was just getting up. After four days of working the late shift, he didn't have to report for duty until 10:00 a.m. so he was sitting at the breakfast table with his wife, Katelin. She had already fed Erica and Doug and was on her third cup of coffee. The kids had finished and gone outside to play.

Katelin had just poured Ken a cup of coffee and handed him the box of Wheaties. "How was your patrol last night? Anything interesting going on in the wee hours?"

Ken filled a bowl with flakes, added some milk and was slicing half a banana into disks, adding them to his bowl. "No. It was pretty quiet. I saw Heloise and three young men driving around. I guess she was showing them around town—giving them a guided tour." He looked up at Katelin and smiled.

Katelin raised her eyebrows, "That's kind of strange, driving around in the dark late at night. Seems like that would be better to do in daylight. Who were the boys, teenagers?"

Ken took a sip of his coffee and said, "I don't know. We didn't stop and talk. They just drove past me in the opposite direction."

"Hmm, I'll have to ask her about her new friends. Maybe she met them at that girls' camping trip last week."

"Yeah, that's probably the case." He shoveled a heaping spoonful of cereal into his mouth.

Katelin sat across from her husband, nodded slowly, and said, "I think I'll pay Heloise a visit today. It's been more than a week since we talked."

CHAPTER 23

The city records office opened at 9:00 a.m. Mrs. Darlene Bauman had arrived at 8:30 and prepared coffee for the office staff, a task she had carried out five days a week since graduating from high school. Darlene was six-feet tall, about forty-five years old, a picture of authority, and could have been a staff sergeant in the military. She was a no-nonsense official and knew just about all there was to know about Timberville. Aside from two people, the mayor and the sheriff, she ran the entire city office building of eight employees, seven being women.

As near as she could tell, all of her coworkers were present and in their normal positions when she unlocked the building for daily business. She stood inside the heavy glass front door watching the clock and when the seconds counted up to 60, she turned the key to unlock the door. She noticed three young men standing just outside the blue-tinted glass waiting for the building to open.

Only twelve feet from the welcoming counter, she turned from the door, walked quickly to her station, and watched the trio enter the building. She wondered what the college-age boys were going to ask her. Was it going to be directions or vital information of some sort?

The tallest of the three approached the counter. "We'd like to rent an old barn at the southern edge of town. Could you tell us if that's possible?"

Barry stepped beside Jeff and said, "I believe the barn belongs to a Mr. Wieselman." Barry whispered into Jeff's right ear, "I saw a shipping tag for hay stapled to the wall inside the barn door."

Jeff nodded and watched Mrs. Bauman enter something into her desk computer. She then reached under the counter and placed a small metal box beside her keyboard. She pulled a card from the container and read it aloud, "My barn may be used by any adult or adults free of charge as long as some upkeep is performed on the premises. Such upkeep must be verified by the city planner or a representative of the police."

Mrs. Bauman continued, "Signed: Dr. Daniel Wieselman, June 3, 1997." She replaced the card in the file and handed Jeff a printed form. "Each of you young men must sign and date the document. That's all there is to it." She handed Jeff a pen and watched as he and his buddies signed the official paper. After Barry signed, he slid the paper and pen through the opening in the glass shield and smiled, "Thanks. That was easier than we thought."

"Good luck with your enterprise. A city delegate will visit you within a week to observe your compliance. He or she will set up a monthly time for review."

As the three left the building, Barry said, "Let's get the upkeep done right away so we don't violate the agreement. Let's each do something to improve the place, okay?"

Leeray added, "Make up a list of chores, kind of like on a farm. You can be the daddy." He gave Barry a big grin.

Barry tried to cuff him on the back of his head but missed. "All right Leeray, my boy, your first job is to clean all the bear and cow shit off the barn floor."

Laughing, the guys climbed in the pickup and headed to the Wieselman barn, now legally their temporary home.

Lt. Ken Sanders parked in the city lot behind the Police Station and entered through the back door, the normal entryway for officers reporting for work. It was exactly 10:00 a.m. Sarah Turner handed Ken a cup of coffee and they took seats in the break room to discuss the day's shift.

Sarah took a sip of her coffee and said, "We've got some info on the drug traffic coming into town. Scuttlebutt has it that two local boys are selling illegal weed. If we can corral them, maybe we can get some better leads to the source of more potent drugs.

"Somebody called it in?"

"Yeah. Mr. Gehring over at Puff's Weed Supply called me at home last evening and reported he had heard rumors about some high school kids finding a package of grass. They're selling it to their friends and neighbors at below wholesale rates. Gehring's afraid it's cutting into his business."

Sarah observed, "I'll bet it is. I suppose we should interview Gehring and see if we can backtrack through the grapevine and see who's making easy money."

Ken said, "That's what I figured. I met Art in Portland a couple of years ago, he's a good man." Sarah slid back her chair and started toward the parking lot. Ken took a last swallow of tepid coffee, folded the cup and tossed it in the trash as he followed his partner.

Sarah had the motor running and studied Ken as he climbed in the front passenger seat. "You seem a bit sluggish today, Ken. That midnight shift mess up your system?"

Ken nodded, "Yeah. I guess readjustment to regular hours will take a few days. I feel like I had a bad dream. I have this odd image of two young men with a bear and the boys' mother." He shook his head and said, "Strange—oh well, let's go talk to Mr. Gehring about some weed."

Puff's Weed Supply was the next-to-last business on the west side of town neighboring the Timberville Shell service station. The building had been converted from a Chevrolet Dealership allowing two businesses to occupy the large structure. Art Gehring had rented half the building, installed a partition, new windows, and repainted the exterior in two shades of green. He hired a local artist, one of his frequent customers, to paint 'Puff's Weeds' above the windows.

Sarah pulled into the Shell station and had the attendant fill the tank. The kid cleaned the windshield and handed her a receipt. Sarah drove the cruiser to a parking spot in front of Puff's. Ken had never been in the cannabis outlet and was curious to see the owner again. When the officers entered the store, Sarah waved to the clerk, apparently the owner, Art Gehring, and smiled.

Art smiled and returned an acknowledging wave as he waited on a customer. He was weighing a pot sample taken from a large cylindrical glass container. Ken felt like he had been transported to the late 1800s as he scanned the interior of the little store. Art was dressed as a turn-of-the-century pharmacist and was weighing pot on an antique analytical balance. He was picking up brass weights with forceps, adding them to the right pan opposite the weed placed on a piece of wax paper on the other pan. When the pointer quit oscillating and pointed vertically, Art packaged the weed and handed it to the patron, a large, bearded man wearing boots, a yellow T-shirt and overalls. The big fellow gave Art a twenty, said "Thanks, Art. See you next week," turned and limped out the entranceway. He paid little if any attention to the two officers.

"Good morning, Sarah. I think I know your handsome companion."

Sarah made the introductions. Art said, "I remember officer Sanders." The men shook hands.

Sarah continued, "We'd like to know more about the rumors of cheap weed being sold in town. Who told you about it?"

"Dirk Taylor came in yesterday for his normal prescription. After Dirk paid his bill, I followed him outside where his daughter, Lynn, waited. Lynn mentioned she knew of a kid selling weed much cheaper. That grabbed my attention and I asked her if she knew who was selling." Frustrated, Art sighed, took a deep breath and continued, "Dirk looked questioningly at his daughter and asked her who might that be? Lynn said he was an older kid, named Dennis. She didn't know his last name."

Ken glanced at Sarah and said, "I think I know Dennis. I've talked to him before."

The officers thanked Art for the information and left the store. When they were seated in the cruiser, Ken typed 'Dennis Michaels' into the computer to get his address. "The Michaels reside at Hall's Trailer Park." Ken looked up from the screen at Sarah and said, "Let's pay the young Mr. Michaels a visit."

"Sounds good. Maybe we can scare something…other than the usual, out of him." Sarah snickered and stepped on the gas.

It only took ten minutes for the cruiser to arrive at the trailer park. They had radioed their intentions to the chief so he could follow their progress. The mobile home park's capacity was two dozen trailers but only about half the sites were occupied. The Michaels' home was parked in location 21 near the eastern edge of the rectangular grounds.

Sarah followed the location numbers and direction arrows, parking behind an old pickup with one front wheel missing. The almost horizontal axle was resting on a stack of four by fours. Two legs protruded from under the engine compartment. The officers stepped from the cruiser and approached the partially exposed form. Ken said, "Mr. Michaels?"

"Who's asking?"

"The police. We'd like to ask a few questions. Could you please come out from under the truck?"

The legs bent, boot heels dug into the ground and a shirtless, middle-aged man in overalls gradually appeared. He stood and with his wrist, wiped a grease spot from his forehead, blinked and asked, "All right, what can I do for you?"

Sarah said, "Actually, we'd like to talk to your son, Dennis."

"Dammit! What's he done now to bring the cops out here to question him? By the way, he's not here."

Sarah glanced at Ken and got a nod. "He's suspected of selling marijuana, but we need his side of the story. It could just be a rumor passed around by some kids."

Ken added, "We'd like to talk to him. Do you know where we can find him?"

Michaels scratched the back of his neck and said, "He took off on his bike to go to his buddy's house."

"So, he went over to see Roger Swartz," Ken stated.

"That's right, but he said he'd be back for lunch." Michaels looked at his watch.

Ken glanced at his wrist and saw that his digital watch displayed 10:58. It made more sense to go to Dennis rather than wait. They thanked Mr. Michaels and left the trailer park. A few minutes later, they entered the lane to the Swartzs' log home.

"I hope those boys are here. I'd like to get Dennis's side of the story before twelve o'clock," said Ken.

Sarah looked at him, surprised. "Katelin expects you home for lunch? When on patrol, don't you usually grab a burger?"

"Yeah, but she wants me to help her plan a birthday party for Erica. When I get home at night, we're both tired, so she wants us to plan something when our minds are more productive."

Sarah cut the engine and the officers approached the front door. Ken reached for the brass knocker, but the door suddenly opened. Dennis and Roger stepped back into the house, surprised by the police.

"Who is it, Roger?" Footsteps from the interior of the house could be heard coming across the hardwood floor.

"It's a couple of cops, Mom."

"Well, have them come inside. They must be here for a good reason. Maybe they found out more about that owl attack."

Ken and Sarah followed the two boys into the living room where Mrs. Swartz gestured for the officers to sit at the sofa and she sat down on a large recliner across the room. She motioned to Roger, "You can go."

Ken quickly reacted, "No, we'd like the boys to stay."

"Oh! All right. What is this all about?" She glanced at the boys.

Sarah leaned forward toward Mrs. Swartz, "Actually, we want to ask Dennis a couple of questions. His father told us we might find him here."

"So, this doesn't concern Roger?"

"Ah, we're not sure." Sarah nodded towards her partner, "Go ahead, Ken."

Ken stood up towering over Dennis, who was about five or six inches shorter. Intimidated by the large officer, Dennis took a step toward the front door.

"Have you been selling marijuana?" Ken stepped closer.

Dennis froze for a second, looked at Roger and said, "Yeah. We found a package along the road, opened it and could tell by the odor what it was. We sold about a pound to friends."

"How much was in the package?"

Roger spoke up, "It was a big lump in a plastic bag. I'm guessing less than two pounds. Den and I pulled off some pieces and started selling it in smaller lumps of about an ounce. We didn't weigh it, we just guessed how much was in each piece. Marijuana isn't illegal in Oregon, is it?"

Sarah stared at Roger, "Do you have a license to sell it?"

Roger stammered, "A…a license?"

Dennis was also confused, "Wait, isn't it legal here? You mean we need a license?"

Sarah nodded and said, "Only licensed dispensaries are allowed to sell marijuana. We have to confiscate the weed. You'll need to give us the rest of it and any money you got from the sales. We'll have to cite you for this and the judge will be in touch with your parents. Unfortunately, this will be on your juvenile records."

Mrs. Swartz hurriedly interjected, "Look officers, the boys have cooperated with your investigation. Can't this be overlooked?"

Sarah replied, "I'm afraid not. This is too serious of an offense. Please get the bag and any money."

The boys disappeared into the back of the house and Sarah gave Mrs. Swartz her police business card. "You will be receiving court documents to schedule an appointment with a judge at the courthouse. If you have further information about the marijuana, call the station."

Ken and Sarah moved toward the door, waiting for the boys to return. When the boys came back, Roger carried a bag of the remaining grass and each teen handed him nearly eight hundred dollars in bills. He quickly counted the money and gave a receipt to Mrs. Swartz.

Ken and Sarah thanked Mrs. Swartz and the boys for their cooperation and left the house. When in the cruiser, Ken placed the money and the marijuana in an evidence container.

CHAPTER 24

Ken took over driving the cruiser and as they moved slowly down the dusty lane back to the highway, Sarah turned to Ken and asked, "Do you really believe those boys found the marijuana along the road?"

Ken laughed, "Nope! I think they took it from someone, maybe somebody that lives close by the Michaels' or the Swartzs', somebody that doesn't want to report the theft to us."

Sarah suggested, "Since the Swartzs' property is almost outside the city limits, why don't we ask those guys at the Wieselman barn if they know anything about a package of weed? There's a pickup parked next to that sad looking structure; somebody must be there. I saw that blue pickup when we came out here to talk with Dennis."

When the police car stopped at the Swartzs' turnoff, Ken made a right and drove to the Wieselman property. He coasted the last ten yards to the pickup and turned off the motor. Sarah was out and walking quickly to the open barn door before Ken unbuckled. As he got out of the patrol car, three young men came from the barn holding yard tools. Two of the three men seemed familiar, but he couldn't recall where he had seen them. He had a sudden flash of memory of a bear in a wire cage.

The tallest of the three young men greeted Sarah, "Howdy officers. What can we do for you? Are you here to check on property improvements so soon?"

"No, nothing like that. We're from the Timberville PD. I'm Sarah Turner and my partner is Ken Sanders. We wanted to ask if you knew of a recent marijuana theft. Have you fellows lost or misplaced a package recently?"

Barry stood next to Jeff and had to answer the officer without acknowledging they were illegally transporting relatively large amounts of weed with intent to sell. Barry laughed, "Someone stole some weed? What'd they get—a few ounces?"

"No, a little more than that. We recovered nearly a pound of marijuana and about sixteen hundred dollars."

Barry and Jeff both appeared surprised and Leeray, carrying a shovel, came forward slightly. "What's all this about pot?"

Jeff said, "The cops want to know if we heard about some stolen pot. They've recovered nearly a pound of grass and a wad of cash."

Leeray acted dumb and said, "Who's selling that stuff around here? Isn't there a dealer in town selling pot legally?"

Sarah nodded and scanned the faces of the three young men. She motioned to Ken to return to the cruiser saying, "Well, I guess you guys don't know anything about Timberville's illegal marijuana trade. Let us know if you hear anything, okay? Say, can I get your names for our report?"

Barry said, "Sure. I'm Barry Nexly. The tall guy is Jeff Wheldine and the guy with the shovel is Leeray Brown."

"Well, thanks for talking with us." Sarah gave Barry one of her business cards and commented, "You can call those numbers any time of day or night."

Sarah drove on the way back into town. Ken was silent for several seconds and then said, "What do you think about those three? I had a strange feeling that I met two of them before, but I can't place where. Even weirder, I keep getting a flash of a wire cage."

Sarah glanced at her watch and stepped on the gas. "I'd better get you home, it's damn near twelve o'clock. I don't want Katelin to accuse me of keeping you from planning a party for Erica. I'll drop you off at home and pick you up at one o'clock."

When the police cruiser was out of sight, Leeray vented his rage, "Son of a bitch! All this drudgery, hiking hundreds of miles over mountains, getting turned into an animal, and I've got nothing to show for it! How did you guys let some asshole kids get my weed? What's your explanation?"

Barry reacted, "Take it easy, Leeray. When you were a bear and got shot, Jeff and I were watching you chase the shooter down the road. We had no clue that other kid was in the barn going through your backpack. At least that's what we think happened."

"Exactly," Jeff agreed. "Then Heloise showed up with you in her SUV and we watched her investigate your injury. We were so involved with you and Heloise we didn't know your stash was gone. It had to be Roger who took your weed, there wasn't anybody else around."

Irritated, Leeray said, "You guys told me all this before, but what are we gonna do about it? This Roger kid, lives right over there, doesn't he?" Leeray pointed at the Swartz's home. "Let's pay him a visit."

Barry objected, "We can't do that, Leeray. Attention will be drawn to us and we'll be robbed or searched. The cops might find Jeff's and my weed. Look…Jeff and I can each give you one third of our profit and we'll still come out ahead." Barry looked at Jeff for assurance, "What do you think, Jeff?"

Jeff nodded, "That's right. We're buddies, so when we sell our pot, we'll split the profits three ways. Each gets a third. I think that's fair. We'll each make about twenty-five hundred bucks."

"Thanks guys, but I'd still like to beat the crap out of that pissant Roger kid. He should have to pay for taking something that wasn't his."

Barry calmly replied, "Be patient, Leeray. We might get a chance to teach him a lesson if we stay around this town very long, but we can't afford to draw police attention right now. You guys recognized that cop from the power station, didn't you?"

Doug and Erica had gone to Heloise's to pick berries, so I was doing some cleaning around the house. I had taken some trash out and washed the coffee maker, expecting Ken any time. I glanced at the clock on the kitchen wall above the sink when Ken hurried in the front door. I smiled and we both said "Hi." He had no reason to apologize, as he had done many times, but he was home for lunch and on time. He sat down on one of the kitchen chairs moaning, "I feel like something is out of phase. Maybe going back to a regular shift has messed with my biorhythm."

I smiled, started giving him a neck massage, and asked, "Did Sarah drop you off?"

"Yeah, she'll be back at one o'clock. We've been alternating driving around for the last couple of hours. Remember those two boys, Roger and Dennis? They found a package of weed and sold some of it. Sarah and I confiscated the weed and the money."

"So, you had a pretty good morning. Want a sandwich or soup, or both?"

"Give me a couple of minutes with your magic fingers. You're doing a great job. I'm already feeling more relaxed. You'll have me groaning before long."

I kept kneading Ken's neck and shoulders and asked, "Have you thought of what to do for Erica's party?

Ken suggested, "How about hiring a clown?"

"I don't think so. Some kids that age are afraid of clowns. All they usually do is make balloon animals and talk funny. Kids want more than that these days. What about renting one of those inflatable bounce houses?"

"Hmm. That sounds like a good idea. How much would one of those set us back?"

"Well, cost and safety are important factors; we might have to dig into our savings account. I think we could do it for less than five hundred dollars. Maybe we can rent one from Portland or Eugene. It might be a little cheaper from Eugene. I'll ask around locally to see if anyone has one we can rent."

"Sounds like we have a plan. Now what's for lunch? Thinking about birthday cake has made me hungry." Grinning, he stood and gave me a long kiss and encircled me in an embrace.

I pushed him away and said, "You're hungry all the time, just like Doug. You know, he's gonna be as big or bigger than you are before long." While massaging Ken's neck, I decided to make some toasted cheese sandwiches and tomato soup."

Ken kissed my forehead and turned around. "I'll be right back." Ken went to the bathroom and washed while I assembled all the ingredients for lunch. The only thing I forgot was the grape jam, but when Ken saw what we were going to eat, he reminded me about the jam. Whether we were having toasted cheese or peanut butter sandwiches, he had to have grape jelly or jam. He told me once that was the glue that held the sandwich together. Doug had adopted that tradition, or was it inherited?

"Hey, where are the kids? Aren't they having lunch at home? Did they take Sasha to the park?"

"No, they're over at Heloise's. She called earlier and invited them over to help pick raspberries. She has a bumper crop this summer. I thought it would be a good activity for them. They'll eat lunch over there."

"Say, that gives me an idea." He winked at me.

"You want to pick raspberries?" I grinned, ignoring the inuendo as I handed him a spoon and a large bowl of soup.

Ken laughed, "No. There are five young men, including Roger Swartz and Dennis Michaels, who are probably involved with the illegal drug trade in town. The department could use some help acquiring information about the recent pot influx."

"You want Heloise to assist you? Those guys won't pay any attention to an old woman, Ken."

"But didn't Heloise just have a camping experience for about a dozen teenage girls? Maybe she could get one or two of them to visit our fair city and gather some evidence for us. I don't want to use local girls."

"Yes, she had ten girls at the camp. She told me they had a very interesting time near the Pacific Crest Trail and the Three Sisters mountains. I didn't press her for any details. She seemed pleased that the outing was over."

"Well, would you ask her if one or two of her girls could help us. You'll see her when you pick up Doug and Erica, right?"

"That's correct, Lieutenant. I'll be going over to Heloise's at two o'clock and will talk to her then. How's that cheese sandwich?"

Ken dunked the last piece of sandwich into his soup, took a big bite, and exclaimed, "That was the best lunch I ever had, pretty waitress. We'll have to do this again." He pushed his chair back, stood and kissed me. "I've got to go back to work. I'll be home at five. Thanks for lunch."

I realized Ken must have known the time but I hadn't noticed him looking at his watch. I knew how prompt Sarah was. I watched as he straightened his uniform, tightened his belt and started toward the front door. Ken stopped, turned around and said, "Don't forget to ask Heloise if she can give us some assistance. Tell her we would really appreciate the help." I heard two beeps of a car horn and Ken disappeared out the door. I was following him to the door and watched as he got in the front passenger seat of the cruiser. I couldn't see Sarah. Ken waved to me as they drove away.

The dirty dishes from lunch didn't amount to much. I stuck them in the washer and wiped off a few crumbs from the counter tops. I rinsed the empty soup can and tossed it in the recycle bin. I was ready to pick up the kids, but it was only 1:30, so I sat down at the computer and looked for a bounce house provider. Erica's birthday was only a few days away, but I thought I still had time to find a rental Ken would approve of.

I found a site in Eugene: Parties for Kids to Grannies, PKG INC. Only thirty-five miles from Timberville and for an extra fee, they would transport and inflate the bounce house. However, there was an instructional sheet available for anyone that wanted to transport the unit in their car. The house was contained in a bag about the size of two large suitcases. I decided Ken could pick up the unit on Saturday before Erica's birthday next Sunday. I'd talk with Ken this evening after the kids were in bed.

I put the computer in sleep mode, went in the bathroom to make sure I looked presentable and set off on foot to Heloise's. None of my nearby neighbors were outside, probably due to the bright sunlight and high humidity. But then I thought retirees were most likely on vacation or enjoying their air-conditioned homes. Only three minutes of brisk walking took me to Heloise's. I climbed the front steps and rang the doorbell.

I heard Erica's muffled voice and then the door opened. Heloise smiled and invited me inside. Doug and Erica were sitting at a card table eating ice cream sprinkled with raspberries. Erica looked up at me and asked, "Hi, Mom, are we in trouble?"

CHAPTER 25

"Why would you think you're in trouble?"

Erica swallowed another spoonful of ice cream and she waved her spoon. She confessed, "'Cause we're having dessert in the afternoon!"

"I'm sure you earned it. I'm not mad. Finish up while I speak to Heloise for a minute."

"They did a good job picking berries. I had to reward them. Should I have asked you?"

"No. Don't worry about it."

Taking my cue, Heloise led me down the hallway. The kids were engrossed with their treats so I felt I could leave them alone for a few minutes. We entered the kitchen and she poured us each a cup of tea. We sat at a small table pushed against the wall and she said, "What can I help you with?"

"Ken asked me to consult with you about a difficulty the police are having." I explained the problem with marijuana creeping into town and told her that Roger Swartz and Dennis Michaels were involved.

Heloise's eyes twinkled with excitement, "I'm familiar with those boys. They are headed for major trouble."

"Well, Ken thinks they have been lying about finding the marijuana. He believes they took it from someone."

"Huh! I'm sure they did and I know where it came from. I wasn't going to rat on the young men just because they have a quantity of grass. I haven't had the time to formulate my own plan. I was going to see if I could convince them to do the right thing. I believe they have only one goal, money."

My jaw dropped open. "You said you know where the marijuana came from?" Stunned, I had to ask, "You know who has the illegal marijuana?"

She nodded, looking over my shoulder to see if Doug and Erica were listening. "Yes. They are living out at the old Wieselman barn. Their names are Barry, Jeff, and Leeray. We met on the Pacific Crest Trail and I searched their belongings when they were distracted." Heloise leaned back and sighed, obviously bothered by divulging what she knew. I had to assume she didn't want to get the trio in trouble with the police. She continued, "Each of the boys had a large plastic bag of pot in his backpack. I'm thinking one or more of the containers was stolen. You might not know; Roger Swartz lives close to the Wieselman barn."

I didn't tell Heloise that Ken suspected that Roger and Dennis had stolen the marijuana they had been selling. I asked her if she thought one or more of the girls from her recent camping excursion might be able to help get a confession from the boys.

Heloise didn't blink an eye and answered immediately, "Yes, I know just the right young lady. She's very capable. I'll communicate with her this evening to see if she will help the police."

"Thank you, Heloise. I'll tell Ken tonight that he might have some help with the marijuana problem. Shall I have him come see you tomorrow?"

"That would be fine but make it in the afternoon. I'll have some company in the morning. And thank you for letting your children help me with the berry picking. They did a good job. I'm giving them some berries to take home. Does Ken like raspberries?"

I had to laugh. "Ken will eat anything, Heloise."

We finished our tea and I could see the kids were getting antsy. I caught sight of Erica with her face in her ice cream bowl licking the last remnants. Doug was sitting there looking up at the ceiling. They were ready to return home, so I thanked Heloise for the tea and the conversation and said, "Kids, thank Heloise for the treat. We've got to be on our way now. I'm sure Heloise has other things to do."

After I wiped Erica's sticky face with a wet paper towel, we were out the door and on the way home a few minutes later. Erica was skipping ahead of Doug and me, but suddenly stopped, turned around, and asked, "Mom, why does Heloise collect twigs?"

I was taken by surprise. Where had that come from? "I'm sure she was just cleaning up her yard, dear."

Doug touched my arm to get my attention, "No, Mom, she took them in the house. She wasn't throwing them in the trash. I was wondering—the same as Erica, but I didn't think it was important."

We continued walking and I began to think that maybe Heloise's actions were a bit strange. I'll have to ask her, but I don't want to appear nosey. I'll mention the twig collecting to Ken. He'll probably laugh and tell me who cares, it's not something that would concern the police.

As we walked, the warm afternoon sun on my shoulders made me drowsy. When we got back home at three o'clock, I set the sprinkler so Erica could have some fun getting wet and burning off some calories from the ice cream. Doug hopped on his bicycle and rode off to the park to meet his latest buddy who flew gliders there. I sat down for a few minutes and planned dinner, but I was interrupted when Erica came running into the house screaming, "A bee stung me!"

I asked, "Where?"

She pointed to her left thigh a few inches below her shorts. A red spot had already formed. I sat her down on the sofa so I could inspect the wound for a stinger but I couldn't see anything; I concluded she had already rubbed it away. I took Erica into the bathroom and retrieved a sting relief pad from the medicine cabinet. I allowed her to rub the inflamed spot with the medicated wipe.

She glanced up at me, tears in her eyes, and said, "Mom, it still hurts. Can't you make it go away?"

"You have to give the medicine a chance to work, dear. Come into the kitchen and we'll put some ice on it. That will help with the swelling."

By the time I had an ice cube wrapped in a washrag and applied to the sore spot, Erica looked at me and said, "It doesn't hurt anymore. I want to go out and pick more dandelions."

I felt like laughing, but I realized it was best to minimize the impact of the bee sting and let her resume her outdoor activities. She would come back inside before long anyway. I had forgotten my disrupted thoughts about dinner, so I wrote some things down on a pad next to the telephone. I checked in the refrigerator to make sure everything I needed was present and started peeling potatoes. For some unknown reason Ken enjoys mashing the boiled potatoes. He claims it's therapeutic after a long day at work. When he arrives at home, I'll get him busy in the kitchen. We've got plenty of milk and butter.

Barry, Jeff, and Leeray had spent the morning working in and around the barn. Jeff began building an outhouse concealed from the road by the aging structure. The internal bathroom was beyond repair. Barry began investigating the property for a source of water. He'd found essential parts of a windmill in the barn's rafters and wondered if he could pump water. Leeray took the truck and went to the library to find directions for windmill construction. Following the morning's investment to improve the Wieselman property, the trio left for Eugene. They needed to establish potential contacts and customers for marijuana sales. They took an ounce of grass with them so interested parties could evaluate the weed's quality.

None of the young men had ever been to the University of Oregon campus before but they thought they had concocted a plausible explanation for their visit. If someone asked, they were thinking of enrolling in the fall. Going to college had never crossed any of their minds and as soon as they were on campus, they felt completely out of their element. When they arrived at the university, Barry took the wheel and the pickup meandered through the campus streets looking for likely customers.

After fifteen minutes of cruising the grounds, a policeman in a yellow and green golfcart pulled them over.

The university cop tapped on the driver's window and Barry lowered it. "Are you fellows lost? I've seen you driving around without an apparent destination in mind. Maybe I can help you find something or someone."

"We're just looking around. We're thinking of going to college here. This looks like a nice place."

As Barry talked, Jeff and Leeray nodded. Jeff leaned toward the window and asked, "Can we watch the football team practice?"

"Fall practice hasn't begun yet and you would have to check with the athletic department about that. Some practices are closed to the public. There is a break between summer school and fall classes right now. If you want to apply for admission, you need to pick up forms at the Admissions Office. I'll show you where that is on this campus map." The cop pulled a map from his breast pocket and handed it to Barry. Then he pointed to their present location and moved his right index finger along the route to the Admissions Center.

Barry's eyes followed the route, but his mind was in another place. He had been given information that explained the lack of students moving to and from buildings. He was ready to return to Timberville and plan to return to the university when classes were in session.

"When will classes start again?" He asked.

The campus cop glanced at a card pulled from his breast pocket and replied, "September 27."

That was all Barry needed. "Thank you for giving us directions. We'll pick up the forms."

"Have a nice day, gentlemen." The cop returned to his cart, made a U-turn and sped away.

Barry started the engine and drove back to the highway. Leeray sat quietly until they were travelling back toward Timberville. "We've got nearly a month to kill. What are we gonna do for income? Your credit card won't last much longer, will it?"

"You got that right. We've got about a hundred bucks left before it maxes out."

Jeff laughed, "I think we'd better find some jobs to tide us over. A hundred smackers won't buy enough food for a week, maybe a bit longer if we eat nothing but peanut butter sandwiches and pickles."

"And I'll die without a burger for a whole month," said Leeray.

Barry hadn't commented for several minutes but then said, "We have another option, guys.

One of us will have to wear a disguise and talk to the owner of Puff's Weed Supply. Maybe we can sell him some of our grass."

Jeff snickered, "That just might bring the cops down on us. We've gotta be smart about this."

Sitting between Barry and Jeff in the truck, Leeray mulled over the idea of getting a job. The only real job he ever had was as a laborer with his father's roofing company. He worked one summer when he was nineteen and after six weeks of backbreaking, dirty work on roofs tearing off old composite shingles, he swore to never do that job again. He looked for easy money ever since. He mowed lawns, pumped gas, and twirled advertising signs on street corners but those had short lives. Selling pot was his type of business, but so far easy money alluded him. He sought a profession that paid well but didn't require sweat, danger, and filth. He hadn't considered going back to school.

Watching telephone and power poles flash by as they drove toward the mountains, Jeff got an idea. When he was growing up, a neighbor was a telephone lineman. Jeff decided he would contact the telephone company or power company to seek a job climbing power poles and towers. Those guys had to be making good money and he wasn't afraid of heights. He leaned back in his seat and relaxed, having made up his mind to see what his options were with two big companies.

Barry thought of his last real job. He worked in the apple orchards near Yakima, Washington, driving a forklift to move apples from one location to another for storage. Before that, he worked in the vineyards in Walla Walla and became interested in the fermentation process. Just as he was going to receive training, the Covid pandemic shut down the school he was to attend. Depressed, he became a drifter, selling used cars, and delivering advertising for a radio station, any temporary jobs that kept his credit card balance manageable. But now it was out of control. He decided to see what job openings were posted at the city services office. He could at least pick up dog poop at a park, making a minimum wage and not overexerting. He wasn't too concerned; it would only be temporary, a few weeks or a couple of months at most. As soon as the grass was sold, they would be forever gone from Timberville. He imagined seeing the town receding in his rearview mirror.

CHAPTER 26

Heloise, a vegan, ate dinner at her small kitchen table and planned an evening trip to Boise, Idaho and Reno, Nevada. She would need two young women to help her reveal the shadowy undertakings of the two local teens, Roger and Dennis, and the three slightly older young men residing at the Wieselman barn. Jean Moberg lived in Boise and Frankie Vox was in Reno. Jean was one of the youngest, but smartest of the novices and Frankie was the eldest, but still a teen, and most sophisticated of the ten girls that took part in the Wickon summer camp.

Heloise was planning for Jean to become friends with Roger and Dennis and she felt Frankie could hold her own with Barry, Leeray and Jeff. But how was she going to get the girls in contact with the young men? Perhaps the girls would have some ideas. But first, she had to explain the situation and see if the girls would want to assist the police. Heloise consulted her maps and at seven o'clock she left for Boise, 508 miles away.

Slightly over an hour later, she arrived in the Mobergs' backyard. Jean, her sister, Joan, and their mother were enjoying the evening seated around a firepit roasting marshmallows when Heloise abruptly swooped out of the sky. The Mobergs gasped and huddled together next to the fire nearly dropping their snacks. A rush of wind stirred the flames and set the marshmallows afire. Heloise apologized and then said, "I've come to ask for assistance."

Mrs. Moberg tossed her blackened treat into the fire and asked, "How can we help you, Heloise?"

Heloise explained the situation with illicit marijuana in Timberville and mentioned the boys, Dennis and Roger.

Joan exclaimed, "Oh, those are the boys who caused trouble when I bought straw. They're both despicable characters. I'll bet they'll be in prison before long."

Jean said, "You didn't tell me about them, Joan. Why not?"

She raised her right eyebrow and grinned, "Well, I kind of beat them up. I didn't want the girls and the mentors to think I did something bad. Heloise knew what happened. That was the end of it."

Mrs. Moberg anticipated what Heloise had in mind. "You want Jean to get those boys to incriminate themselves?"

Heloise nodded, "I would be nearby to guarantee her safety."

Joan reacted immediately, "I'd like to help, too." She looked at her mother. "Can I go along with Jean? We could work together…there are two boys. They wouldn't have a prayer with our combined powers."

"That's for sure," Ursula agreed. "All right, Heloise. How long will they be gone? School starts before long. I don't want them to miss anything."

Heloise was very confident. "I can't imagine they will be gone for more than a couple of days. Like Joan said, those boys won't have a chance."

The sisters were huddled together talking in whispers. When they had an opportunity to speak, Joan said, "When would you like us to come to Timberville? We could follow you back if you like."

Heloise replied, "I still have to go to Reno, but you can fly to Timberville tonight without me. It will take you a bit over an hour if you don't go supersonic. Get your brooms so I can transfer directions to my home."

The girls darted into the house and returned with their flight sticks. Heloise grasped all three brooms together and said, "Copy directions home."

She looked at the girls and said, "I'll be home in a couple of hours. You don't need to wait up for me." She turned to Ursula and commented, "Thank you for the assistance, Ursula. You will receive accolades in the next issue of Wickon Quarterly Northwest. I must be off. Good night."

Heloise waved to the Mobergs and vanished into the night sky.

The sky above downtown Reno was brightly illuminated and Heloise landed on top of the Lucky Break casino after flying for about forty minutes. At twenty stories high, the Lucky Break hotel/casino was an older building and Heloise had no trouble bypassing the roof security system. She entered the nearest ladies room and changed into a purple jump suit extracted from her cape. She stashed her broom and flight clothing in a utility closet, washed her face, applied makeup and left the bathroom.

As she passed the top floor security office, she checked for occupancy. In an adjoining room one employee monitored card games on the first floor and watched multiple TV screens intensely. The outer office was dimly lit and nearly empty, except for two benches of computers, so Heloise decided to use one of the machines to search for Frankie Vox.

Her search took only a fraction of a second. Frankie Vox had been let go from Harrah's security and had gone to work for a motel on the eastern edge of town, Eastside Suites. Harrah's had given Frankie a sterling recommendation. She had been terminated as a reduction in force due to COVID. Heloise smiled and turned off the computer. As she moved toward the door, it unexpectedly opened and a large man dressed in a guard's uniform asked, "Who are you and where is your ID lanyard?"

He held a gun and entered the room. Heloise had no choice but to back up a couple of steps. She lowered her arms to her side allowing her wand to drop from her sleeve into her right hand. She said, "I was just delivering a message next door to Sharon. It's from her husband."

The security officer moved to the adjoining room door, tried to open it as he watched Heloise. He abruptly realized he had to enter a code on a keypad. As soon as the officer turned his back to Heloise to enter a code on the door lock, she waved her wand over his head. He then had trouble with his code, pressing random numbers in frustration and she quickly exited the room. He didn't follow. She returned to the ladies' room, recovered her belongings and left through the door to the roof. Deciding to keep on the jump suit, Heloise donned her flight gear and swooshed away to the eastern edge of town to the Eastside Suites Motel.

She stored her broom and flight clothes behind a large trash container and walked to the front office door. She noticed the neon NO VACANCY sign but paid little attention. As she entered, a gong sounded and a middle-aged overweight bald man appeared at the check-in counter. Something reddish was dripping from his chin. It looked like ketchup to Heloise. He wiped his chin with his left hand and smiled. "Sorry, I'm eating a burger." He wiped his hands on his trousers and said, "We have no rooms available tonight, madame."

"That's okay, I'm not looking for a room, I'm looking for a young woman, Frankie Vox."

"Are you a relative? Her grandmother?"

"No, just a close friend. I need to ask her a question."

The gentleman glanced at his watch. "She's on tour with my daughter."

"Tour?"

"Yes, a security walk-around. Checking for any problems on the premises. She should be back in a few minutes. Difficulties are quite rare around here."

"If it's all right with you, I'll just wait for her here in the office."

"No problem. I'm going to finish my dinner. There are some magazines on display." He pointed at periodicals on two shelves beside the office door. There was a chair below the shelves. Heloise sat and said, "Thank you, I'll wait for her."

The man disappeared through a plaid curtain into a back room. Heloise heard some non-English spoken words she couldn't understand. She waited for about a minute before the door gong sounded and two women entered the motel office. Heloise could only see their backs. She stood and said, "Frankie?"

The taller of the women turned around and said, "Heloise! I thought I recognized your things, but I couldn't figure out why you would be in Reno. What's going on? Why are you here?"

"I've come to see you, Frankie. I need your help in Timberville."

Frankie looked at her young companion and said, "My friend and I have to talk. I'll see you again tomorrow evening. You are almost ready to do walk-arounds by yourself."

Her associate nodded and backed away, disappearing into the rear of the office behind the curtain.

Heloise said, "Let's go outside where we can't be overheard." She turned toward the office door. First to the door, Frankie reached up and silenced the gong mechanism. Heloise remarked as she went outside, "Thanks, I could only reach that using my wand."

When the two were outside and leaning against the office wall, Frankie uttered, almost whispering, "I don't understand what I can help you with. You have much stronger powers than I. Please clarify."

After a few minutes of explanation, Heloise asked, "Do you think you can help me and the police in Timberville?"

"Sure. I'd be glad to, but I can't leave until tomorrow evening… about this time. I'll have Saturday and Sunday off. Do you think the job can be completed over the weekend? I have to work here on Monday."

Heloise smiled, "I'm so glad you will help. Flight time to Timberville is less than an hour. Wear some student clothes under your cape. Something that won't confuse the young men."

"Gotcha. A sweatshirt and jeans should do, and a pair of boots. What do you think?"

"Sounds good. You've got the right idea. I'll expect you on Saturday. You know my address."

"Bye Heloise. Your things are where you left them. Take care."

While Heloise was flying back to Timberville pleased with her successful recruiting trip, the two girls from Boise had spent the last hour at Heloise's house planning. Jean was relaxing on the sofa with Amos in her lap and Joan was sprawled on the floor reading aloud from the Wickon source books. Astrid was on the floor curled up beside her, as though asleep but purring loud enough for Heloise to hear as she entered the back door.

The girls jumped to their feet disrupting the cats when Heloise entered the house and whisked into the living room. Joan said, "I hope it was all right for us to consult your reference works."

Heloise chuckled, "I'm happy to see you went right to work. The manuals are available to all levels of Wickons. Have you found anything useful?" She put her cape in the hall closet.

"Oh, we sure have. Jean and I plan to visit with Roger and Dennis tomorrow. We've been rehearsing our back story."

Jean asked, "How was your trip to Reno?"

"Just as I hoped. Frankie Vox will be joining us on Saturday. You remember Frankie, don't you?"

Jean glanced at her sister, smiling, "We sure do. We've talked about her several times since the retreat. She's a ventriloquist and can do several different voices. She's very clever and really funny. I hope we can learn a few things from her this weekend."

Patting her cats good-night, Heloise said, "Well, I'm very tired and must get to bed. Flying my old bones around the country at night wore me out. I'll see you ladies in the morning. The guest bedrooms are ready for you. Good night."

The girls spoke in unison, "Good night, Heloise."

The cats curled up on the sofa and went back to sleep, following their normal routine, after Heloise had turned in. Jean and Joan retired within a few minutes of midnight. The girls had yawned occasionally but talked over Friday's plan one last time before going to bed. They thought they would be able to sleep in Friday morning but they didn't realize Heloise had other plans.

It was a couple of minutes after 7:00 a.m. when the house shook from what sounded like dynamite exploding but it was Mother Nature announcing Friday morning with a thunderstorm. Rain mixed with hail pummeled Timberville for an exciting five minutes. Then the sky cleared and the sun began to evaporate the fresh precipitation. Jean and Joan had been rudely awakened but after Heloise calmed her cats and assured the girls the Russians hadn't attacked; the twins went back to bed for another half-hour of slumber.

By eight o'clock, Heloise and the girls were eating breakfast and planning the course of action for the afternoon. Heloise informed the girls that Lieutenant Sanders wanted to meet with them after lunch and prior to any conduct that might violate police guidelines.

Joan reminded Heloise that a confrontation with the boys had taken place when she obtained straw for repairing the Wickons' brooms. Jean said, "Joan, do you really think those boys will remember you?"

"I'm not sure, but I did give them trouble. I accidently knocked Dennis in the head. They might remember me because of that. Since we look alike, they might get suspicious when they see both of us."

Heloise chuckled, "I have just the solution." She went in her bedroom and came back with a small black briefcase. She undid the two clasps and flipped the lid open to expose a costume/makeup kit. The girls thought it was going to be a simple change of eye shadow and lipstick.

"Will makeup be enough to change my looks?" Joan asked.

Heloise smiled, "I'm going to give you a broken nose. That will certainly change things."

Jean excitedly contributed, "Put a pimple on her dimple, and put a brown mole on her chin."

Joan objected, "Hey, how would you like something put on you, like a black eye?" She shook her fist at her sister.

"Now girls, this is just for fun, but the pimple is a good idea."

Jean smirked, "Make the pimple look like she just squeezed it, kind of a big irregular red spot in the middle of her cheek."

Heloise looked at Jean, "I've changed my mind. You will both have to adopt a phony look tomorrow. The boys won't remember any previous encounters with either of you."

Jean chuckled and commented, "This is going to be fun. I can hardly wait for tomorrow."

CHAPTER 27

Heloise wanted the twins to be aware of the two boys' ruthlessness with defenseless animals, so she told Jean and Joan about the death of Specter, her favorite and special cat. Warning the girls would hopefully prevent them from getting into any trouble. She told them how she had terrorized the boys when they were camping, which initiated a round of laughter.

Joan asked, "Can Jean and I ride bikes to the Swartzs' property?"

Heloise replied, "Good thinking. Swartzs' home is on the edge of town. It would be an easy ride. I'm sure the police have some bikes we can borrow. They usually have a number of them in the impound lot or the lost and found. I'll call the station and have Lieutenant Sanders bring them when he meets with us later."

While Heloise contacted the police department, Joan and Jean applied rubber appendages to their noses, ears, and fingers. Their experiments lacked realism and when Heloise returned from phoning Lieutenant Sanders, all three women had fits of laughter. Heloise took over and in a short period of time did an expert job making Jean look as if her nose had been recently broken. Then she began working on Joan adding a scar, a mole and acne blemishes. As she worked with their make-up, she told the girls, "Lieutenant Sanders will bring two bicycles for you this afternoon. A mechanic will make sure they are in good working order."

Jean smiled, "I get first choice. I want a brightly colored one. Joan, if there's an ugly bike, you get it to go with your broken nose."

Joan responded, "Let's get some zit cream that you can apply when we see the boys. That will surely pique their interest."

All three women laughed. When the laughter subsided, Heloise said, "Officer Sanders wants both of you to wear a wire so the boys can't deny anything incriminating. He wants everything to be based on facts, no hearsay evidence."

"This is starting to make me feel like we're working for the FBI or CIA," observed Jean.

"I know. It's getting kind of exciting," Joan added, raising her eyebrows.

By one o'clock, the three Wickons had finished lunch, cleaned up the kitchen and were waiting in the living room. Joan looked at Jean and started laughing. Jean turned away and looked out the window towards the street, saying, "If we are going to laugh when we look at each other, this isn't going to work. Only one of us will do the job." Jean then saw a large dark-blue SUV pull up to the curb and noticed POLICE displayed on the side panels.

She announced, "Lieutenant Sanders just arrived. Time to get to work."

The trio met Ken Sanders when he was halfway to the front door. Heloise introduced the girls and commented, "Jean and Joan are identical twins. Can you tell them apart?"

Ken became flustered. He couldn't help but notice the two girls appeared very different. Before he could think of anything, he looked at Heloise and saw a big smile.

Ken chuckled, "Oh, you're putting me on. They're wearing makeup. You had me for a second. I didn't know what to say."

Joan volunteered, "I met the two boys a couple of weeks ago when I was here for the campout. If both Jean and I look the same, we thought the boys might remember seeing me. Heloise gave me a broken nose and a pimple."

"You and Joan are no longer identical twins, that's for sure. I spotted the difference right away…police training sure comes in handy."

Everyone laughed and Heloise said, "Were you able to get some bicycles for the girls?"

"I've got two bikes in the squad car. Let's get them out and then go in the house. I need to get the girls wired and they can tell me what they've cooked up with to engage the boys."

As the group started toward the SUV, they heard a door slam and Sarah, Ken's partner, appeared at the back of the big vehicle. Sarah introduced herself to the women and lifted the cargo door to expose two well-used bicycles.

When Jean saw the obviously worn bikes, she began to giggle. Joan, after a quick look at the two-wheelers, took a deep breath and sighed, "I guess our make-believe parents don't have much money."

Sarah smiled and said, "The bikes are a bit rusty, but they should withstand a good day's riding. Here's a city map. Let's go inside so I can wire you up. Ken will give you the addresses where the boys live." She went back to the driver's door, reached in the open window and retrieved a small, unmarked cardboard box. Ken followed the women to the door where Sarah put her right palm against his chest and said, "You'd better stay outside while I wire the girls. We don't want to embarrass anyone."

"Okay. I'll be in the vehicle and listening to the receiver. Have them say a few words to test the hookup. Make sure to tell them to conserve the batteries. Oh, I want to talk to them before we leave. They need to know everything that Dennis and Roger told us."

Ten minutes later, Joan and Jean both spoke into their transmitters. Ken could hear them clearly. He secured the police car and entered the house. After a short discussion with the girls, Sarah and Ken left the house and drove away.

The twins wore matching short sleeve sweatshirts, shorts and hiking boots. They hadn't ridden bikes in several years, but after riding a few blocks, both felt comfortable and confident as they traversed Timberville's predominantly vacant streets. They encountered only one streetlight in the downtown area and walked their bikes through the intersection after a motorcycle assaulted the crosswalks with loud noise and streaks of rubber.

They stopped for a moment after crossing the street, referred to the city map and then continued on to the Swartzs'. Only one hill had to be ascended, but without a low gear, the girls walked the bikes a short distance to the top. The descent was enjoyable, wind in their hair, coasting and exceeding the speed limit for nearly four blocks. The girls began to pedal again when they saw the Swartzs' house come into view. They decided if the boys weren't there, they would ride on to the trailer park and find Dennis's home. As they turned into the dirt and gravel lane leading to the house, Jean put on her brakes, stopped and surveyed the area. Joan stopped a few feet ahead of her sister.

"Do you see the police vehicle?" asked Jean.

Joan swiveled her head and remarked, "Nope. The last time I saw it was when we walked to the top of that hill. It was pulled over on the shoulder."

"That's what I remember. That's good, the cops are supposed to be out of sight. Let's see if the boys are here."

They rode toward the front of the house. Since no kickstands were available, they leaned their bikes against the flower garden fence, walked to the front door and rang the bell. When the door opened, an older woman appeared. The girls assumed Mrs. Swartz was on the other side of the screen door. "Can I help you?"

Jean answered, "We're looking for Roger. Is he home?"

"Yes. He's out in the barn with Dennis. They're working on their bikes. You can go out there." She made a sweeping motion with her right hand and said, "Just follow the gravel road leading behind the house."

Joan sang, "Thank you."

The girls walked around the side of the house and found the boys sitting on a concrete slab leading to a modern barn. The boys were sprawled beside two worse-for-wear bicycles with chains removed. Smudged with dirt and grease, the boys' T-shirts looked as if they had been used to wipe their hands. Dennis and Roger were engrossed with repairs and didn't notice the girls until the sisters stood within a few yards.

Dennis suddenly issued a warning, "Hey, we've got female company."

Roger looked up, dropped his bike chain and struggled to his feet.

"Which of you is Roger?" asked Joan.

Dennis got up and motioned with his right thumb, "He is."

Jean said, "We heard you had some grass for sale."

"We did, but the cops took it and all the cash we had."

"We heard you had more than a pound. It's all gone?" Joan threw her hands up and turned to walk away.

Dennis reacted, "Wait a sec! We think we know where there's more weed. How much do you want?"

Jean glanced at Joan and shrugged, "At least half-a-pound, maybe more."

Roger shook his head. "Jesus! Where can you use that much grass?"

Jean answered, "On campus…at the university. We're gonna be freshmen next semester and want to make a good impression."

"That would do it," laughed Dennis. "One weekend of that and you'd be out on your butts. But the university won't stand for that activity on campus."

"Jeez, you had a lot of weed," Joan said. "So how did you get more than a pound?"

"We found it on the side of the road." Dennis pointed toward the paved roadway.

The girls looked at each other and frowned. Jean stared at Dennis and replied, "Sure you did. We don't believe you. Who in their right mind would lose more than a pound of pot along the side of a road? Especially on the outskirts of Timberville, which isn't a real hotbed of marijuana traffic."

Joan added, "Yeah, I'll bet there is only one local dealer and he probably just makes ends meet."

"What's the real story, guys?" quizzed Jean.

Roger and Dennis used a moment to study the girls and then moved toward the barn. As they walked away, Roger turned his head and said, "Just a minute. Me and Dennis have to talk."

While the boys were conferring, Jean smiled and whispered, "I think we might be getting some results soon."

Joan whispered back, "I hope so, these guys are a little spooky."

The boys were gone for less than a minute. When they returned from the barn, Roger looked at Joan and said, "You've been here before buying some hay and you attacked us with a broom. What's the real purpose of you being here? Did you think we wouldn't recognize you?"

"We just want to buy some weed. If you can't help us, we'll take off and leave you to your bike chains. Come on, Jean, these guys don't have anything for us. Let's go." The girls started to leave, but Dennis had taken up a position to block their exit. Joan recognized that Dennis might try to grab one of them, so she purposely stepped on the rear wheel of one of the bicycles, damaging several spokes.

"Damn! I don't have any replacement spokes. You broke one of them and bent two others." Dennis was incensed and yelling at Joan. She peeled away the nose appendage and said, "I'm the one that knocked you on your ass, not my sister."

Joan recognized the opportunity to gain an advantage over the boys and said, "We carry extra spokes on our bikes. We'll give you a replacement. We'll even install it for you."

Jean said, "Take us to our bikes so we can get the spokes. Our bikes are in front of the house."

"Okay, but don't try anything crazy. We'll run you down." Dennis indicated the girls should start walking around the house.

When the girls arrived at their bikes under the watchful eyes of Roger and Dennis, they removed their wands taped to the bikes' seat tubes.

Dennis rubbed the back of his neck and said, "Those don't look like spokes to me."

Joan replied, "Well, you don't know everything about bikes. Have you been to Europe? These are universal replacement parts made in Finland. They'll fit any bike made. They're very expensive."

Jean quickly added, "We'll show you how to install the new spokes; it's not an easy job, but they'll last forever."

The girls marched back to the boys' bikes and Joan knelt beside the wheel containing the damaged spoke. Jean stood holding her wand as the boys dropped to their knees to watch what Joan was doing. She began to remove the old spoke and Jean stepped closer. She waved her wand over the boys' heads and said, "You will now tell us the truth how you obtained the package of grass."

Joan used a pair of pliers and removed the broken spoke as Roger started talking. He told the girls when Dennis was being chased by a bear he shot with his twenty-two rifle, Roger sneaked into Mr. Wieselman's barn, rummaged through a backpack near the door and found a package of grass. He hid the pot and got it later when the older boys were gone from the barn. When Dennis and Roger retrieved the package and unwrapped it to see exactly what they had, they started selling it around town an ounce at a time. They each spent about fifty dollars of the proceeds before confiscation by the police.

Jean waved her wand over the boys, engrossed with the repairs taking place but not noticing the broken spoke had not been replaced. Joan had just rotated the tire to a different position. The boys' eyes were fixed in one position and seemed happy with the apparent repair. The girls said, "See you later." The sisters moved away from the boys, returned to their bikes and started back to Heloise's house.

As they left the Swartzs', Jean smiled at Joan and said, "That wasn't so bad. I think we got what we came for. Remember to turn off your transmitter to save battery power."

Joan laughed, "I turned mine off after Roger spilled his guts. The batteries will be recharged anyway, won't they?."

CHAPTER 28

Now that their job was complete, the girls rode back to Heloise's at a leisurely pace. When they arrived, Sarah was parked at the curb waiting for them. She had anticipated their timely return and had popped open the cargo hatch. Lieutenant Sanders sat in the passenger seat and was nearly asleep listening to music from a Eugene radio station. He heard voices as the bikes approached, shook off his drowsy feeling and exited the vehicle to greet the girls.

Sarah joined him and waved to the girls as they rode toward the police vehicle.

The girls, exhibiting expectant expressions, slipped off their seats and stood beside the bikes. Joan asked, "Did you get the information you needed?"

Ken said, "Yes. Good job, ladies. Now we know for sure where the pot came from. That was one of our big questions."

When Heloise saw the girls talking to the officers, she came out of the house carrying Astrid with Amos following close behind.

"How did the girls do, Lieutenant?"

"*A+* work. Thank you all for an awesome job. If you don't want to do any more riding, we'll take the bikes back to the impound lot. Would you like to buy them?"

Joan looked at Jean and grinned. They said in unison, "No thank you. We have other modes of transportation."

Lieutenant Sanders said, "Oh, I forgot. You're old enough to drive. You probably both have licenses now."

Sarah commented, "I have one question. How did you girls get Roger to talk and tell the truth?"

Jean replied, "Oh, that was a sleight of hand, a bit of magic. When Joan spun the bicycle wheel, he got a little hypnotized by the light reflecting from the rotating spokes. He was so interested in fixing the spoke, he didn't think of what he was saying. He started spilling everything. We just let him talk."

"I should learn your method of interrogation. Our cases might be solved more quickly," said Sarah.

Ken said, "I have one last question. My daughter's birthday is Sunday. Could you ladies come and help with entertainment?" He looked at the girls, and before they had a chance to react, he said, "I can pay you for your trouble."

Heloise said, "You can stay with me over the weekend. Ken's wife told me they will have a bounce house. She could use some more supervisors."

Jean and Joan looked at each other, shrugged, grinned and Jean said, "That might be fun. Sure, we can do that." Joan added, "But we'll have to go home right after. Mom expects us back."

Ken said, "We'll expect you about one o'clock then. Thanks, girls, and thank you for your help today." Ken loaded the two bicycles into the big police SUV while Joan and Jean followed Heloise into the house.

When the women were inside, Heloise reminded the girls that they had planned on being gone for only two days. If they were to stay for Lt. Sander's daughter's birthday, they needed to inform their mother of the extended stay in Timberville. Jean called her mother and explained. Mrs. Moberg agreed to the girls' extended time in Oregon.

Late Friday night, two light taps were heard at Heloise's front door. Heloise and the twins were playing Parcheesi and Heloise was behind. The players almost ignored the sound, thinking it was just the house reacting to a change of temperature. Heloise had just moved one of her pieces and Jean tossed the dice. Heloise walked to the door to check on the noise, flipped the porch light on and took a look through the peephole. "Oh, it's Frankie!" She stepped back from the door.

The girls watched Heloise wave her wand at the door and it swung open. Frankie Vox entered and embraced Heloise when the older woman moved forward to greet her. Frankie saw the girls sitting at the card table.

"Oh! You have company!" she exclaimed. "I thought I would surprise you. I left Reno right after work and hit the sky. Where should I park my broom?"

"You must remember the twins from camp. Give me your device and I'll store it in my closet. You look cold. You must have flown fairly high over the mountains. Come on in and warm up. I'll get you some hot chocolate. Say hello to the girls."

Following the greetings and very warm drinks, the women outlined what Frankie might contribute to solving the marijuana infiltration in Timberville. The source of the recent pot explosion had been identified by the twins to be Wieselman's barn. Heloise admitted that she had known about the grass for some time but didn't want to intervene unless police were involved. Frankie was to wander onto the Wieselman property and try to discover where the boys hid the pot. The potential saving of time for the police searches would be tremendous. Heloise would drop her off about a quarter mile past the barn and wait for her return.

Frankie commented, "I could fly out there and you wouldn't have to waste time waiting around for me, Heloise."

Heloise shook her head and said, "No. We can't fly during bright daylight here. There are too many guns and people ready to shoot at anything flying. This is still fairly primitive country in and around the forests. I'll drive you to the area and wait. I can pass the time reading. I'm planning on pursuing a new hobby and I've got plenty to learn."

"Okay, we'll do as you say. What time should I be ready to go out there?"

"Tomorrow, right after lunch. I hope at least one of the boys is at the barn. I heard they were looking for jobs…I believe they're running short of money. But since it's Saturday, I hope they'll be hanging out at that old structure, maybe doing some tidying up." Heloise took a deep breath and sighed, "I'm very tired, ladies. I think I'll go to bed now. Frankie, you'll have to sleep on the sofa or the recliner, I don't have any more beds. I'll get some linens and a pillow for you. Blankets are in the hall closet."

Saturday morning seemed to leap from the eastern forests, promising to be a sunny and cloudless prelude to Erica's birthday. Ken had the weekend off and was on the road to Eugene by 8:00. He had to pick up the bounce house, transport it to Timberville and assemble it in the back yard. Doug had reluctantly gone along with him due to my encouragement. Erica and I stayed home in the kitchen baking and decorating cupcakes for Sunday's party. I expected the men to be back home for lunch.

My trusty helper had finished putting a dozen of the pink, yellow, and blue fluted cups in the tin and we filled the paper containers two-thirds full of batter. As I slid the muffin tin into the oven, an excited Erica asked, "When will they be done, Mom?"

I grinned and said, "In about twenty minutes. I'll show you how to test the cakes to see if they're ready to frost. We'll make some frosting while the cakes are baking."

Erica was anticipating licking the bowl of excess frosting when the doorbell rang and Sasha barked.

"See who that is, dear. I want to stay in the kitchen while the cupcakes are baking."

I watched as Erica ran to the door with Sasha following at her heels. She turned the knob and swung the door open to see two older girls. She picked up Sasha and cradled the dog as a safety blanket.

One of the girls said, "Heloise sent us over to see if we could help get ready for the party. Are you Erica? We're Jean and Joan. I'm Jean."

Erica stepped closer to the screen door, squinted and exclaimed, "You're twins!"

The twins laughed and one said, "That's right and tomorrow you'll be eight. Right? We've come to help you and your mother."

Erica put Sasha down and opened the screen door. "Come in, we're cooking cupcakes in the oven. Follow me!" She turned and skipped into the kitchen with Sasha sniffing at the twin's legs.

Erica pointed at the new arrivals, "Mom, this is Jean and this is Joan, they're twins. They've come to help. Heloise sent them."

"Hi, girls. Thanks for coming over to give us some assistance. I'm Katelin. Can either of you make frosting for the cupcakes?"

Jean replied, "We can do just about anything in a kitchen. Our mother started us baking things when we were about Erica's age. We'll frost the cakes as soon as they cool. What flavor do you have ingredients for?"

"I'd planned on vanilla and Erica can add the sprinkles. Take a look in the cupboards and you'll probably find what you need. If you don't find anything, we can borrow it from neighbors, and I'm sure Heloise has everything. She's full of surprises."

The twins chuckled and said, "Yes, she sure is."

By eleven o'clock the house was permeated with the odor of baking cupcakes. My crew and I had baked four dozen, frosted and sprinkled them, quite an undertaking. We baked another half dozen to use all the batter and they were frosted and decorated with M&M's. We had run out of sprinkles due to Erica's liberal use of them on the first four dozen cakes.

We were looking at our messy countertop and admiring our creations when Erica asked, "Can I have one, Mom?" I had expected that request to come much sooner, but she had been absorbed with the twins' activities and had been wearing out the kitchen floor, darting everywhere.

I almost said "No," but I couldn't disappoint her after all the energy she had expended. I said, "All right, but just one until tomorrow. We've got to get the kitchen cleaned and start preparing for lunch. The men will be home before long. I'll bet when they smell the cupcakes, they'll be very hungry. Doug will probably try to get a cupcake as soon as he comes in the house. You might have to guard the cakes, especially the ones with M&M's."

I offered the twins cupcakes and they didn't refuse. In less than a minute, Erica had them sitting in the backyard at our picnic table eating, with Sasha looking on with great interest. I had just leaned against the kitchen counter thinking of preparations for lunch when I heard a familiar noise in the driveway. Our car possessed a peculiar, but identifiable squeak when Ken hit the brakes, no matter what the speed. I often wondered if some parts had been borrowed from his police cruiser.

I started to unwrap a loaf of bread to make sandwiches when Doug came in the front door carrying two large pizzas. I think the odor of pizza had prevented him from smelling the cupcakes, because he hadn't noticed them. Ken was right behind Doug and dropped his keys on the little hallway table. He said, "We're back with the bounce house!"

I added, "And two large pizzas. What made you buy pizza…and two large ones for heaven's sake?"

He looked a bit puzzled. "When Doug and I got back in town, I thought I saw Heloise's SUV. For some reason I got the idea that I should buy two large pizzas. Was that strange?"

"Come here and take a look in the backyard." I motioned him over to look out the kitchen window. He put his arm around my waist and gave me a peck on the cheek. He took off his sunglasses and surveyed the yard.

"Hey! I know those girls. They're twins, Jean and Joan. They were at Heloise's camp."

"Humph! You never mentioned them to me."

"Don't worry, it was police business and not a big deal."

"Tell me."

"Later tonight after the kids are in bed. Let's get the pizza into some mouths, okay? Then I would like one of those cupcakes."

"Well. You can have one of the cakes after you inflate that house… after we have lunch. We'll make the bounce house a group project if you can't handle it by yourself."

"You think I can't do it myself?"

I laughed and said, "I don't want to inflate your ego, but I bet you can do it…with directions."

Ken tried to tickle me, but I grabbed the pizzas, a stack of napkins, and ran into the back yard. I yelled back, "Make sure you wash your hands!"

CHAPTER 29

Frankie admitted she had a few butterflies when she climbed into the front passenger's seat beside her mentor. Heloise pointed out Wieselman's barn as they drove by leisurely. Frankie briefly surveyed the area and began to think about her back story. She really wanted it to be believable so no suspicion would be aroused.

They drove on for a quarter mile before Heloise stopped to let her passenger out. Frankie said, "Take me another half mile please."

Heloise frowned and asked for clarification. "Why so far, dear?"

"I want to look tired and a little dirty from hiking so far. I want them to believe my story."

Heloise nodded and stepped on the gas. After thirty seconds she pulled over and stopped. She asked, "Is this good enough?"

"This is fine." Frankie got out, slipped her oversized backpack on and gave Heloise a wave. "Thanks for the lift! I'll be back to your place in a couple of hours."

Heloise turned her car around and started back to town, but when she was just about to pass Frankie she stopped and rolled down her window. "How would you like a walking stick? It might come in handy."

"What have you in mind?"

"I have an old flight stick that has been out of service for many years. I carry it around with me as a reminder of old times. It's almost an antique and is warped…never did fly straight. I'll pop open the cargo door. It deserves some last excitement. It served me well for many years at Halloween before it became so distorted I could no longer use it."

"I'll treat it right."

When the cargo door opened, Frankie saw the crooked wooden staff, leaned forward and withdrew the gnarly but still solid branch. She gave it a test bang against the ground, stepped away from the car and said, "This is perfect. Thanks, Heloise."

Heloise beeped her horn and drove away. Frankie watched the car disappear around a curve in the road and started hiking toward the Wieselman barn. She assumed the barn would be visible after about twenty minutes at a fast walk. At almost six feet tall, she had a long stride. When she turned onto the lane to the cow barn she would start limping. Heloise had prepared her for the three young men she would be meeting. She had high hopes of having some fun.

The first thing Frankie noticed as she turned toward the barn was a blue Ford pickup. Someone was home. As she limped closer, she heard sounds of hammers and saws. At least someone was close to if not in the building. Peering into the structure with caution; she saw no human presence. But several voices could be heard, apparently outside and behind the old timbers.

She walked to the side of the building and limped around the corner. The three young men were constructing an outhouse; it was obvious, one of them had drawn a half moon on a board, apparently destined to be a door. They hadn't noticed her, so she said, "Hello," and leaned against her walking stick.

Their heads swiveled and the tallest one dropped his hammer. He said, "Hello. Who are you and where have you come from?"

"My name is Frankie Vox and I'm a member of Pacific Trail Hikers. I got separated from my group a day ago and I've been walking to get to State Route 126. If any of us got lost we're supposed to get in touch with them day after tomorrow. My phone is dead. I'm really beat, I messed up my knee a couple of hours ago. Do you guys have anything to eat?"

Barry said, "You done?"

"Oh, sorry. I haven't talked to anyone for a long time."

Leeray put down his saw and said, "I'm Leeray, Barry just spoke to you and the tall guy is Jeff." He pointed to his buddies. "We don't have much to eat, we just ran out of cash. Our credit is shot, but we've got some apples and peanut butter sandwiches. Are you interested?"

"That would be awesome. I had a candy bar for breakfast and nothing since."

Jeff took a sudden interest in Frankie and followed up with what Leeray had said. "Come with me and I'll get you something." He took a few steps and glanced back to see if Frankie was following. He noticed her limp and commented, "You can wait here if you like. I'll come right back."

Frankie wanted to isolate at least one of the guys, so she remarked, "No, I'll come with you. I don't want to eat next to an outhouse." She followed Jeff around the barn and sat on the bumper of the Ford. She watched Jeff vanish into the barn's shaded interior, pleased that the other two guys hadn't followed.

Jeff reappeared holding an apple in one hand and a bulging sandwich bag in the other. Frankie stood and moved forward, letting go of her walking staff and falling in the dirt. Jeff rushed forward, placed the food on the Ford's hood, turned and helped Frankie stand.

"You all right?"

"I guess. I think my knee is weaker than I thought. I just did more damage. Do you have any pot? I could sure use a joint now. Smoking a little grass helps with the pain."

Jeff stepped back and replied, "Ah, maybe. Let me talk with my buddies to see if they have any. Can you get to the food without my help?"

"Not a problem. See if you can find me a joint." She shuffled to the pickup and took a bite from the apple as Jeff walked around the barn. About two minutes later, Jeff and Barry returned. Frankie's evaluation of Barry as he approached suggested he was going to ask some questions. She was prepared.

"What are you doing here, anyway? Why did you stop here?"

"When I saw your truck, I thought I could get a ride into town, but then I thought you might light up once in a while. Ever hit your finger with a hammer? Pot sure helps with pain. You must know that."

Barry was still suspicious. "You know, you don't look like you smoke."

Frankie replied, "Well, you know what they say."

Jeff said, "What's that?"

Frankie smiled, "You can't evaluate a book by its cover."

Jeff continued, "Where are you from?"

"That's easy. Reno. Where are you from?"

"Seattle."

"Oh, U-W. You're a Husky fan. Good luck."

Jeff and Barry stood there looking at Frankie as she unwrapped the sandwich and started eating.

"Who made the sandwich?" she asked.

Jeff frowned, "What's wrong with it?"

"Needs a bit more jelly. It's kinda dry."

"I'll get you some water."

"I'd rather have some pot. But if you don't have any, that's all right. I can tough it out. Can you drive me to the hospital? I'd appreciate it. I'm afraid I won't make it to town without stopping or maybe hitching a ride but I don't like to solicit from people I don't know. There are a lot of weirdoes out there."

Jeff chuckled. "Yeah. One of them lives right over there." He pointed at the Swartzs' home. "The kid took some of our grass." Jeff suddenly realized what he said, but it was too late. He shrugged his shoulders at Barry, turned toward the barn, and said, "I'll get you some water."

Barry glanced at Jeff and whistled. Leeray and Jeff met with Barry at the corner of the barn and started a discussion, but Frankie couldn't hear what they were saying. She finished the sandwich and took another bite of apple before the trio approached. When the guys were huddled, Frankie reached in her pants pocket and removed what resembled to be a cylinder of lip balm. She wanted her wand handy at a moment's notice. In a fraction of a second the telescoped instrument could be extended to its optimum length. She concealed the collapsed wand in her left hand and waited for an opportune moment.

The three guys returned to the front of the truck and Barry said, "Jeff is going to cough up some pot for you. Leeray and I are going back to work."

Frankie edged closer to the trio and as they turned away, she extended her wand and waved it over their heads, commanding, "Show me your pot."

Jeff twisted at the waist and motioned, "Come with me. I'll get you some grass. You won't need much, just a pinch or so."

Frankie followed Jeff into the barn and watched him climb into the rafters. She heard some rummaging around and then Jeff's head appeared looking down at her. He said, "Here, catch," and a small white envelope floated down from above. She caught the cover, folded it and stuck it in her pocket. Barry suddenly appeared behind her and said, "I'll show you my package, but you have to keep it a secret. Okay?"

"Not a problem. Who would I tell?"

She followed him into the back of the barn and watched him move some hay with a pitchfork and expose a stack of burlap bags. Using the hayfork, he lifted the bags to reveal a good sized brick of pot.

"How much is in that package?"

"Seven tenths of a kilo…about one- and a-half pounds. I figure I might get seventy-five hundred for it, maybe more. I'll net at least four thou."

"Wow! That's impressive. Whose brilliant idea was it to buy pot and resell it?"

Barry scratched his right cheek and said, "We were brainstorming one night and I can't remember who thought of doing it, but it was probably Jeff or me. Leeray isn't very imaginative, but he's dependable."

"Good luck. I hope the cops don't bust you."

"The cops around here have no idea we have pot. I'm not worried. Just keep quiet about it. Okay?"

"Mum's the word. I promise not to tell the cops." She motioned like she zipped her lips. "Could you give me a ride to the hospital so I can get my knee checked out?"

"Aren't you going to smoke a joint? Didn't Jeff give you some pot?"

"Yes, he did, but if the nurses smell pot on me they might not give me proper attention. I'll save the joint for later."

Barry nodded and said, "Hop in the truck. I know where the hospital is, it's not far."

In less than ten minutes, the blue pickup was stopped on the curved driveway at the front of the hospital. Barry said, "I'll park and help you into admissions."

Frankie was already getting out, leaning on her walking stick and holding onto the open door. She looked up at Barry through the cab and said, "I'll make it without help, thanks. Thanks for the ride. I might not see you again, so, goodbye."

She shut the door and watched Barry drive slowly away. When the blue truck turned onto the street, Frankie took a few slow steps, did an about face and began walking normally away from the hospital in the direction of Heloise's home. She passed a waste container when she reached the sidewalk and stood for a moment thinking. Should I throw this stick in the garbage or give it back to Heloise? A second later, she decided to return it to her mentor; it wasn't very heavy. Heloise might use it in her garden.

Frankie took a zigzag course to avoid walking through the downtown streets. Several homeowners stopped and stared at the young woman carrying a walking stick, but not using it.

Frankie waved to people as she passed by and was back at Heloise's in about twenty minutes.

She estimated the distance traveled was about half a mile. She hadn't tried to set any records and walked at her normal pace.

Heloise and the twins were sitting on the front steps waiting for Frankie to return from Wieselman's barn. Jean saw Frankie approaching when the Reno recruit was about a block away.

"There she is," Jean pointed down the street. "She's carrying a staff."

"That's the walking stick I gave her," said Heloise. "I didn't care to get it back. I guess she didn't want to litter and decided to return it. I'll put it in the closet with some of my other souvenirs."

Joan said, "I hope she found the hiding places for the pot. Lt. Sanders will be happy to get that information."

As Frankie came closer, she was smiling, so the twins and Heloise knew Frankie had good luck. She dropped the staff on the lawn and sat next to the other women.

Heloise asked, "Did you have to walk from the barn? That's a long way."

"No, just from the hospital. Barry gave me a ride so I could get medical attention."

"You were hurt?" quizzed Joan.

"No, I had an imagined twisted knee. Look what I have for the pain." She showed the women the joint Jeff had given her and laughed.

"Were you successful at finding where the pot is hidden?"

"Uh-huh, but I promised I wouldn't tell the police. But I can tell you." She told Heloise and the twins where the pot was hidden so they could inform the police. "I need a drink of water, I had a dry peanut butter sandwich, skimpy on jelly."

CHAPTER 30

At breakfast Sunday morning, Heloise and her three recruits celebrated their successful missions assisting the police investigation. Anticipating a busy afternoon at the Sanders' protecting eight-year olds from injury at Erica Sander's birthday party. The three young women were looking forward to a reward of cake and ice cream. Heloise hoped that Katelin would have something like strawberry frozen yogurt for the adults, since cake and ice cream upset her stomach. She also wanted to talk with Katelin about a witch's retirement project, something she considered but was still in its initial stages.

The novice witches and former campers decided to get Erica craft making gifts and Heloise was going to present Erica with a yellowish-green peridot necklace. The necklace was guaranteed to grant Erica a future wish, but only if she made it before she turned nine. Heloise and the girls went shopping an hour after breakfast. Fortunately, the young women found gifts in stores open seven days a week. When they returned with their purchases, Heloise excused herself and went into the basement while the girls wrapped their gifts.

On the top shelf of Heloise's cellar cabinet was a small metal box about the size of a shoebox. She reached overhead, grasped the box and blew off the dust, which caused her to sneeze. With a few deft motions of her hands and a short incantation, the necklace was prepared. She closed the box, returned it to the cabinet and went back upstairs to her bedroom. She emptied a small white jewelry gift box and placed the silver chain with peridot stone inside. She would have one of the girls wrap the gift; her arthritic fingers lacked the necessary dexterity.

Following a light lunch, the Wickon women, all in magically prepared colorful dresses, walked to the Sanders' for the party with their gifts. As they approached their destination, several cars loaded with children lugging presents were parked at the curb. One vehicle had already parked in the Sanders' driveway. The Wickon teens followed the children into the house and Heloise, trailing the others, watched a police cruiser park across the street.

I was pleased when Heloise and her young companions arrived. The dozen youngsters in the backyard needed more supervision than the few mothers accompanying some of the children could handle. Each of the four women carried a gift and I had them place the packages on a card table in the corner of the living room. I hadn't met Frankie before, but on the way to the backdoor, she slowed at the kitchen and asked, "How can I help you, Mrs. Sanders?"

"Oh, please call me Katelin." We had a brief conversation. I was impressed with this young lady. She seemed far more cultivated than the twins. When I discovered she worked as a security guard in Reno, I understood how she had gained so much self-assurance.

The doorbell rang again. I threw up my hands, grimaced at Frankie, and rushed to greet the next arrival. Fortunately, I didn't have to explain anything. It was dependable Sarah, Ken's partner. She had a small gift for Erica which I accepted and added to the growing pile on the card table. I introduced Frankie and Sarah, then we went to the backyard. Ken had just started cooking some wieners and hamburger patties on our borrowed barbecue. Our neighbors, the Stebbins, loaned us their portable grill.

Joan and Jean took over monitoring the bounce house activity and made sure each kid wore head gear. Ken rented a dozen head protection helmets from Bob Burn's Bike shop just to make sure all the kids were safe. The triple-B bike shop personnel had questioned why he needed a dozen headpieces. Ken explained the predicted activity of the youngsters in the bounce house. Bob gave Ken a reduced rate since they were to be used for only one day.

Following nearly an hour of the kid's feverish activity and a few bumps and bruises, Ken blew a whistle and rounded up the children. The twins started singing "Happy Birthday," and everyone joined in. Self-conscious Erica generated enough lung power to extinguish the eight candles on a large devil's food cake. While nearly everyone ate cake and ice-cream, Erica opened her gifts.

Erica was unexpectedly orderly at unwrapping her presents. She started with the largest and ended with the smallest. The wrapping of each gift was torn open with great enthusiasm and I noted the items and givers for later thank you notes, much like on Christmas morning when we all opened gifts in near abandonment. Erica thanked each person as she progressed through the pile. She was extremely happy when she opened Sarah's present, a small digital camera. I was selected to take the first picture; Sarah and Erica eating cake. She gave Sarah a big hug and almost forgot there was one more even smaller present. I had to remind her, "Erica, you have one more to open. It's from Heloise."

I scanned the onlookers and couldn't see Heloise. I thought she might be in the kitchen getting something. The wrapping paper came off without much of a fight and Erica hesitantly lifted the lid on the little white gift box.

"Oh, Mom! Look! It's a necklace. It's beautiful!" Erica tilted the jewelry box so I could see. Immediately, I thought it was too expensive and I didn't even know the chain was silver. Erica wanted me to help her put it on and she came closer to me and lifted her long hair. I undid the clasp, reached around her raised arms and closed the clasp at the back of her neck. She smiled at me and said, "How does it look?"

As she spoke, the yellowish-green crystal briefly pulsed three times. At the moment, I thought it was just sunlight reflecting off the facets, but I found out later it was more than that. I told Erica, "You look beautiful with the necklace. Be sure to thank Heloise before she goes home."

The activity in the backyard calmed down and a few of the children left the party with their parents. I took a break from the dwindling festivities and looked for Heloise. I didn't have to search very far; I found her sitting at our kitchen table, humming, drinking tea and eating red delicious-apple slices.

When I entered the kitchen to discard some soiled napkins in the under-sink garbage can, she looked up and said, "I hope you don't mind, I helped myself to one of your apples and made some tea. My stomach can't tolerate chocolate cake and ice cream anymore."

"You can have anything you like, Heloise. Help yourself. If there's anything I can get you, just ask."

"Thank you. I have some information for you or Ken from Frankie."

"Oh, should I get Ken? Is it something he should know?"

"Yes, but Frankie promised she would not tell the police, so she told me. If I tell you, Frankie is able to further insulate herself."

I was intently focused on Heloise when she mentioned it was something the police should know. I didn't want to relay something to Ken that would not be correct because of my misinterpretation.

Heloise was watching me to be sure she had my full attention.

She said, "The marijuana is hidden at the Wieselman barn in two places. There is a pile of burlap bags in the back of the structure where one package of pot is hidden. The other container of pot is hidden in the attic. That's what Frankie found out." She smiled, "When you talk to your husband, you might want to tell him about our conversation."

"I'll do that. He'll be happy to get that information, so will Sarah." I was sure I could remember what Heloise told me and I asked her if there was anything else.

She nodded. "Yes, but it's not about police matters."

I hadn't the faintest idea what she was going to ask me. I scooted my chair closer to the table and said, "Shoot."

"Do you think there is a market for rustic furniture for Barbie dolls?"

I held back a laugh when I realized she was seriously interested in my opinion. I thought for a brief moment and said, "I think so. What do you have in mind?"

"Well, I'm going to retire in time for Christmas and I want to make a few dollars to enhance my checking account. I want to start off with something that doesn't require a large investment and I've been thinking of source materials that are free. All one does is pick things up from the ground."

I was frowning, not knowing just what Heloise had in mind. She had mentioned furniture but I still hadn't caught on.

Heloise explained, "I was looking at a real estate advertisement the other day and I saw a cabin for sale in the mountains. There was a wrap-around porch. On the porch was some furniture made from tree branches and other natural materials. That's when it hit me; I could make furniture for girls that would be just right for their Barbie dolls. I could use twigs! All I need is a hot glue gun, some garden clippers and a small ruler. I made a foot stool the other day. Maybe you could come over and take a look."

"What a great idea! You could market them at the gift shop on Main Street."

"Oh, thank you, Katelin. I was hoping you would say that was awesome."

I grinned, "I haven't used awesome recently, but it is an appropriate word for your idea. That sounds like something your young house guests might have said."

"No, they don't know anything about it. I haven't told them I am going to retire. I am learning some of their vocabulary."

I heard the back screen door bang and Ken's voice talking to Sarah. It sounded like they had entered the house together.

Ken came into the kitchen, went directly to the sink and began washing his hands. Sarah drifted closer to Heloise and me and said, "That sure was a nice party. The youngsters really had fun, especially with the bounce house. Those three young women did a great job keeping an eye on the kids. No injuries at all." She paused for a moment, looked at Heloise and me and asked, "What have you gals been cooking up?"

Heloise replied, "Oh, nothing much. I need to talk with Erica about her necklace, though. Have all her guests gone?"

Ken answered, "I have to clean up the barbeque. I'll send Erica in if all her friends have left. The three young ladies you brought with you are walking back to your place, Heloise. I thanked them for helping out. They did a fantastic job. Thanks for bringing them."

As Heloise said, "You're welcome," she stood and started toward the back door following Ken.

She looked back at me and commented, "I'm going to speak with Erica outside." When the screen door banged shut, Sarah and I were left alone in the kitchen.

"Can I get you something to drink, Sarah?"

"No thanks, Katelin. I'd better be going. I've got to get some clothes ready for my husband before he leaves for work this evening. He's got a two hour drive ahead of him. I hate for him to drive at night in the mountains."

"I understand. Thanks so much for the camera you gave Erica. She's going to have a great time with it."

"No problem. Tell Ken I'll see him in the morning. Bye." She walked quickly to the front door and let herself out before I had a chance to accompany her. I said "Bye" and waved as she hurriedly crossed the street to her little green Kia hatchback. I don't think she heard me. She got in and drove off as if she was late for an important meeting.

I returned to the kitchen and emptied the dishwasher, then looked around to see if I had missed putting away anything. The countertops were clean so I went out to find Erica and Ken. Doug had come in earlier with a slice of cake on a paper plate and announced he was going to his room to read. I think he meant to say he was going to eat. The backyard was vacant except for Heloise, Ken and Erica. I noticed a few bits of napkins and plastic forks on the ground but those would be picked up using our lawn mower.

Ken was busy scraping and hosing off the barbeque, so I joined Erica and Heloise. I heard Heloise say, "When you are wearing the necklace, you may make one wish that will come true in your future. There is no telling when it will happen. But you must make the wish before your next birthday. Oh, if the peridot stone occasionally sparkles, that is normal."

Erica was listening intently, standing with her mouth open, not knowing what to say. She glanced at me and then at Heloise, "Thank you for the beautiful necklace. I think it is the best gift I've ever had." She stepped up to Heloise and gave her a hug.

I wondered if what Heloise said about the wish could actually come true or was it just an imaginary story from an elderly woman. I hoped Erica didn't take making the wish too seriously.

CHAPTER 31

Erica had become worn out after carrying her gifts to her bedroom. She walked around like she had feet made of lead. I asked her where she was putting all her loot and she replied, "Under my bed. I'll figure out where to put things tomorrow. I'm out of energy to even think." She said, "Good night" and trudged off to her room. Doug and Sasha had gone to bed a little earlier.

It was nearly nine o'clock when Ken finally came in from cleaning up the backyard and deflating the bounce house. We sat down together on the sofa to reflect on the day's activities. We both sighed and looked at each other, smiling. He put his arm around my shoulders and exclaimed, "What a day!"

The house was silent except for an occasional noise from the attic as the roof cooled from the sun's heat. We sat without talking for a couple of minutes. I broke the calm with a question, "When you and Sarah came in the house, were all the kids gone?"

"Yeah, but we didn't come in together. Sarah was in the utility room watching out the back window."

"Really? I didn't hear her come in. She might have heard Heloise telling me about the marijuana."

"What's this about pot? If she heard something, she didn't say anything to me about it."

"Well, then, she must not have heard what Heloise told me. Heloise said the pot was in two places at the Wieselman's barn: under some burlap bags and in the attic." I told him how she got the information.

Ken said, "I'll contact Chief Watters in the morning and he can set up a raid. I'm sure Sarah and I will be taking part."

Ken and I talked for half-an-hour about the activities during the party. He had watched the kids jump around in the bounce house while he cooked wieners and hamburgers. At ten o'clock I began to yawn and felt like I might fall asleep. Ken noticed my eye lids drooping and said, "Let's go to bed, it's been a long day."

Ken was up early Monday and already started Mr. Coffee. The brew was ready, but two mugs sat empty on the counter next to the sink. I drifted to the back door and saw Ken packaging the bounce house in its travel container. It looked like he was nearly finished, so I poured the coffee and sat down at the kitchen table to wait for him to finish bundling the deflated plastic. He joined me in less than a minute and as he washed his hands, said, "I need to call Chief Watters but I didn't want to disturb him too early. He might be surly all day if I wake him up." He gave me a wink to show he was joking.

I motioned to his coffee mug. "Have some coffee. Do you want toast and an egg, or some cereal?"

"Just some toast this morning, thanks. Sit still, I'll get it."

Ken put two slices of bread in the toaster and joined me at the table.

"Have the kids got anything planned today? I'd like to have Doug ride with me to return the bounce house. I figure I'd come home at four. That way we'd be back in time for dinner."

"Well, I won't need the car. Doug will probably ride his bike with some buddies. I'm taking Erica and Sasha to the park this morning. She can take some pictures with her new camera and Sasha can chase squirrels."

"Sounds good. Tell Doug to be home at four o'clock if he wants to ride with me to Eugene."

The toast popped up and Ken said, "Could you please butter that for me? I need to call Watters."

I buttered his toast and topped off his coffee as he was on the phone. It was a quick call. He rejoined me at the table and hardly breathed as he hurriedly ate his toast. He took a big swig of coffee and was out the door after giving me a quick kiss. Ken announced, "Watters wants me there right now! He's got something planned. See you later."

He rushed out the door, was in the car in a flash and rolling down the street before I could say, "Have a nice day."

I returned to the kitchen to find Doug and Erica sitting at the table rubbing their eyes free of sleep and looking around, probably scanning for evidence of their father's breakfast.

Doug said, "What did Dad have for breakfast?"

I smiled, "Toast and coffee. Want some?"

"Gross, Mom. I'll get some Wheaties." He pushed back his chair and went for the cupboard.

Erica mumbled, "Get me the Corn Flakes, please."

I got the milk from the refrigerator, two plastic cereal bowls and spoons, and the sugar container. Doug almost threw the cereal boxes at the table, but it was a controlled toss and the boxes remained upright. I was mildly shocked at what he had done. It was something that must have been practiced, but I decided not to reward him with any praise. He was getting to the age when activities and manners needed to be a bit more thoughtful and controlled.

As they began eating, I asked Erica, "How would you like to take some pictures at the park this morning?"

Before she answered, Doug said, "I'm going to go riding with Jimmy Garcia, if it's all right with you."

I looked at him, "Sure. Where are you going to go?"

Erica was watching Doug and me. Then she answered, "That's a good idea. Sasha can go too."

I was having to carry on two conversations simultaneously. The kids weren't helping.

"We were thinking of riding to the creek to see if we can spot any fish. Jimmy said someone saw some salmon."

"You want to take lunch?"

"No, Mom. We'll be back before noon."

"Your dad wants you to ride to Eugene with him at four o'clock to return the bounce house. If you want to go, be home so he doesn't have to wait or look for you."

Doug sat there for a moment, probably weighing his opportunities for the afternoon. "Yeah, I'll go with him. We might see some of the football team."

"OK. But if you change your mind, you need to let me or your dad know."

While the kids ate, I poured three glasses of orange juice and got myself a bowl of Grape Nuts cereal. Doug was anxious to get on his bike and quickly finished eating. He was up and out of his seat before I sat down.

"Your dishes, Doug," I reminded him.

He turned around, retrieved them and mumbled, "Sorry Mom." He waved as he went out the door.

I swallowed some juice and reacted with, "Be careful and be back home before four o'clock."

As soon as Erica finished her orange juice, she went to her room and came back wearing her birthday outfit, new necklace and carrying her camera.

I had to warn her, "Do you think you might lose the necklace?"

She thought for a second, turned around, retraced her steps to her room and reappeared without the peridot jewelry. I finished my bowl of crunchy breakfast food, placed all our morning dishes in the washer and said, "Get Sasha and let's head for the park."

Four police vehicles converged on Wieselman's barn, three cruisers and the big SUV driven by Sarah. Chief Watters led the caravan down the lane to the old structure with his lights flashing. Ken followed closely and narrowly avoided back ending him when he slammed on the brakes and skidded to a stop a few feet from the open barn door. He stepped out of his car carrying his bullhorn and announced, "This is the Timberville Police! Come out with your hands up!"

Sarah, Deputy Larry Lancaster, and Ken exited their cars and joined Chief Watters. Deputy Lancaster drew his sidearm. Watters repeated his command and a long minute passed, but no one appeared from the barn.

The chief motioned with his bullhorn to Deputy Lancaster. The deputy entered the barn and called out, "Anyone in here?"

Silence.

Watters stepped inside the barn opening. Ken and Sarah followed. A quick search ensued and clearly the police were the only people present. Lancaster climbed the ladder to the loft and carried out a search, while Ken and Sarah discovered a pile of burlap bags in the back of the barn. With the aid of a pitchfork, the stack of gunnysacks was inspected. No pot was found.

A complete search of the premises came up negative, no people and no marijuana. Ken even checked the outhouse but had nothing to show for his effort. The chief gathered his crew and said, "Let's get out of here and back to our regular jobs. Apparently, we received some bad information."

As Ken reached his cruiser and started to open the door, Chief Watters called to him, "Ken, I'd like to talk with you later today…in my office."

When we reached the park, I saw a woman about my age sitting adjacent to the jungle gym watching a youngster hanging upside down with her knees draped over a horizontal pipe about six feet off the ground. The adult acknowledged us with a reserved wave and polite smile. I took a seat a couple of feet from the woman and we introduced ourselves.

Aubrey Conners was a substitute fourth grade teacher. Her husband, Tom Conners, owned a fleet of trucks that hauled timber for regional forest harvesting. Their upside-down daughter Marcy, an almost nine-year-old, spotted Erica and her camera and dropped to the ground.

The youngsters seemed to have an instant attraction for one another and were soon meandering the borders of the park looking for objects to photograph. Aubrey and I watched our daughters as they alternately took pictures of flowers and apparently insects, things too small for us to identify.

Aubrey pointed far to the right of the girls, "Who is that old woman?"

I recognized her immediately, it was Heloise. We watched her as she seemed to randomly retrieve items from the grass and save them in a small bag hanging from her waist. I didn't know if Heloise wanted the public to know of her hobby at this time so I didn't explain her actions.

Aubrey said, "Do you think she's picking dandelions?"

I felt like saying something, but my thoughts were interrupted by the girls. They were running side-by-side toward us as if racing. Erica was falling a little behind Marcy, probably because she was carrying her camera. Erica was naturally competitive and would have been putting all her effort into running.

Marcy was out of breath, but she managed to blurt out, "Mom, we have to go. If we don't, I'll miss my violin lesson." She was looking at her wristwatch, panting.

"Oh, you're right, let's go! I'll talk to you some more, Katelin, bye."

I watched the mother and daughter hustle off to a small red SUV and zip off down the street.

Erica stood in front of me holding her camera with both hands. Once her breathing returned to normal, she said, "Mom, I really like Marcy. We might become best friends. She didn't know that was Heloise picking up twigs. We decided to call her the twig lady."

A CRYSTAL FOR CHARITY

CHAPTER 1

When my alarm went off at 6:00 a.m., I tossed back the sheet and comforter and swung my big feet out onto the cool hardwood floor. I pressed the alarm button to silence the beeping. I sat there a few seconds trying to focus without glasses. Blinking and squinting didn't help so I put on my bifocals. I contemplated buying a new alarm clock without those devilish looking big red LEDs that flickered every minute all night long. I had grown to dislike that alarm clock, but it did its job. During the last couple of years, I had thought about getting a new clock but what did a seventy-year-old man need snooze alarm, music, news or any other conveniences on a clock for more expense. I just wanted a reliable noise to wake me to get up at the same time every day to stay on schedule. I actually enjoyed being able to read the big LED numbers without my glasses.

I muttered, "Oh yeah, it's Wednesday, trash pickup day." I slowly climbed into my clothes. As I dressed, Foxy, my cute gray and white cat with a little four-inch tail appeared at the bedroom doorway. She was twelve years old but regal and delicate as one of the neighbors had observed. Foxy must have been the runt of a litter and not gotten her fair share of feline growth hormone. She was small, never weighing more than six pounds, and never lost the appearance of a young kitten.

"Hello Foxy. How's my girl? Did you have a good sleep?"

She jumped up beside me and I scratched her back and covered her with the corner of the comforter. A second later, she poked her head out and dropped to the floor.

It was mid-September and the noisy Waste-Management trucks would be in the neighborhood before long. I wrestled the three containers out to the front curb before the trucks arrived. While I moved the containers, Foxy checked out the good-neighbor fence searching for unsuspecting birds. She seemed to know which ones were pests.

I went back in the house to the kitchen and started a pot of decaf. From the kitchen window, I saw the neighbor's two dogs chasing each other and barking. Seemed like no matter where one was in the Portland area, there were barking dogs. I took my insulin from the refrigerator, went into the bathroom and took my daily shot.

One look in the mirror was all it took. My hair was hiding most of the temple pieces of my glasses. I needed a haircut. After lunch I would pay a visit to the barber. That would be my afternoon activity. I returned to the kitchen to get some breakfast.

The trash trucks always scared Foxy, as did the big yellow school buses. I went to the slider that led to the second floor deck, pushed back the vertical blinds and let Foxy in the house. She let out a little squeak as she came in as if to say, "Thank you." I heard the trucks proceeding down the street stopping at each house, lifting the containers and banging hell out of them.

I ate a couple of waffles warmed in the toaster. They were made more enjoyable with some spray-on butter and maple flavored sugar-free syrup. A soy burger nuked in the microwave and adorned with some ketchup joined the waffles. I got a mug of decaf and returned to the dining room table. Looking outside through the slider, I was reminded the deck needed some stain and sealer. That would be a project for next summer.

When Foxy rubbed against my leg, I reached down, scratched her back and lightly pulled on her short little tail as she walked over to the slider. She never objected to the slight tail pulling. One of the series of trucks had passed by and it was momentarily quiet outside.

"So you want out again?"

I let Foxy out and she headed to a cedar planter on the deck and gave it a good scratching. I refilled my Santa Claus mug with coffee and joined my feline. I watched limbs on the big pine trees across the street swaying in the usual East wind coming down the Columbia River gorge. That meant there was a low-pressure area off the west coast and in a day or so there would probably be rain. But, right now, the sun was out and the sky was a cloudless beautiful blue. It seemed like the beginnings of a nice day.

The rest of the morning went quickly. I wrote checks to pay bills and put several low value stamps on the envelopes to make up the current postal rate. I checked the Internet for email and deleted spam before teasing Foxy with one of her mouse toys for a few minutes. She molested that plastic feather like it was a real mouse. She loved to attack that toy attached to a string as I pulled it around the floor. Following play time, I returned the empty waste and recycling containers from the front curb to the shed behind the house.

Lunch was at 11:00, as usual. Then I showered, shaved and put on some clean clothes. I had to make a deposit at the bank and pick up cat food, but those errands could wait until after the afternoon haircut.

A few minutes after 1:00 p.m., I climbed into my Subaru Forester and backed slowly down the sloping driveway. I drove to Troutdale Road, turned and started toward the downtown area. Troutdale Road became Buxton about a half-mile from the business area of town. After a few blocks, I descended the steep hill toward the old Columbia River Highway, the main drag of Troutdale. A block before reaching the old highway I made a left turn and parallel parked. Across the street was the police station and a few police cruisers were parked next to the building.

I opened the door and stepped into the street. As I pocketed my keys, I noticed the front driver's side tire looked like it might need some air. I made a mental note to get the gauge out of the glove box and check the tire pressure when I returned to my car. That old bicycle tire pump in the garage would be put to good use when I got home.

I walked about ten yards to Buxton. After two cars passed going uphill, I crossed the street diagonally and walked down to the business district. I stopped at the corner and looked east down the old Columbia River highway. Downtown Troutdale had been improved in recent years and many colorful restaurants and shops lined both sides of the occasionally busy two-lane street. Cars were parked on both sides of the highway; currently, there wasn't any traffic. I noticed the new artistic metal arch over the highway about a block to the left, announcing the gateway to the gorge.

I crossed the highway and walked toward Tina's barbershop. Her "OPEN" sign was prominently displayed on the sidewalk. When I entered the shop, no one sat in the barber chairs so I assumed I could get sheared right away. The warm sunny room sported three barber's chairs. Tina was sitting on a brown leather-covered couch in the waiting area with her feet up on a large coffee table about half covered with magazines. She looked up from her laptop and smiled.

"Go ahead and sit in the first chair, I'll be with you in a sec. I have to close down my email." She motioned for me to take a seat in the leather covered padded chair nearest the door in front of the shop.

I grinned, "You don't need to hurry. Remember, I'm retired and have plenty of time."

Tina stood up and put away the laptop. Her five foot nine slender frame and pretty face always attracted my attention. Tina's full name was Tina Nancy Templeton. I fleetingly thought, if I were twenty years younger, I would ask her out, but she smoked. That was a deal breaker.

"Haven't seen you in a while," commented Tina.

"I should have come in about a month earlier. I'm more than shaggy. My eyebrows are growing over my glasses," I replied with a smile.

I slid into the chair and stored my glasses in my shirt pocket. In a few seconds, Tina was standing behind me putting a drape around my shoulders and fastening it at the neck. She had a nice touch.

"You've been busy working on your house?" Tina inquired.

"A little bit, but mostly just being lazy. Hobbies and yard work seem to eat up most of my time. Outside of work, what have you been doing?"

She picked up her clipper and eyed my hair. "I went to the coast last weekend with a girlfriend. I don't like the smell of the ocean though. But it was a good ride through the mountains, not too cold yet."

"Your car doesn't have a heater?"

"Oh, we took our motorcycles. My friend went to the ocean several times this summer, but I've been too busy to go."

As they were talking, Tina's little dog Brutus, a Yorkie, appeared from the back of the shop curious about the new voice. I didn't seem to be of much interest to Brutus. The mini dog turned around and quickly scampered out of sight, nails clicking on the linoleum floor.

"Cut it pretty short," I requested. There were still some warm days left in September and some dirty yard work had to be done before it got too cold. Short hair was easily washed and dried quickly.

Tina picked up a comb, started the clipper, and began to cut my hair. I closed my eyes and relaxed in the warm room and comfortable chair as the clipper buzzed in my ears.

A screech of brakes and a loud car horn invaded the barbershop. Tina paused cutting and we looked out the windows. A man ran across traffic between a sports car and an older model pickup. The runner had startled the pickup driver and he had slammed on his brakes. The jeans and yellow T-shirt-clad runner clenched something in his right hand. Having crossed the street, he ran up the hill next to a two-story building partly covered with ivy on the side open to a large empty lot. The building that had been there was torn down when the downtown area was being resurrected. Shrubs at the bottom of the ivy extended up the hill to the next street, just a half block away. A large public parking lot occupied half the block.

I thought I saw the runner drop something in the shrubs but without my glasses, I couldn't be sure. When the runner had nearly reached the other end of the building, another man came running by the shop waving an ugly looking handgun.

"Up there," he yelled, pointing up the hill next to the building. He joined another man and they quickly climbed the hill and disappeared behind the two story brick structure.

"I wonder what that was all about...who would need a gun in Troutdale?" I asked Tina after watching the strange event take place.

"In twenty-two years, I've never seen anything like that," Tina exclaimed as she resumed cutting my hair.

Some muffled sounds like firecrackers echoed through the downtown streets.

A few minutes later, Tina and I heard an ambulance siren.

As my trim was about finished, a police officer came by the barbershop. Tina recognized the officer who daily checked the businesses along the street and asked him what had happened.

"Two guys chased a man and killed him in front of the police station. Some of my fellow officers were just leaving the station to go on patrol and they shot it out with the two men," he replied.

"Who were those guys?" Tina asked.

"We think they were thugs from Portland," the officer replied.

He continued, "One of them was killed and the other was wounded and unconscious. One of the officers was grazed in the shoulder. Both of the thugs were carrying nine millimeter handguns equipped with silencers. I'll know more when they question the survivor at the hospital."

The radio on the officer's shoulder came on. He listened for a few seconds and said, "The guy taken to the hospital died. He never came to." He looked frustrated. "Well, I have to finish my beat. I'll see you tomorrow Tina."

"See you Bill."

I got out of the barber's chair, put on my glasses and handed Tina a twenty from my aging leather wallet. "Keep the change. The haircut and commotion were worth it!"

"Thank you, Ned."

"I'll be back for another trim in a couple of months. Can you guarantee some more excitement?"

"No guarantee, but I'll be here," Tina commented with a smile.

I exited the barbershop and hurriedly crossed the street, not bothering to go to the crosswalk. My intention was to see if the runner had really dropped something in the shrubs.

I found climbing the incline along the wall of the building was not so easy for a man pushing seventy. The grass and shrubs had been watered the night before and the ground was still a bit wet. As I climbed, I looked closely around the shrubs, being careful not to slip and fall. I realized I wasn't in great shape and was glad I didn't have to run all the way up the hill. I wouldn't have made it without resting and slowing my heart rate.

A little over halfway up the slope, I spotted a small brown paper bag on the ground next to one of the shrubs. The crumpled bag was about the size of my fist. I bent over, picked it up, put the bag in my pants pocket and stepped out from the shrubs. I carefully climbed the hill to the sidewalk.

When I reached the concrete walkway, I could see my car. I started toward my SUV, parked near the police station. When I got to Buxton, I had to wait for traffic before crossing. As I waited I heard a yell.

"There he is!"

I looked around to find the source of the voice and saw two husky men about half a block away running toward me. No one else was in the area and the police cruisers were gone. Buxton was clear of traffic so I quickly crossed the street and ducked into the large brick building on the corner. I saw a stairway to what might be a large basement. Why was I being pursued? What did those men want? Could they be after the wadded sack in my pocket? I had to assume they were after the paper bag I had retrieved from under the bushes.

I nearly ran down the stairs hardly worrying about tripping. The unlocked door led to what reminded me of an old bomb shelter. There were lines of lockers on both sides of a dimly-lit long hallway but I couldn't hide in them. The lockers weren't very big and when I had initially tried to open a couple of them, thinking I might squeeze in, I discovered they were locked. I assumed they were all locked. It would have been a tight fit anyway. Broad shouldered and six feet tall, getting into one of the lockers would have been like putting ten pounds of flour in a five-pound bag.

At the end of the hallway was an unlocked gray-green janitor's closet with a door ajar. I heard footsteps on the stairs so I pushed aside the mops and buckets, got in and pulled the doors shut.

I had to check out what was so important in the paper bag. Light from the hallway ceiling fixtures filtered through the louvers in the closet doors so I could see fairly well. I opened the bag and peeked in.

A milky-white crystal wrapped in plastic gave off a faint light-blue glow. The crystal was about the size of a jumbo chicken egg. I fished the crystal out of the plastic and tightened my fist around it. I was going to slug anyone right in the kisser if that closet door opened.

I could hear voices of at least two men and footsteps as one of them approached the closet. The doors were flung open. Petrified, I could hear my heart beating faster than if I had just run a mile.

The muzzle of a nine millimeter handgun was pointing right at me. I wanted to hit him but I was frozen in position. I closed my eyes expecting to be shot. The guy looked right at me but turned and yelled down the corridor, "He's not here!"

I couldn't believe it! I was right in front of the guy!

I thought, "This guy must be blind!"

Disgusted, the thug slammed the closet doors and hurriedly walked back down the hallway.

I felt a hand on my shoulder and heard a female voice from behind me. "We're all done."

Startled, thinking I was in a basement closet, I swiveled my head to see Tina's smiling face. I had fallen asleep in the barber's chair!

She said, "I noticed you were asleep but I tried not to wake you until I was finished."

I replied, "I was having a terrible dream. You saved me from getting shot."

Tina snickered, "I can't have a homicide in my shop. I'm glad you're all right."

"Yeah, me too. Thanks."

After she removed the drape, I retrieved my glasses from my shirt pocket and got out of the chair.

Two young men were sitting on the couch waiting for haircuts. I hadn't even heard them come in the shop. They were talking about NFL football players mentioned in one of Tina's magazines.

I fished my wallet from my left hip pocket and handed Tina a twenty. "Keep the change, the haircut and dream were worth it. I'll be back again as soon as my eyebrows start creeping over my glasses."

"Thank you very much," Tina said with a big smile. "I'll see you in a couple of months. Hope you have better dreams."

I left the barbershop and went down the sidewalk to Buxton where I crossed the highway at the intersection. The dream seemed so real I couldn't help but look around to see if anyone was following. Details from the dream kept flooding through my mind, especially the invisibility experience.

I went up the hill to my car and opened the door on the passenger side so I could easily get the tire pressure gauge from the glove compartment. I remembered to check the pressure on the driver's side front tire. I got into the passenger side front seat and flipped the lever to access the glove box contents.

When it opened, a small crumpled up brown paper sack tumbled out and fell to the floor with a thump.

"What's this?"

I didn't remember having anything but maps, the car registration, an insurance card and the tire pressure gauge in the glove box. I picked up the bag and cautiously opened it. Inside the paper sack was a plastic bag containing a rough milky-white crystal just big enough to fit in the palm of my hand. "Humph! Just like in the dream."

CHAPTER 2

I removed the crystal from the plastic bag and laid it down on the passenger seat. I fished the tire gauge from the glove box and checked the pressure in the front tires and decided to inflate the tire at home. I got in the driver's seat and tossed the pressure gauge on the seat next to the crystal.

I made a U-turn and went back to Buxton, turned right and went up the hill. I had to stop at the light where I could make a right to go to the post office. When I turned, the crystal and the pressure gauge both rolled off the passenger seat onto the floor. I decided to pick the items up when I dropped off the mail.

I entered the drive-through at the post office, lowered my window and dropped two envelopes into the mailbox. Two cars were behind me so I continued on and drove back onto the street.

Cherry Park mall was my next stop at the bank. After obtaining cash from the ATM and depositing a check, I returned to my car but had forgotten about the gauge and crystal on the floor. My mind was focused on finding the tire pump in my garage. I tried to recall where I had last seen it.

When I neared home, I halted for a red light on Stark. As I waited for green, I bent over and stretched to pick up the crystal. I transferred the crystal to my left hand. When the light turned green, I drove through the intersection. Several cars sounded their horns, but I didn't pay attention. I had done nothing wrong. I was almost home, only a few blocks to go. I stuck the crystal in my pocket. Pulling into the driveway, I saw Foxy sitting in the picture window watching for me. I smiled and shut off the engine. I leaned over, reached as far as possible to pick up the gauge from the floor and absent-mindedly stuck it in my pocket.

When in the house, Foxy greeted me, rubbing against my ankles. I had to go to the garage and find that tire pump, but first, Foxy had to be given some loving. Just as I scratched behind her ears and tickled her stomach, the doorbell rang. I hoped that it wasn't another person trying to sell him new windows or talk about Jesus. Couldn't people read the NO SOLICITORS sign? I went to the door and could see a large, uniformed man through the small decorative glass window. With my foot as a doorstop, I slowly opened the door.

"Is that your SUV in the driveway?" quizzed the police officer.

I answered, "Sure is. Is there a problem?"

"We received a couple of reports that your car was being driven without a driver. Two people called the department on cell phones and said there was no driver in your car."

"What? You're joking! That's ridiculous!" I continued, "Why don't you come in and explain." I had to hear what the cop had to say.

The tall muscular officer stepped into the living room. He was over six feet tall and probably outweighed me by at least sixty pounds. I have never been a muscular individual or well padded. The tag on his chest said Bill Watson.

The officer asked, "Did you stop at the red light at the top of the hill about ten minutes ago?"

I replied, "Yes sir, I did."

I thought about my actions at the stop light and suddenly realized I had picked up the crystal when I waited for the light to change. I must have been invisible to other drivers! Just like in the dream when I was in that closet! When I held the crystal, no one could see me.

I had to think fast to explain. "When I was stopped at the light, I leaned over to pick up my tire pressure gauge that rolled off the passenger seat when I stopped. Someone must have thought no one was driving because I was bent over and out of sight."

I reached in my pocket, retrieved the pressure gauge and showed the officer.

"I need to put this back in the glove box."

The officer said, "Okay, that makes sense. But remember, you need to give driving your complete attention at intersections. Lots of fender benders happen at cross streets." The officer looked around my living room. "What is your name, sir?"

"Ned Franks," I extended my right hand to the officer. As we shook hands, the officer replied, "Bill Watson. We have to check out all reports, no matter how strange they might be," Bill said as he opened the front door to leave. "It was nice meeting you."

I said jokingly, "Let's not make this a common occurrence."

The officer grinned, turned and walked to his patrol car, climbed in and slowly drove away.

I couldn't believe it! In the dream I was invisible in the closet and now in reality, when I held the crystal, no one could see me.

It was almost time for dinner, but I took a few minutes to search the garage for the air pump. I inflated my front tire to normal pressure and put away the pump, this time on a peg-board where it could be easily found.

As I was eating dinner, I decided to go over to my friend's house in the evening and tell him what happened. Steve Jensen was another retiree, married to Donna. They lived a three houses away across the street.

Steve was a biochemist and his wife worked for years with the police department in the chief's office. She retired a year after Steve quit his teaching and research position at Portland State University. Steve had retired at sixty-two, the same year I retired. I called Steve, Old Man, because he was two years older than I. Steve referred to me as Junior.

I taught Chemistry for twenty-five years at Eastern New Mexico University, a small university in New Mexico. Steve and I didn't know each other until we met at a stamp collector's show in Portland. We are both avid philatelists.

We started talking to each other at the show when we were looking at exhibits. Curiously, we discovered we lived near each other on the same street. So, in the past few years, we had become fast friends. Donna called us "Ned and Steve, the nutty professors." Donna thought it was funny that two highly educated scientists collected little bits of paper. Donna apparently didn't have the "collector's gene."

It was about seven in the evening when I stuck the crystal in my pocket and walked over to the Jensens'. They were almost always home in the evenings.

I climbed the five steps to the porch and rang the bell. Donna answered the door and smiled when she saw me through the screen door.

"Hi, Ned. Come in. Steve is in his stamp room. He got something in the mail today. He's in the guest bedroom, it's his stamp room now."

"Thanks Donna. How have you been?"

"Just great! I've been going down to the department to help the secretaries set up records on the new computer system. It's very sophisticated. We have access to the national fingerprint and facial recognition system, hot stuff with the FBI."

She yelled down the hallway, "Steve, your nutty buddy is here. I'm sending him down the hall."

As I ventured down the hall to the open doorway he said, "You're gonna like what I've got to show you."

I walked past the den situated between the two bedrooms and entered the last bedroom. It was a fairly good size room with an executive desk, a table with two chairs, and stamp albums nearly covering one wall from floor to ceiling. There was no space available for a bed. The floor was covered with a thick light-gray carpet and an electric heater rested in the far left corner. A computer and printer sat at one end of a large table along the wall to the right.

Steve was a well-fed biochemist. Donna was a good cook and Steve's inseam was now smaller than his waist size, but he wasn't fat, just a little bulky. I thought Steve looked like he had never passed up a doughnut or candy bar but I kept my thoughts to myself.

"Hey Junior, take a load off. I've got something to show you that arrived in the mail today…insured."

Steve pulled another chair over near where he was working and said, "Have a seat."

Steve had his United States stamp album in front of him. He pointed at the set of airmails he had just gotten in the mail. "Look at these babies!"

I sat down and looked with a little jealousy at the expensive set of stamps. I nodded, "I'll bet those set you back a few bucks."

"Not as much as you'd think. I found a dealer, Ben Schvindell in Vancouver, going out of business and he sold them to me very cheaply."

I couldn't help myself, "So you didn't get schvindelled?"

Steve shook his head, "That was bad, Junior." He looked like he wanted to pock mee with his stamp tongs. "You said you had something to show me. Let me see what you have."

"You're not gonna believe it, and it's not stamps…not even close," I replied.

I reached into my pocket and pulled out the plastic bag containing the crystal.

Steve exclaimed, "Jesus, that is one petrified egg! Where'd you get that?"

I told Steve about my dream and the incident with the police officer earlier in the afternoon.

"Hey, we're both scientists. Let's figure this out."

Steve took the plastic bag and held it up to the light to give the crystal a better look. I think he was a bit fearful to touch it. It seemed to have a pinkish glow, not blue as in the dream.

We talked over a plan to investigate the properties of the crystal. Unfortunately, we didn't have laboratory instruments for basic analysis. After a few minutes, Steve said, "You take the crystal out of the bag and I'll observe."

I removed the crystal and quickly disappeared.

"You're gone, except for your shoes." Steve laughed.

I placed the crystal back in the bag and instantly reappeared.

Steve was intrigued. I could see it in his face. He said, "How did the crystal get in your car glove compartment? Did you leave your car unlocked?"

"Hell if I know. I always lock the doors. I locked the car when I got out. I stood there and watched the lights flash and the horn sound."

"Well, the crystal didn't get there by itself. Someone put it there. Someone with a master."

"So, you think I was selected to get the crystal. That never crossed my mind."

"Who else knows about this? Must not be the police."

I replied, "No one, just you and me."

Donna stood in the doorway with her hands on her hips, "What are you guys hatching? Can I bring you something to drink?"

We both chuckled after glancing at the egg shaped crystal.

I shook my head and Steve replied, "No thanks, dear. We don't want to get anything on the stamps."

"Okay. I'm going to watch a movie." She disappeared down the hallway.

Steve went to the door to check to see if his wife was still listening. He returned to his chair at the table.

"O.K. Ned. Take off your shoes and socks. I hope you don't have stinky feet."

I caught on immediately.

As I took off my shoes, I replied with a smile, "I took a shower today so my feet shouldn't smell. You know, I take at least one shower a week whether I need it or not."

After I removed my socks, I slipped into my shoes but left them unlaced. I grabbed the crystal and vanished again.

"Now I can't see your shoes. You're totally invisible," stated Steve.

I reappeared after putting the crystal back in its plastic housing.

Steve commented, "We need to keep notes about this. Let's put our notes on the computer. We can password protect the file." Steve went to the computer and started using some software that he had used for writing research papers.

"Junior, what shall we use for a password?"

"Eggsperiment," I quickly replied.

"Good choice! We won't forget that!"

As we were looking at the crystal, it began to emit a bluish glow.

"What do you think that means, Ned?"

"I don't know. Maybe it's reading our minds. That's what the crystal did in my dream."

"Have you tried to say anything when you were invisible? That would really be creepy if someone heard a voice but no one was there."

"Nope. Why don't you try it and I'll watch this time. When I was invisible I didn't notice anything different. I could hear just fine."

"Okay, I'll say something to you when I'm invisible. Here goes."

Steve picked up the crystal and disappeared. I had to laugh. I could still see his shoes and belt.

"I can see your shoes and belt. Say something to me," I said.

I listened closely but couldn't hear anything except Donna walking around upstairs. She was probably cleaning up in the dining room and kitchen before starting a movie.

"Calling Steve. Put down the crystal."

Steve put the crystal in the bag, reappeared and typed some more notes into the computer.

"What did you say to me, Steve?' Ned asked. "I didn't hear a peep."

He grinned, "I said your feet do stink…just kidding." He continued, "No, what I really said was, 'Can you hear me?' So, you couldn't hear anything?"

I smiled and shook my head, "Nothing. I could hear Donna upstairs walking around but not a chirp from you. I've been thinking about your belt and shoes. For the clothing to become invisible it must have to be touching some skin."

"That's what I thought when I told you to take off your shoes and socks and then put your shoes back on. But I didn't see your belt," Steve stated.

"I'm not wearing one," I replied.

"That explains it."

We sat there staring at the crystal for nearly a minute and then at each other for a few seconds without speaking. Then, Steve said, "I'm a biologist, so where do you think this thing came from. Did an alien chicken lay it?" At first, I thought he was serious, but then he grinned.

I smiled and then said, "There might be cobalt in the crystal. It can be blue or pink, depending on its environment…its coordination number."

"Do you think it might be something from Area 51?"

I frowned, "You mean recovered from an alien spaceship?"

"Or maybe something developed at the Skunk Works?" added Steve.

"Well, it wouldn't surprise me if it came out of California," I observed.

Steve heard some movement in the hallway and made a motion to me to zip it. Donna yelled down the hallway, "Steve, I'm going to bed early and read some more of my novel. Tonight's TV movies are all crappy. Good night boys."

"Good night!" We yelled back.

I looked at my old dependable analog watch and saw that it was after nine o'clock.

"I'd better be going, Steve. We can continue this tomorrow. Why don't you come over to my place after dinner? Are you going to tell Donna about this?"

"I don't think so. She might blab it to someone and create a problem."

"Well, come on over unless you have something else to do."

"Are you kiddin' me? I'll be there. I'll take notes and add them to our computer file when I get back home. Donna has a women's group meeting so I've got a free night."

I picked up the plastic bag containing the crystal and stuck it in my pocket. We went to the front door and said good night. I walked home consumed with thoughts trying to analyze what we had discovered.

CHAPTER 3

When I got home from Steve's, I decided to go to bed early so I would be fresh the next day to do some deep thinking. However, I had difficulty going to sleep. I kept recalling the events of the day. I also had to contend with an annoying itching sensation on my fingers and the palms of my hands. Counting sheep was a dumb idea that never worked.

When I woke up, I noticed the skin on my palms looked burned. I applied lotion to my hands and got busy with the day's plans. I spent Thursday morning trying to think of other experiments with the crystal. That's when I realized handling the crystal must have caused the inflammation on my hands.

I went to Home Depot and Lowe's during the afternoon to check out prices of lumber and light fixtures. I already had stain and sealer. I thought I could do some work on my deck before the weather turned bad.

At about 4:00 p.m., I headed to Walmart to pick up some diabetic supplies. I always parked at the outskirts of the large parking lot and walked to the store. There were two benefits; I got some needed exercise and there was less chance of another car bumping my SUV than if I parked among the dense cluster of vehicles nearer the store.

I habitually checked out my surroundings when I left my car. I noted a fancy red sports car parked a few spaces on the other side of my car. The driver looked well-groomed and was probably just waiting for someone. Perhaps his wife or girlfriend was in the store, but that didn't seem quite right. A female would want him to park nearer the store entrance. There were several spots available.

I visited the pharmacy and then checked to see if any Blu-ray disc prices had dropped. I refuse to pay thirty bucks for a movie. I gave up, frustrated with the high prices.

On the way back to my car, I saw a big old gray van parked next to the bright red sports car. A man stood next to the car talking to the driver. As I approached my Subaru, the driver of the sports car handed the other man something. The sports car driver backed out of the space and drove slowly away. The other man climbed in the big van.

I thought it reminded me of something I had seen on TV. It was one of the police dramas and a similar event took place during a drug deal.

I got home, had a microwave dinner and played with Foxy for about ten minutes. I turned on the computer and checked my email but didn't have anything but the usual junk mail. I hadn't played chess in several weeks, but I wasn't in the mood for a game, the computer usually won. I put the computer on sleep and turned on the TV. The only thing on was the news. It was about politics, too boring, so I turned it off.

Shortly after 7:00 p.m., the doorbell rang.

I raised my voice, "Come on in Steve, it's unlocked."

Steve joined me in the kitchen where I was loading the dishwasher.

He watched me add soap and said, "I spent most of the day having my car serviced. I had to drive to the dealer, wait in the showroom for an hour and then talk to a serviceman about getting a new battery. Then, as I drove home, I discovered the clock on the dash was not set properly. It took another twenty minutes to figure that out. Damn cars are more trouble than they're worth. And they cost too much." Steve vented.

"Yeah, I know what you mean. I always feel like they're ripping me off."

I turned the dishwasher on and we adjourned to the living room.

Steve took a deep breath and sat on the sofa. "Are you ready for some deep investigating?" he quizzed.

"Yeah. I spent much of the night and all morning thinking about the crystal. I've got a couple of ideas." I paused for a second and held up my hands. "Take a look at my hands." I turned my palms toward Steve.

He remarked, "Hey, they look sunburned."

"It's from handling the crystal," I commented. "Last night they really itched but they feel better now."

"Well, my hands are okay. But I only touched the crystal for a short time," Steve replied.

I said, "I estimated that I held the crystal for more than five but less than ten minutes during the day."

Steve wrote it down under "Time of Exposure."

"Anything else?"

"One other thing. The crystal glowed pink last night," I replied.

"Let's try an experiment with the crystal. I'll handle it so you don't have to," Steve stated.

I set the plastic bag containing the crystal on the dining room table. I closed the vertical blinds so no one could see from outside.

"Got a mirror?" Steve asked.

"Sure." I retrieved a small mirror from the bathroom.

"Okay, let's see what happens when I hold the crystal and you grab my hand."

Steve picked up the crystal and disappeared so I couldn't see his hand.

"You'll have to grab my hand Steve; I can't see yours."

I looked in the mirror and only saw my reflection. When Steve touched my hand nothing dramatic happened except Steve's image started to flicker in and out of visibility like erratic TV reception.

"Whoa, I think we have exceeded the power of the crystal!" I exclaimed.

Steve put the crystal down and scribbled in his notebook.

I suggested, "Let's see what happens if you pick up something metallic when you are invisible."

Steve picked up the crystal and then a fork from the kitchen table.

"That's strange, Steve. I can see the fork hanging in the air."

Steve reappeared and put the fork down. The crystal was back in the plastic bag.

"Well, that was interesting!" Steve exclaimed. "I wonder why your glasses become invisible?" he questioned.

"Most of my glasses is plastic, not much metal present," I replied.

"We have to assume a small amount of metal is okay; a few grams is probably the limit," Steve concluded.

"Let's talk these things over and see if we can use the crystal to do something beneficial," I stated.

"Yes. The big picture," grinned Steve.

We discussed our findings for half an hour but couldn't come up with anything legal we might do using the crystal. Then I related my observations at the Walmart parking lot.

Steve was excited, he blurted out, "Robin Hood!"

"Oh, I get it," I declared. "We take money from drug dealers and give it to charities. I like it, but we'd better have a fail-safe plan. Those guys carry guns."

My phone rang, startling both of us.

"Excuse me." I answered the phone. "It's Donna. She's home from her meeting."

"Okay. It's about time for me to go anyway. Let's think of a plan that we can check out on Saturday. I have to visit some antique stores with Donna tomorrow. We'll probably drive to Hood River."

"Let's go to the stamp store in Vancouver on Saturday," I said winking my right eye.

"Okay. I'll come over after lunch. Take it easy, Junior."

Steve headed home and Foxy came out from the bedroom to get her late night back scratch. She almost always hid in the bedroom when someone rang the doorbell. It took her a long time to trust anyone, even when it was Steve.

I spent Friday working on the house. I did some drywall repairs in the utility room and started tearing down an old hot tub building behind the house. I was intent on building a wood shop in its place, probably next summer. I usually had more new projects than I had time to accomplish and some unfinished ones.

Steve came over a little after 1:00 p.m. on Saturday. He drove over and parked at the curb.

"I've been thinking about the automatic doors at Walmart, Steve. Do you think they will be activated when we are invisible," I quizzed.

"Hey, you're the chemist. What do you think?"

"Maybe the crystal only affects visible light. I believe the automatic doors are activated by radio waves, much longer wavelengths." I stated.

"We can try it when we get over there. Let's see what happens. We can take my car. It's out front. Have you removed your socks?"

"Yep. I'm ready to go," I replied.

When we arrived at the big Walmart parking lot, we left the car far from the store and walked to the sprawling building. We went in the men's room and found it unoccupied. I took out the crystal and became invisible.

"Okay Junior, follow me. Wait until the automatic door is closed and then try to go through," stated Steve. "I'll watch for the door to open with nobody there."

"Oops! I can see your belt. We forgot about your belt. You'd better put it on under your pants, or at least under your shirt," Steve instructed.

A man entered the bathroom and Steve stepped in front of me to hide the action.

Steve pretended to be drying his hands. We exited the men's room and walked through the store to the automatic doors. No one was leaving the store. Steve whispered, "Try it now."

The door opened, apparently by itself, and the lady checking receipts seemed surprised.

"Must be a malfunction," Steve commented to the lady as he proceeded through the doorway.

We walked to the car and Steve opened both front doors pretending to look for something. I got in the car and put the crystal away, reappearing in the front passenger seat.

I glanced at my wristwatch and commented, "It took us about 45 seconds to get here from the men's room."

I had started the timer on my watch when in the men's room. It was a nearly all-plastic Superman watch I had purchased at a garage sale. It used batteries like a kid eating Halloween candy. My regular watch contained too much metal to become invisible when holding the crystal.

"So we have about four minutes to carry out a heist," Steve commented.

"Heist? You're really getting into this, Steve," I commented with a big smile. "I'd rather call it a donation." I had no idea what procedure he was estimating that would take four minutes.

"When we were in the store, I thought of something else, Steve. What if I accidentally drop the crystal if someone bumps into me?"

Steve quickly had a suggestion. "How about wearing a glove? You can stuff the crystal in the palm of the glove. That should hold it tight to your hand so you can't drop it."

"Hey, great idea. I knew you were good for something, old man."

On the way home we stopped at a local stamp dealer's shop and bought some stamp mounts. We spent about an hour looking at stamps and I found some items for my collection in the dealer's bargain box. We destroyed our receipts so Donna wouldn't become suspicious. A round trip to Vancouver would have taken at least two hours.

As we drove to my place, we planned for the coming Tuesday evening. Donna had a meeting for the Red Cross at the VFW armory Tuesday night.

Tuesday arrived and so did rain clouds. Bad weather put off our excursion to Walmart. Further planning took place and we checked out sport cars on the Internet.

The red car I had seen at Walmart was a corvette. We planned to visit a Chevy dealer and find out if we could reach into the car and open the center console without getting into the car. We found locations for three Chevy dealers where we could experiment.

The sun reappeared on Wednesday. We went to one of the car dealers, but no corvettes were on the lot. The second dealer had just what we needed; several older model corvettes were parked just outside the showroom. As we were reaching into a corvette that I thought looked like the one I had seen at Walmart, a salesman approached and said, "Can I help you gentlemen?"

"We were just trying to see how the center console opened," Steve stated. "Are all Corvettes about the same?"

"Yeah. They're pretty much all the same," answered the salesman as he reached into the car and opened the console from the driver's side.

"Are you looking for a new corvette?" asked the man.

"Well, I had a ninety-two but it hadn't run in a couple of years," Steve answered. He continued, "I took the engine apart to work on it but I was too busy to get back to it. I sold it three years ago. It would be nice to have a new one though."

"What's the price of a new one?" I asked.

"Basic models are about sixty thousand…depends on what you want in it. The high end ones are about twice that," the salesman answered.

"Well, that's too much for either of us," Steve commented.

I said, "Thanks for showing us the car. We'd better go Steve."

As we walked back to our car, I said, "I didn't know you had a corvette."

"I never did," Steve replied with a smile. "A little fib never hurts when you're not buying a car."

CHAPTER 4

As Steve and I drove home, we made plans to pick up our first donation. We both had afternoons free from one to four o'clock. Steve would drive my SUV and I would be in the back. I would have plenty of room to crouch down out of sight. Steve's car, a sedan, wouldn't work as well as the Subaru and this way there was more time available to pick up the donation. We didn't plan to enter the store. When we discovered a deal going down, I would insert the crystal in my glove and climb out of the car after Steve opened the cargo door of the SUV. But how would we keep the drug dealer from backing out and driving off without giving us time to take the money from the console? We needed a diversion.

"I've got it!" I exclaimed. "We put something in the back of the SUV that needs two people to lift it out. Steve, you can go over to the corvette and ask the guy for help. That should give me enough time to reach in and pick up the donation."

"What if he says no?" asked Steve.

"Well, stand behind his car so he can't back out. It should only take a couple of seconds," I speculated.

"Okay. If he yells at me, I'll yell back at him. He can't afford to cause a problem in the parking lot."

"Sounds good, Steve. There is only one problem."

"What's that?"

"We have to wait around in the parking lot for the drug dealer to show up. It could take days. It will be a stake-out," I replied smiling.

Each afternoon Steve and I went to the parking lot with some reading material, crossword puzzles, cookies and two Thermos's of coffee, one high test, and the other decaf. After the first day of no results, we took a pair of binoculars with us.

We observed from the lot for nearly a week before we spotted the bright red corvette parked at the outer edge of the Walmart lot. The driver was smoking a cigarette and apparently listening to music. It was about 3:00 p.m.

I was scanning with the binoculars. "Hey! I think we have a donation pending," I had spotted the red corvette from the back of the Subaru and alerted Steve. He was working on a crossword puzzle.

"Where is it?" Steve inquired looking around the lot.

"About twenty yards from the entrance to the parking lot on the right," I replied.

"Oh, I see it. Time to move our car into position."

The SUV came to life and Steve slowly drove to within three or four parking spaces of the corvette, maneuvering to the left of our target. No other car was near the corvette but we decided to go ahead and see if our plan would work. Steve pressed the hatchback button on the ignition key and the rear door popped open. At the back of the Subaru Steve pretended to lift a heavy old electric motor we had loaded in the rear of the car. I was invisible and climbed out of the vehicle.

"Here we go!" commented Steve. He walked to the corvette and asked the driver, "Sir, could you help me?"

"What do you want?" the well-groomed driver asked.

"I could use some help lifting an old motor from the back of my car," Steve replied.

"Sorry, I don't want to get dirty. I've got nice clothes on," the driver stated.

"I have a pair of gloves you can use. You only have to grab the shaft, I'll get the dirty end," Steve responded.

The driver looked around. No one was nearby so he said, "Well, okay."

Our plan was going great!

After the driver got out of the corvette and was walking toward the SUV, I leaned over, reached in and opened the center console. I saw a gun and a big roll of money bound tightly with a rubber band. I grabbed both. I suddenly realized the gun was not invisible so I tossed it into some dense bushes in front of the parked cars. I quickly shut the console and walked back toward my car.

I watched Steve retrieve one of the orphaned shopping carts nearby. Steve and his recruited assistant placed the heavy motor in the cart.

"Thanks for the help," Steve said, extending his hand to the driver. They shook hands.

"No problem," the driver commented.

The man turned and walked back to his fancy car.

I had climbed back into the Subaru through the rear hatch just before Steve slammed the cargo door shut. Steve began wheeling the motor toward the store. When Steve got near the store entrance, he stopped and took out his cell phone and called me. My phone was on "vibrate" so no one could hear it ring. We planned for me to take my car and pick Steve up near the store entrance. I watched the driver in the corvette. He seemed preoccupied with his music, completely unaware of the theft.

With some difficulty, I climbed over the backs of the seats and got in the driver's position. Five minutes had elapsed so I took off the glove and put the crystal in the plastic bag in the glove box. I started the car, backed out and drove to meet Steve. We quickly loaded the motor in the Subaru and Steve took over driving. I moved to the rear of the SUV and observed some activity around the corvette.

The corvette driver was stomping around his car excitedly, talking into a cell phone, probably yelling. As we left the parking lot, we observed a large gray van pulling up next to the corvette.

Steve drove to my place while I counted the donation money.

"Hey Steve. We've been in the wrong professions for years. There's over two thousand dollars here," I joked.

After we got to my place, we cleaned up the car and stored the motor in my garage. We thought we might need it again. Once in the house, we sat at the kitchen table and Steve recounted the money to ensure an accurate total.

Steve questioned, "Did you see a gun in the console?"

"Yeah. I threw it in those bushes in front of the cars," I answered.

"Oh no! We have to go get that gun. What if some kid picks it up?"

"Jesus, I didn't think about that," I replied. "I've been thinking about our donations."

"Me too. What charities should we support?" asked Steve.

I suggested, "How about the ASPCA and Make a Wish?".

"Okay. Let's include the Red Cross, too," added Steve.

"We'd better get that gun, Steve," I said with a concerned look on my face.

We walked over to Steve's house and got in his car. We didn't want anyone to notice the Subaru returning to the parking lot, especially not the corvette driver. He might be hanging around watching for my car.

When we arrived back at the parking lot, I asked Steve, "Do you remember where the corvette was parked?"

"Exactly. It was the fifth spot in from those small trees that line the entrance to the lot," he replied.

We pulled up next to the bushes. I got out and quickly found the gun. It was a small caliber, probably a twenty-two. There was a clip in the handle, which I removed. I checked to make sure no bullets remained in the gun. When I was in college, I took ROTC as an undergrad and had learned quite a bit about firearms. I got back in the car and we went back to my home.

We put the gun in one of the cupboards above the refrigerator and the clip in a drawer behind the silverware tray in a base cabinet next to the dishwasher.

"Sit down at the table, Steve. I'm about ready to pop."

I went into the master bathroom. Steve got a glass from the cupboard and filled it with water. Just as he started toward the dining room table to sit down, the doorbell rang.

"Hey Steve, would you get the door?" I yelled from the bathroom.

"No problem."

Steve put the glass of water on the table and walked to the front door. He opened the door and to his surprise, he saw the driver of the corvette.

"I want my money and my gun," he demanded.

"What?" Steve answered.

"I want my money and my damn gun," he repeated.

"You're the guy that helped me at the Walmart parking lot," Steve stated.

The man at the door said, "And you're the guy that took my money and my gun!"

"How could I have taken anything of yours? I wasn't even near your car." said Steve.

"I don't know how you did it, but your car was the only one near mine in the lot."

He pulled a gun from behind his back and Steve stepped away from the door into the living room. The corvette driver entered the house, looking around.

"You the only one here?" he quizzed.

"Yes." Steve lied.

I had overheard the confrontation from the hallway so I ducked back into the bathroom. I picked up my plastic lancing device from the top of the vanity. It was used to prick my fingers to measure my blood glucose. The end of it was about the diameter of a thirty-eight caliber gun barrel. To keep it visible, I wrapped my hand with a washrag and then regripped the device. I had the crystal in my pocket, which I retrieved and held in my left hand. Now invisible, I went into the living room with the lancing device in my right hand, floating through the air as I walked.

I stepped behind the corvette driver and stuck the lancing device in the middle of the guy's back. I quickly put the crystal in my pocket and said, "Drop the gun or I'll put a bullet through your spine!"

The gun made a loud thump as it hit the floor.

"You said you were home alone," scowled the driver.

"A little fib. I don't even live here." Steve replied as he bent down and picked up the gun.

He gave the gun to me. I put the lancing device in my pocket.

"Steve, call nine-one-one."

Steve punched in 911 and asked for help. In about twenty seconds, two police officers were at the front door.

The front door was open and I asked the officers to come in. They opened the screen door and came into the living room with guns drawn. They were pointing their revolvers at me since I was holding a gun.

"Sir, put the gun down."

I noticed the officer speaking was Bill Watson. I turned the gun so I had the barrel in my hand and gave the gun to Bill.

"Hi, Bill," I greeted the officer I knew.

"What's going on here?" the other officer quizzed.

Steve explained what had happened earlier at the parking lot, leaving out the part about the donation and my invisibility. Then he explained that this guy had come to the door and wanted money and a gun. I had gotten behind him and forced him to drop the gun. Then Steve called nine-one-one.

The corvette driver stared in disbelief. He couldn't say anything in his defense. He would have been arrested for possessing another illegal gun. And what about having over two thousand dollars cash? Both of his guns had probably been obtained illegally. He also would have lost the corvette since he had drugs hidden in it. The car would have been confiscated. Bill questioned the driver to get his name. It was Adam Bruker.

Bill handcuffed Bruker. The other officer, Jim Jenkins, put him in the back of the patrol car.

Bill emptied the handgun and commented, "Twenty-two caliber Beretta ten plus one."

"How long will Bruker be in jail?" Steve asked. He was worried about retribution.

"It will depend on his rap sheet but attempted armed robbery will probably carry a sentence of several years," Bill replied.

"So we won't see him again?" asked Steve.

"I doubt it," Bill replied.

Steve introduced himself to Bill, mentioning that he and his wife, Donna, lived down the street.

"Jensen?" quizzed Bill. He continued, "Oh, your wife is Donna Jensen, the former aid of the Chief of Police."

"That's right," replied Steve.

"She's a real pro with the department's new computer system."

"Can you gentlemen come down to the department tomorrow and sign statements?" asked Bill.

Jim had returned from the patrol car and said, "It should only take a few minutes."

"Sure, we'll be there," I replied.

"I guess we're done here. We'll escort Bruker to jail," Jim stated.

"Thanks, officers. You sure got here fast," Steve commented.

The officers left the house, got in their patrol car and drove off down the street with their prisoner.

"Wow! That was kind of scary, Ned," Steve exclaimed.

"Piece of cake," I replied.

CHAPTER 5

Following the home invasion, Steve and I decided we had enough excitement for one day and he went home. I took the money from its temporary hiding place, a big cookie jar in the corner of the kitchen and divided it into two smaller rolls. I then put the rolls in empty pill containers and placed them in the medicine cabinet in the hallway bathroom. I thought the pill bottles were a less obvious hiding place than the cookie jar.

It was 5:30 p.m. and time to eat. I popped a 310-calorie frozen turkey dinner in the microwave and sat down to watch the news.

Foxy came out of hiding and rubbed against my leg uttering a little squeak so I wouldn't step on her.

"Did those men scare you, Foxy? You're a good girl," I stated as I reached down, scratched her back and gave a slight tug on her miniature tail. She walked into the living room, vaulted onto the back of the sofa and looked outside.

I ate dinner in the living room while watching the news. The anchorwoman mentioned a drug dealer was arrested for a home invasion and according to the three strikes law, Bruker would be in the state prison for a long time.

The phone rang. It was Steve.

"Hey, did you see the Channel 2 News?" Steve asked.

"Yep. We won't have to worry about him coming back," I replied.

"Let's not do anything for a few days and then we can make our donations to charity. How about getting together on Saturday, or are you going to watch football,"

Steve queried.

"Nope. My teams are terrible this year. Saturday's a good time." I paused for a couple of seconds. "I was thinking about buying money orders at the post office, but the post office is closed on the weekend."

Steve stated, "That's not a problem. We can get money orders at any of the supermarkets."

I suggested, "Let's meet in the Safeway parking lot at 1:00 p.m."

Saturday arrived and so did rainy weather. There had been an east wind for two days. Friday night clouds signaled a wet Saturday was a few hours away.

Steve and I went to Safeway and ordered coffee at the Starbuck's kiosk. We sat down at one of the small tables and talked over the routine for getting money to the charities. I usually shopped at Safeway and Steve frequented Albertsons. I would go to Albertsons for a money order. Steve would get a money order at Safeway. That way, the transactions would be less memorable to the staff. We would also go to Bi-Mart, Walmart and other supermarkets on the east side of Portland. We didn't want to draw too much attention to ourselves, so we decided to limit the money orders to two hundred dollars.

"I'll make a two hundred eighty cash donation at the animal shelter. They have a donation box that would be easy to drop a wad of money into. No one would even notice," I grinned, "especially if I'm invisible."

"Okay. Then we'll need ten money orders to use up the money," stated Steve.

Steve and I spent about two hours obtaining money orders and met back at my place.

We sat at the dining table, nursing diet colas.

"Okay, junior, where are we sending the money?" asked Steve.

"Just a minute," I replied.

I walked down the hall to one of my extra bedrooms. I returned carrying a large box crammed full of unopened mail. I stated, "These are requests for money I received during the past year."

"Jesus! There must be hundreds of them. If you sent twenty dollars to each of those charities, you'd be in debt up to your eyebrows," exclaimed Steve. "Why did you save all these?"

"I was curious to see how much of this type of mail I received during one year. A lot more will come by the end of the year. I'll probably have another box half full," I answered.

I started combing through the unopened mail and found the charity addresses we needed.

As Steve watched, he saw that some of the envelopes contained money.

"Is it okay if I open these?" Steve asked as he began separating out the envelopes containing nickels, dimes and a few pennies.

"Sure. Help yourself."

"Where's your letter opener?"

"I'll get one for you," I grinned. "Are you afraid of paper cuts?"

I went into my stamp collection room and returned with a letter opener, which I handed to Steve. I sat down, picked up a ballpoint and started addressing envelopes for mailing the donations. I avoided putting a return address on the envelopes.

Steve started opening the charity requests and removed dimes, nickels and an occasional quarter. A paper dollar made the total nearly four dollars. We would use the cash for the money orders fees. He also found about twenty dollars of return postage, which he tore off the corners of the envelopes.

"I'll take these home and soak them. If they don't soak off, I'll warm them with the heat from my toaster and peel them off." Steve stuck the chunks of paper in his shirt pocket creating a good sized bulge.

"All right. We can use them for our charity mail. Keep half of what's left over and buy a Glue Stik if you don't have one." I instructed. "Hey, what's Donna doing today?"

"Remember when she and I went antique hunting several weeks ago?" quizzed Steve. He continued, "Donna found some small brass vases at a garage sale on our way back from Hood River. She's polishing them with some Brasso. She wants to use them on the mantle as candleholders for Christmas; says they'll look nice with red ribbon on them. I think she's right."

Smiling, I asked, "Are you sure those vases aren't cremation urns?"

"Boy, Junior, you come up with some of the damnedest ideas. Have you checked your blood sugar recently? Maybe it's a little low?"

I laughed and said, "Maybe you're right. It's time for me to eat dinner. Bring those stamps you're going to soak off with you tomorrow and we'll get our donations in the mail."

"Okay, junior," Steve replied, "see you tomorrow."

On Sunday, I felt lazy so I lounged around in a robe and slippers until 10:00 a.m., when the phone rang.

"Hello. Hi Steve. I've got some yard work to do, too. I have a dental appointment tomorrow, so my whole afternoon will be shot. I'll check with you on Tuesday."

I dressed, went outside and started the lawn mower. As I cut the grass, I mulled over the incident with Bruker and the police officers. Something just wasn't quite right. Steve and I noticed Bruker didn't have a car and the officers had arrived within about twenty seconds of Steve's 911 call. Also, there was no siren from the police car. It seemed to me the police always used their siren to help clear the streets and perhaps scare off the bad guys. I was going to mention this to Steve on Tuesday. I finished the lawn and put the mower away, still wondering.

After lunch I watched TV for a short time. Professional football only interested him if a Cowboys' game were being televised, and the five-minute spans of commercials were very irritating. I didn't need anything on my body made bigger, muscles or otherwise. I didn't need insurance or a new car. I channel surfed but couldn't find anyone playing Dallas.

I turned off the flat-screen and went to my stamp room. Just as I sat down and opened my Great Britain album, the doorbell rang. Foxy jumped down off a heavily padded chair and streaked into my bedroom. I assumed she was going under the bed. I got up and went to the door.

"Hi Gloria," I greeted my next-door neighbor, who owned ever-barking dogs.

Gloria was the self-appointed queen of the neighborhood watch. She owned a handgun. From what she said, she knew how to use it. Gloria Rodriguez was fifty-seven years old and lived alone. She had two big dogs and a gun for protection. Her husband had died of cancer two years ago. She was a watchful neighbor.

"Ned, have you noticed a dark blue SUV in the neighborhood lately?" she asked.

"No, I haven't." I rarely pay attention to cars in the neighborhood unless they stop at my place.

"I've been noticing that car around the neighborhood for the past week or so. I thought maybe they were selling something, but they never get out of the car."

"They?" I quizzed.

"Two nice looking young men," Gloria replied.

I suggested, "Jehovah's witnesses, Latter Day Saints?"

"No, they're dressed too casually and they talk on cell phones all the time," she replied. "I've been watching them with my binoculars," she said sheepishly.

"Have you talked with them?" Ned asked.

"Oh, no! I mind my own business."

"Well, thanks for the info Gloria. Let me know when you need your lawn cut."

"Thanks Ned, but I have my nephew mow my lawn. I give him ten dollars each time he mows it. He's earning money for a new computer game."

"Okay. See you later, Gloria."

I closed the door and returned to the stamp room. I found Foxy curled up and sound asleep on the chair where I had been sitting. I guess she hadn't gone under the bed. I smiled, reached over to the stamp album and closed it. I had some thinking to do.

I went in the living room and sat down in my recliner to cogitate.

What if Bruker had a partner who was watching the drug transactions from another location in the parking lot? But the partner would probably have seen the gun flying through the air into the bushes. So Bruker wouldn't have been asking for his gun. Maybe the partner didn't see the gun? The partner could have driven him to my place and when the police arrived, he drove away. That could explain why Bruker had no car. Now, how had the officers shown up so quickly? Maybe the men in the blue SUV had contacted the police when they saw Bruker approach my home. That meant the people in the SUV were probably police. But why would they be stationed on my street?

I had even more things to mention to Steve. This type of analysis was almost like writing a thesis based on unsupported experimental evidence. The experiments created many more questions than answers.

My shoes and socks contained pieces of grass from mowing and my pants had green stains from the knees down. I decided to take a shower and change clothes. Something about showering caused my thinking to become clearer. While in the shower, I realized Steve and I needed an accomplice if we were going to pick up more donations. Someone in the parking lot may have noticed the 'help me with the motor' routine. We better not repeat the scheme. We needed a different distraction.

Around 4:00 p.m. I decided to walk to the park. It was about a half mile round trip and only took twenty minutes unless I stopped and talked to neighbors. When I started my walk, I saw a dark blue SUV parked two houses away on the other side of the street. I could see two people in front, so I decided to ask what they were doing. As I approached the car, the engine started and the occupants drove away. Gloria's tip about the dark blue SUV took on more importance. I finished my walk, ate dinner and worked on my stamp collection until bedtime.

I went to bed still thinking about all the different explanations for what seemed to be irregularities in the day's events.

Monday arrived and I busied myself around the house doing things I neglected while Steve and I carried out the first donation exercise. The afternoon was spent at the dental office and doing some shopping. I went to Walmart, parked in my usual place, went in the store and bought a Blu-ray Star Trek DVD.

As I returned to my car, I saw the same red corvette Steve and I took the donation from the week before. It was unoccupied, parked at the outer edge of the parking lot. I knew it was the same corvette because I had memorized the license plate. I got close enough to read the license plate: PCH 314 was easy to remember. It was "peach pie," PCH for peach and 314 for pi. I decided to keep an eye on the corvette. I watched it from my car for half an hour. Dinnertime was approaching so I had to return home. I didn't want to risk driving while possessing a low blood sugar. I had some candy with me, just in case, but a balanced meal was much better than hollow calories. I left the lot without seeing the driver of the corvette.

I spent an uneventful Tuesday morning at home. After breakfast and playing a little bit with Foxy, I sat down with a pad and pencil and made a list of things to talk over with Steve.

After lunch, Steve came over and we sat in the living room discussing the previous week's activities. I related seeing the red corvette in the Walmart parking lot.

"Are you sure it was the same car?" asked Steve.

I told Steve how I memorized the license plate number.

"And you didn't see the driver?"

"Nope. While I was there no one was near the car."

"The driver was invisible!" Steve joked.

"Come on, Steve. Sometimes your jokes need resuscitation."

I suggested that someone was in the lot watching the red corvette to see if anyone would prowl around it. The prowler might be the thief. He would be grabbed and pressured to give back the money and the stolen gun.

"How far were you parked from the corvette?" asked Steve.

"I was about thirty yards away on the opposite side of the entrance to the parking lot," I continued, "There was a row of cars between my car and the corvette, so I doubt if anyone saw me. Too bad I didn't have the crystal with me, I could have checked out the corvette while invisible."

"But would you have remembered to take off your socks?"

I gave him a dirty look. Then I brought up the idea of acquiring an accomplice.

Steve asked, "Anybody in mind?"

"Yeah. Donna."

"You're joking."

"Yep!" I said smiling. "Do you have anyone in mind?"

"Well, I don't know her very well. How about your barber, Tina?" Steve replied.

I reacted, "Hey, that might work. Tina has a motorcycle. She could pretend she was having trouble with it and park the bike next to the corvette on the driver's side."

I added, "I don't think she would tell anyone about our escapades. She is quiet and reflective rather than gregarious."

"Geez, an ideal woman!" Steve remarked.

Steve also thought about the police arriving so fast and Bruker not having any means of transportation. Those inconsistencies didn't negate our need for an accomplice.

"We'd better get some stamps on those envelopes containing the money orders. Where's your Glue Stik?" Steve asked, as he reached into his shirt pocket and pulled out a small assortment of stamps he had soaked off the charity envelopes.

I got the Glue Stik from my stamp room and we sat down at the dining room table. As we attached the stamps to the preaddressed envelopes, I volunteered to talk to Tina about joining the team.

"I'll go down to her shop tomorrow afternoon. Do you want to be there?"

"Yeah. I think so. It will add credibility to your story," Steve answered.

Recruitment day arrived. It was Wednesday, the outside temp read 90, unusually hot for the end of September. Donna went shopping with one of her girlfriends.

We drove to the barbershop in Steve's car. Steve parallel parked on the street close to the barbershop. It was early in the afternoon and would get hotter.

"Looks like she's pretty busy today," I observed.

"You're going invisible, right?" quizzed Steve.

"Uh huh. When she isn't busy, you can come in. I'll be waiting in back."

"It's too hot to wait in the car. I'll window shop in the shade and keep an eye on the barbershop,"

I clutched the crystal and converted to invisibility. After looking around to make sure no one was watching the car door open and close, I got out of the car and entered Tina's shop.

The barber shop door was open, so I entered and walked to the back of the room. Brutus growled as I walked past the little dog. Brutus was lying under a chair in a small foam rubber cushioned bed not far from Tina.

"Brutus why are you growling?" asked Tina.

Tina laughed and said, "Sometimes that little guy is really crazy!"

Tina kept busy cutting hair. She had three more customers waiting.

Brutus got up and came to the back of the shop. I had become visible and was sitting in a chair. Anticipating dog trouble after the growling incident, I opened a bag of doggie treats and gave one to Brutus. He carried it into the shop, climbed into his bed and began crunching.

"Brutus, where did you get that?" quizzed Tina.

Tina commented, "I guess he found a biscuit on the floor. I must have missed one when I swept."

I smiled and picked up a magazine from a small wall display case. I started reading, occasionally peering out from the back of the shop to see what Tina was doing.

Brutus returned to me to beg. I gave him another treat and the little guy went back to the front of the shop as before.

I heard Tina react. "Brutus, where are you getting those treats?" she asked with some concern.

Tina excused herself from the customer in the chair and went to the back of the shop. I had foreseen the problem and quickly grabbed the crystal and moved away from where I had been sitting. I had put one of the treats under my chair. Tina reached down, picked it up and put it back in the bag.

"No more treats, Brutus. You're going to get fat!" Tina returned to her customer.

I put the crystal in my pocket and waited patiently for the shop to clear.

"I need a break. I've been standing too long." Tina commented after her last customer left.

Tina came to the back of the shop where I was waiting.

"Oh! How did you get back here, Ned?" she exclaimed, mildly in shock.

"Sorry I scared you, Tina. Let me explain."

"Remember that dream I had when I was here last? After I left the shop, I found an egg-size crystal in the glove box of my car. It's not an ordinary crystal. When a person holds it, they become invisible."

"Sure they do," Tina commented, believing I was pulling her leg.

Just then, Steve came in and Tina, thinking it was a customer, started to go back to the front of the shop.

"It's okay, Tina, Steve is with me."

"Hi Tina, I'm Steve Jensen." Steve and Tina shook hands.

As all three of us stood in the back of the shop, I said, "Let me show you what happens when I pick up the crystal."

I reached into my pocket and disappeared.

"Whoa! Where'd he go?" inquired Tina.

"I'm right here, Tina." I reappeared as I put the crystal in the plastic bag and stuck it in my pocket.

"I don't believe this!" exclaimed Tina.

"Can I try it?" questioned Tina as her eyes twinkled.

"Sure. Why not?"

I took the crystal out of my pocket and handed the plastic bag and crystal to Tina.

She slowly opened the bag and cautiously peered inside.

"Don't worry, it won't bite," reassured Steve.

Tina reached in the bag and pulled out the crystal. She was invisible except for her belt and shoes.

Steve told her, "All we can see is your belt and shoes."

Tina reappeared and hastily gave me the bag containing the crystal.

I explained why we could see the belt and shoes.

Together, we told her the story of what we had done.

"Are you guys nuts? You could get in deep doo-doo doing that."

"We told you about it 'cause we want you to help us," I explained.

"Do you have any charities you want to support? It won't cost you a cent," Steve remarked.

"Sure, but it's stealing, and I don't want any trouble. What would my kids think?"

Tina had two children, both young adults.

"We call it a donation. It's like Robin Hood. We take from the rich and give to the poor and needy," I explained with a smile.

She grinned and said, "Well, when you put it that way, what would I have to do?"

"Now you're talking!" Steve quipped.

"You don't have to decide right now, but here's our plan for picking up another donation," I began to explain, paused and then gave her more detail. "It would have to be on one of your days off. We would call you on your cell phone and tell you where to park your bike. It would be in a parking lot next to a drug dealer's car. We know a red corvette has been used in the past. I saw it parked at Walmart recently, but I didn't see the driver. It was the same car that we took money from before. It had the same license plate. All you have to do is distract the driver. You can do that without even trying. I'll bet you look great in your riding gear. It only takes a few seconds for me to reach in the car and grab the money from the console. But, if you can get the driver out of the car, it would be even better. Maybe you can get him to look at something on the bike you suspect is causing trouble."

"That seems easy enough," Tina stated.

"We'll split the money equally. If it's like before, it will be about $700," Steve added.

"The shelter for battered women will like that," Tina replied. "Okay, count me in, but only this one time."

I said, "I hoped you would help us out."

Tina asked, "What if I had said no?"

Smiling, Steve replied, "I would have told you I'd get all my haircuts from you in the future."

"Wow! What a philanthropist!" Tina said sarcastically.

A customer entered the shop and Tina said, "I have to go to work. Ned, give me your phone number. I'll call you and tell you all my days off for the next month."

I wrote my home phone number down on a pad of paper. Steve and I left the barbershop through the back door.

CHAPTER 6

It was mid-October. Steve and I watched the parking lot almost religiously. We saw the corvette a couple of times on Sundays but Tina wasn't available. We checked parking lots and saw the car at Lowe's and Home Depot as well as at Walmart. The driver was a black guy built like a linebacker. If he got hold of one of us, he could snap us in half like a toothpick. The next Sunday was a perfect day for the team since Tina was off work and didn't have any family matters to tend to.

It was about 3:00 p.m. and we watched the corvette in Lowe's parking lot. We saw an older model pickup arrive next to the corvette and a transaction took place. I made a call to Tina and she was in the parking lot in about ten minutes. By the time she arrived we moved my Subaru within ten yards of the corvette. When we saw her coming into the parking lot, I shoved the crystal inside my glove to make skin contact and started toward the corvette.

Tina parked her bike next to the corvette on the driver's side, swung her right leg off the bike and set the kickstand. When she removed her helmet, blonde hair cascading to her shoulders, she glanced at the corvette's driver. He was checking her out as planned. Tina smiled and walked around her bike and over to the corvette.

"Do you know of a bike shop in the area?" she asked.

"Sorry ma'am, I'm not from around here," the driver answered.

"Could you help me then? I feel a vibration when I'm riding and I'd like to see if I can find out what the source is."

"Sorry ma'am, I can't leave my car," the driver answered.

I thought, "Time is wasting and Tina's not going to get this guy out of the car.

I'd better try to get the money while he's talking to her."

"Where are you from?" asked Tina.

"Eugene," he replied.

"I'll bet you played football."

"Sure did, defensive linebacker."

The football talk seemed to get the driver's rapt attention, so I reached into the car and opened the center console quietly. So far, so good. Suddenly, the driver turned and grabbed above the console and came in contact with my gloved left hand containing the crystal. A vice couldn't have been tighter. I tried to pull my hand back but no such luck. I tried to twist away but that didn't work either. Then I reached over with my right hand and grabbed the little finger of the driver's hand and bent it back, hard. The driver winced in pain. I pulled my gloved hand back. But my glove ripped open and the crystal went flying. Time seemed to slow down as I reappeared. I watched the crystal rotating and arc through the air, travel about twenty feet and shatter into hundreds of pieces on the blacktop.

The corvette driver, Tina, Steve and I were all shocked by what had happened. An unmarked police car rapidly approached and came to a screeching stop within a few feet of the sports car.

Bill and Jim scrambled out of the sedan; guns drawn.

Bill announced, "You're all under arrest."

Almost immediately after Bill said, "arrest", a dark blue SUV came to a sudden stop behind the police car. Two well-groomed young men in uniform got out of the car and approached Bill and Jim with their ID's displayed.

One of the men said, "Air Force Intelligence. We'll take responsibility for Dr. Franks and Dr. Jensen."

Steve and I looked at each other in shock. We were surprised the two men knew our names. They seemed to be the ones in charge of the situation.

Who are you?" I inquired.

The slightly older Air Force man said, "I'm Captain Lloyd Andrews."

Captain Andrews motioned to his companion and said, "This is Lieutenant Greg Hamilton."

Jim put handcuffs on the corvette driver and escorted him to the back seat of the patrol car.

Captain Andrews asked, "Where is the crystal, gentlemen?"

Steve pointed to the remnants of the shattered crystal and said, "Over there."

"We were afraid something like this could occur," Lt. Hamilton said dejectedly.

"Well, we still have one left," reminded Capt. Andrews, "but I doubt if it will be of much value anymore. They seemed to function as a pair."

Tina, Steve, and I gathered and watched Capt. Andrews approach the two officers and talk for a minute.

"Professors, you are coming with us to the police department where we will discuss this situation with the police officers in a conference room," informed Capt. Andrews.

He had our rapt attention. "You will drive your car and I will ride with you," commented Lt. Hamilton.

"Mrs. Templeton will join us after she changes clothes," Bill stated.

Bill looked at Tina and said, "You can go."

I had never referred to Tina as Mrs. Templeton. It sounded strangely formal to me.

The group dispersed and reconvened about fifteen minutes later at the police station.

When Steve and I entered the conference room, we were a little surprised at the number of people there. As Steve and I scanned around the room, we were also surprised to see some of the faces. In addition to the two arresting officers, Bill and Jim, there were the two Air Force men. Tina was there, as was Donna, Steve's wife. What surprised us most of all was the presence of the two drivers of the red corvette. There were also some police officers we didn't recognize. The Chief of Police entered the room and stood at the rostrum, apparently in charge of the meeting.

Capt. Andrews was first to speak.

He began, "Two crystals were found in the Antarctic in 1956 with the remains of what was assumed to be a crashed alien vehicle. It was ten feet below the surface and encased in ice. At that time the crystals were discovered and taken to Washington, D.C. They were stored until after the Cold War.

Two years ago, a team of investigators at Area 51 measured the chemical and physical properties of the crystals. The crystals were found to communicate when within about two kilometers of each other. The "talker" would glow pink and the "listener" would glow blue. If a human held a crystal, the individual became invisible. It was our intent to have some professors investigate the properties of a crystal outside the laboratory. We wanted a physical scientist and a biochemist to investigate one of the crystals. Therefore, one of the crystals was planted in Dr. Frank's car. We knew Dr. Jensen, a biochemist, and Dr. Franks were friends. However, we did not think the professors would carry out the type of study they did. But, it is understandable, that, without laboratory equipment, a plan was initiated to put the crystal to good use. We have been observing the professors since the crystal came into their possession."

I raised my hand.

"Dr. Franks," acknowledged Capt. Andrews.

"Where is the other crystal?"

"We have it in the area in a secure location."

"Capt. Andrews, how were the crystals used by the aliens?" asked Steve.

"We assume they were used to communicate and to make themselves invisible, when necessary, when they moved among the human population. We think they died before they had a chance to do that."

Steve asked, "How big were the corpses?"

"They were approximately five feet tall and weighed about eighty-five pounds. Their skin was a bluish green color. Their 'hemoglobin' was based on copper, instead of iron, as ours is. They breathed nitrogen, not oxygen." answered the lieutenant.

He continued, "They looked pretty much like small humans; their heads were elongated, but not enlarged with enormous eyes. Their faces looked normal."

"Thank you, Captain," said the Chief.

"Bill, you're next."

Officer Bill Watson stepped to the front of the group.

"We originated a sting operation several months ago to try to further diminish drug sales in the area," Bill stated.

"However," he continued, "we had no idea the professors had cooked up a scheme to take money from drug dealers and give it to the needy. We were completely caught off guard when the marked money was stolen from Adam Bruker. His real name is John Drummel. He's an officer on loan from the Eugene police department."

Bill took a drink of water from a plastic bottle and continued, "We took Bruker to Dr. Frank's house to try to scare the doctor into giving us back the money and the gun. At that time, we didn't want to reveal that Bruker was an officer, but we were sure the professors had a hand in the theft of our marked money. We just didn't know how they pulled it off."

"When we received the 911 call we had to pretend to arrest our officer," Bill stated.

"Ned and I thought something was fishy, since the patrol car showed up so quickly and without a siren," noted Steve.

"We were concerned about our officer not being in control without his weapon. We were parked a few houses down the street from Dr. Frank's home. We had no idea you gentlemen would be so resourceful," admitted Bill.

Bill continued, "When we got back to the department, we described the theft of the marked money on the new computer system, which is tied in with the government police bureaus. It only took a few minutes for us to get in contact with the captain and lieutenant. They informed us of the potential use of the crystal and mentioned it had been put in Dr. Frank's car."

Officer Hobson joined Bill and continued, "Area supermarkets had deposited the marked money that had been taken from the corvette. We went to the supermarkets and reviewed their security tapes and discovered the professors had purchased money orders that were sent to charities. The professors' fingerprints were on the marked money."

The two officers sat down; the Police Chief stood up and continued, "We wanted to catch everyone involved so we waited until another robbery seemed to be taking place. The Air Force officers helped us watch the two professors, but we didn't know Mrs. Templeton had been recruited to help them as a distraction. Eugene Police loaned us another officer, Henry Buchanan. Officer Buchanan was the driver at Lowe's parking lot."

"Officer Buchanan," please take over.

Officer Buchanan stated, "I was talking with Mrs. Templeton and out of the corner of my eye, I noticed the console start to open, apparently by itself. I moved my hand through the air above the console and when I came in contact with something, I grabbed it. It was Professor Franks' gloved left hand. I held on as tightly as I could until my finger was bent back and I was forced to let go. Dr. Franks suddenly appeared next to the car and then the other officers showed up."

Donna stood and asked, "Steve, why didn't you ask me to help you?"

"We were afraid you might blab about it," answered Steve.

Everyone in the conference room laughed. I felt the mood of the group had suddenly changed.

The chief continued, "We checked for police records for all three of you. You're all squeaky clean; not even a parking ticket. Since no one was injured except for a sore finger, and the money had been confiscated from earlier arrests, we will not charge anyone with any crimes. But, we want the professors and Mrs. Templeton to leave the police work to the police and not get involved in any more hair-brained schemes."

"Will you people guarantee you will not get involved in anything like this again," he asked.

Tina, Steve and I nodded and answered in unison, "Yes."

My right hand was in my pocket and I had crossed my fingers.

"This meeting is adjourned," stated the chief.

"Oh! I almost forgot. Dr. Franks, we need to pick up that gun from you. I'll send an officer over to your house tomorrow."

As everyone started leaving the room, Tina joined me.

"Ned, call me some time," she said as she smiled and handed me a small piece of paper.

I opened the folded paper and saw Tina's name and phone number.

"I'll do that," I said as a big smile spread across my face.